The Collectors

(Finders Keepers)

Book Five

By

Ron A Sewell

ISBN-13: 978-1501053979

ISBN-10: 1501053973

All rights reserved. No part of this book may be reproduced or transmitted in any form or by any means, electronic or mechanical, including photocopying, recording, or by any information storage system and retrieval system, without permission in writing from the copyright owner.

The Collectors – Book Five – Finders Keepers is published by Appolonia Books can be contacted at ras@cytanet.com.cy.

The Collectors – Book Five is the copyright of the author Ron A Sewell 2014. All rights are reserved.

The cover is designed by Berni Stevens Design. All rights are reserved.

All characters are fictional, and any resemblance to anyone living or dead is accidental.

This book is for

Sheila Sewell,

Marlene Lavell

Bev Fisher

With thanks for all their assistance.

Also by Ron A Sewell

A Basketful of Sleepers

The Angel Makers

You Can't Hide Forever

The Collectors Book One

The Collectors Book Two

The Collectors Book Three

The Collectors Book Four

Part One

"Antiquities are history defaced, or some remnants of history,
which have casually escaped the shipwreck of time.

Francis Bacon

Chapter One

Thessalonica, Greece, July 1944.

The streets were quiet, no cars or pedestrians. Abrax Bachis lay on his stomach and studied the rail-yard. From the edge of the damaged roof, he focused his binoculars on the shunting engines. As a railway man he assessed each carriage as it rolled the length of the slope towards a line of waiting trucks. In pencil, he drew diagrams and made notes in an old exercise book.

He froze as an armed German foot patrol sauntered along the street. They stopped, lit cigarettes beneath his position, chatted, laughed, and strolled away. He controlled his nerves and waited.

Stiff, he checked his findings again. His observations complete he shoved the note book inside his shirt. With safety in mind, he spread his weight and slithered across the roof to the rough scaffold supporting the front of the building.

Abrax made sure the patrol was nowhere in sight before he began to descend. Loose debris tumbled to the ground as the scaffold shifted.

On the other side of the street soldiers appeared from behind a building. "Stay where you are," a harsh voice commanded in German. The clunk of steel-capped boots on cobbles came closer.

Fear filled him with adrenalin as he glanced around, searching for an escape route. To his left a floor dropped into the dark.

To break the curfew meant imprisonment but detained with detailed sketches of the rail-yard, after torture and interrogation, the firing squad.

His heart raced and sweat soaked his shirt. He gripped the scaffold, pulled his feet up against the pole, released his grip and pushed. With a crash, he hit the boards. It rocked as his hands reached out. Out of control, he careered towards the void. Desperate fingers found a gap. With straining muscles, he dragged his frame back from the edge.

A bullet ricocheted off the stonework. He did not see who fired but forced his body into a narrow opening in the wall. Damaged stairs descended to the rear of the building. Close to the wall, he scurried like a rat into a space filled with split wooden beams and brickwork. Young and agile, he clambered over and through until a slit into a dark street loomed. He raced away as shouts followed.

Terrified he sprinted and dodged through the jungle of narrow streets surrounded by damaged buildings but the men followed shouting.

Bullets struck the wall; gunshots buzzed past, one caught his right arm, the pain worrying. He reached for the wound, blood covered his hand.

Desperate, he crossed a wide avenue, charged into the desolate Jewish quarter and hugged the dark. Discarded belongings and rubbish lay everywhere.

For a moment, he stopped, ripped off his shirttail and bound the injury. From behind came no sound, the patrol no longer followed or had they stopped to listen? He darted along a passage, took a left turn and then a right. At a slow even pace, he continued to run until free of the city.

He kept running; his heart pounded as he approached a stone built house with a large out-building to one side.

At the front door, he gave the prearranged signal: Two knocks, a pause, and then one. The door opened.

"You made it, Abrax," a bearded man shouted.

"Come, sit, and catch your breath. I bet you ran every kilometre," said Costas.

"It's over thirty," a young looking, dark-haired woman muttered, "impossible."

Costas grinned. "Not for this one. That's the reason I chose him plus he has the brains of a scholar. Tell me, Abrax, are the rumours correct?"

From his shirt he removed the book. "The Germans have marshalled three trains. They've loaded the closed trucks with prisoners. Armoured wagons are located between these. The engines are fully protected." Each one studied his notes and sketches.

Costas rubbed his chin. "Time to gather and position our forces."

"This boy stays here," the dark-haired woman said. "Not one of you noticed his wound."

Costas grabbed and examined the arm. "No problem. The rest of us will ride and gather our armies." He pointed to a map. "At this point, we stop these trains."

The dark-haired woman and Abrax stood at the door and watched the leaders of the resistance ride at a gallop into the night.

The door closed. "Off with your shirt."

Abrax obliged and waited. He made a face as the material glued by the dried blood ripped the wound open. With a clean cloth, she bathed and cleaned the gash, soaking it with a splash of ouzo before applying a homemade bandage.

With a grin, she embraced him. "You were brave tonight. Captured I doubt if you would have survived to see the sun rise."

"I did what had to be done."

"How old are you?"

A nervous smile played on his lips. "Twenty. Why?"

"I am a woman. Our leader tells me he will marry me when the war ends but as a man he lies. I am here for him to use when he wants." There was tenderness in her voice. She held his face in her hands, kissed and pulled him close.

The softness of her body and the warmth of her mouth enveloped his senses.

"They will be gone for days." She grabbed his hand and dragged him into the bedroom.

Chapter Two

The uniformed SS sergeant stared through the windscreen as he drove the Mercedes along the dark, deserted streets to the railyard. Tonight the curfew prevented any unauthorised movement.

In the rear of the staff car, between sleep and awareness, slumped an exhausted Brigadier General Karl Koenig. The vehicle juddered as it struck a pothole and disturbed him. He yawned and opened his window. The car arrived at their destination; the sounds of a railway working, loud and uneven jarred his senses. A thousand lights blazed, steam spewed as hot fog into the air, multiple engines shunted rolling stock into position. Pairs of soldiers armed with light machine guns patrolled.

Karl Koenig's grey eyes studied the sluggish lines of Italian and Greek prisoners herded as cattle into the waiting wagons. He thanked God for the low cloud; no bombers tonight.

He glanced at the red brick building and the Nazi flag that hung limp from its pole. "The first thing the Russians will burn," he muttered under his breath.

An SS guard opened the door and saluted. "They're ready for you, General."

He nodded, pressed his lips into a tight smile, stepped across a puddle and strolled into the building with his aid Captain Spee at his heels. To his left clerks emptied filing cabinets and tossed papers onto an open fire.

Those in the room on the right saluted as he entered. At the rear, a wooden desk piled high with folders and cluttered with half a dozen telephones, each a different colour. On the wall hung a picture of Adolf Hitler in uniform.

Karl slumped in the chair behind the desk, and with a wave of his right hand motioned for a colonel, three majors, and a captain to sit. "What news from Berlin?"

A newly promoted SS captain, with deep shadows beneath his pale eyes, stood. "General, they say the Fuhrer has important matters to deal with but he has not forgotten."

Karl's eyes hardened as he glanced at their faces. "If it hadn't been for that fool Mussolini, Greece could have waited. The Russians are advancing into Bulgaria and Hungary and we wait for them to arrive. The trains, will they be ready? Has the train from Athens arrived?"

"Sir, it's being unloaded and configured for the journey to Berlin," said Colonel Becker.

Karl smiled. "Gentlemen, these three trains, I want the railcars which house anti-aircraft gun turrets and concealed howitzers, in between the wagons holding prisoners."

Select your best NCOs and soldiers as guards. Give them as much food and ammunition as we can spare. The two trains filled with prisoners are to be similar. Our informants tell us the resistance intend to stop Greek treasures leaving the country. These trains will reach Berlin even if you have to battle for every mile. You will have the roofs of each wagon inspected. The French use whitewash to mark special trains. Position a hopper filled with ballast in front of the engine. Forget nothing and you will arrive in Germany. Overlook one thing and... well I'll say no more."

"When do you want these trains to leave, sir?" Becker asked.

Karl rubbed his chin. "I want them ready by morning. I will make the decision on which route later. Gentlemen, go about your duties and Colonel, your officers will check and then double-check the preparations. Remember, any Greek seen in this yard is a spy and is to be shot." He sighed. "I'm weary of being a stationmaster and harbour-master. Dismissed."

The group stood in unison, saluted, and left the room.

Karl opened his briefcase and removed a large map. His eyes scanned the route of the rail lines from Thessalonica to Berlin. "Which one?" he murmured. "Get this wrong and I might as well shoot myself." If he had any regret, it was that no one cared. He glanced at the photo of his wife and two children, a teenage boy and younger girl and remembered the fires of Dresden. Could his life ever be the same again?

Outside the building, Colonel Becker, a harsh and inflexible man, stopped his officers. He stood facing them with his feet apart and took off his cap. From his breast pocket, he removed a sheet of paper. "Major Oskar Berg, train one. Axel Koch, train two. Lars Zimmerman, train three. You heard the general. When you believe your train is ready, report to me and we will check again. When the Russians arrive, you and your men will be in Germany."

"Colonel, sir."

"Yes, Major Zimmerman."

"We are soldiers not railway men. How does the general expect us to know what to check?"

With no emotion the colonel said, "Follow your orders." He turned and marched into the building.

"Stupid question," Koch said.

Zimmerman laughed. "And you are an expert on armoured steam engines?"

"No," Koch said, "but I went through my men's papers and found many of them worked on the railways before this war. I suggest you do the same. I don't care if a corporal advises me on the rights and wrongs. I'll listen to his advice."

Zimmerman scratched his head. "Great idea. Wish I'd thought of it."

Koch placed his arms around the others' shoulders. "Well my friends, standing here is not getting the job done."

They laughed and walked out of the shadows and into the glare of floodlights towards their trains

Chapter Three

> The stately ship is seen no more,
> The fragile skiff attains the shore,
> And while the great and wise decay,
> And all their trophies pass away
> Some sudden thought, some careless rhyme
> Still floats above the wrecks of time.
> William Edward Hartpole Lecky.

Weary, Karl pushed a stack of papers aside and looked up as Captain Klinger Baum entered the room. He motioned towards a chair. "Sit, Captain, you appear as tired as I am."

Klinger grimaced. "That rust bucket I've been assigned should have been scrapped before this war began. The fresh coat of white paint is holding her together but she's ready, sir."

"It may be as you describe but I believe it will be the last ship to leave before the Russians arrive. Your task is of the utmost importance. Should you and your crew fail... You know what I mean."

Klinger raised his eyebrows. "The window for success is fast closing, General. The British Navy rule the sea and the Royal Air Force the sky."

"They will not touch a hospital ship."

"And if we are stopped?"

"You change from hospital ship to an armed merchantman. If discovered you will, without any doubt, be boarded. To make sure there are no survivors I've placed an armed squad of the SS on your ship. You will set the timers on the explosives and scuttle. I am convinced the Russians will be here by the end of the month. You have a chance to go home, albeit slim."

"When shall I sail, sir."

"You said you are ready and the cargo's on board and secure. I do not see any reason to delay. You are on a tight deadline to reach Crete to refuel. What is your best speed?"

"Twelve perhaps thirteen knots."

"With more night hours than day. There's a chance."

Klinger nodded. "I understand my orders come direct from Heinrich Himmler and my cargo is necessary for Germany to win this war."

"Trust me, the demands I ask of you and your crew are no more than I ask of every man I command. Our intelligence is a shambles, my signal room requires spares to operate and the Fuhrer informs me he hasn't forgotten." He stopped when the phone rang.

Klinger watched an old man age.

"I understand. We defend the city until ready to mount a counter offensive." The call ended and he faced Klinger. "Even I have to take orders. Go, Captain, and pray the clouds cover the moon."

***

Captain Klinger Baum stood and stared across the empty harbour as he waited. He turned and his eyes glimpsed a brass plaque on the rear bulkhead, which gave the correct name of his ship. Jupiter. 1927 Built Harland and Wolf Belfast. He smiled, when new she might have been the pride of the company. At six thousand tons, her holds when full may have contained many different cargoes. Now they held wooden ammunition boxes, their contents anonymous but he guessed they were of value.

The direct line to the engine room buzzed. "Bridge. Captain."

"Chief, sir. Ready to proceed."

"Thank you, Chief. You and your men carried out the impossible. I will try to get us home."

"I'll keep the screw turning and you set the course, sir."

"Standby, Chief."

Klinger contacted the harbour officer. "Lift the boom. *Gradisca* is leaving harbour." He watched as the small tug shifted the boom from which steel nets hung.

"Let go forward. Slow astern port – slow ahead starboard."

Unhurried, the bow turned away from the dock wall.

"Let go aft. Slow ahead port." He took a compass bearing on the centre of the entrance. "Steer 160."

In the dark, the profile of the vessel appeared similar to the hospital ship *Gradisca*. The second funnel and wooden framework aft, which concealed two guns bolted to the deck, might give them the edge they needed to survive.

"Steer south."

The middle-aged quartermaster, his hands resting on the spokes, eased the wheel, correcting the course as he glanced at the dimly lit compass card.

Klinger stared ahead, thankful tonight neither the cloud-covered moon nor stars gave any light. The dark was his friend. Daylight his enemy.

"Full ahead both, maximum revolutions." He waited for the engine room line to buzz.

"Chief, to survive I need everything this tub can give." The line went dead as the vibrations through the vessel increased.

"When shall I take over, sir?"

"Bruno, you have the watch but I will stay on the bridge and catnap. Where are the SS at this moment?"

"Leaning over the rail sir, being sick."

Klinger chuckled. "So much for our elite troops."

"Be careful, sir, someone may hear you."

"This war's finished, Bruno. If we make Crete and we might, then I'll navigate us out of the Med and into the Atlantic. What do you believe are our chances?"

"Ten percent if we are lucky, and avoid British warships."

"An ice cube in the fires of hell has more chance. I'm tempted to scuttle this heap of shit when we sight Crete. My crew deserve to go home and see their families. Keep your eyes open, Bruno, and we may yet stay alive. Wake me if you notice anything."

"Yes. Sir."

***

"Sunrise, sir."

Klinger woke, slid from his chair, and walked out onto the starboard bridge wing. He yawned, stretched, and scanned an empty sea and sky. Thankful, he offered a prayer.

"Bruno, it's time you rested. Give me ten minutes to wash and grab a sandwich. If you spot another vessel, alter course as you consider right, and get Hans up here."

Chapter Four

Major Oskar Berg stared at the massive armoured engine in front of him as smoke from its chimney corkscrewed into the night. The steel door protecting the footplate opened and a middle-aged man in overalls jumped to the gravel-covered ground and saluted.

"Sergeant Brock, sir."

Berg recalled Koch's comment and pointed. "You drive this?"

Brock grinned. "I've been with this engine since 1940, sir. There's nothing I don't know."

Berg rubbed his chin. "So each engine has its own crew. Are there any other railwaymen amongst the soldiers?" He saw the man nod, his blackened face giving nothing away.

"There's a few, sir."

"I sense a but."

"It's not my place to tell a officer how to run his train, sir."

Berg left nothing to doubt. "My knowledge of trains is not worth a Reich-mark. I need you to find every man who has worked on the railways. This train has to be ready to leave by first light."

The sergeant saluted as a regular soldier. "What configuration, sir?"

Berg gave him details.

"I'll need ten minutes to give my fireman his orders before I start. Where will you be, sir?"

"In the cab, waiting. No one sleeps tonight."

He clambered up and into the overheated cab and nodded to the fireman. "Can you drive this train?"

The man covered in coal-dust stopped raking the fire. "Yes, sir, but the rules forbid it until I am qualified."

"But you could?"

"In an emergency, sir."

"Have you been told where the train is going?"

The man stared at him in a manner almost insolent. "Sir, I'm a fireman. I tend the fire. It's of no interest to me where we are going but the sergeant will tell me, once the wheels start turning."

"You're not married?"

"A girl in every rail-yard, sir. My sergeant hasn't seen his wife and children for over two years. He should be ..."

The cab door opened. "My apologies, sir, my fireman prattles on."

"Passing the time, Sergeant. You found my men?"

"Eleven, sir, and every one a corporal."

"Good. Let's go and give them their orders."

Throughout the night men and equipment swarmed around the train. With his uniform jacket off and his sleeves rolled up, Berg laboured alongside his men. At 0800 he entered the red brick building with Axel and Lars. The colonel arrived moments later.

Brigadier General Karl Koenig sat with his aid making notes as Colonel Becker and his three majors entered the room.

Karl stopped what he was doing.

"The trains are ready to move when you give the order, sir."

"Then there's no time to be lost. Becker, you will be on the first train with Berg and an explosives team. You will stop before crossing every bridge and check for explosives while in Greece. Gather round." He waited until all movement stopped. "The quickest route is through Albania. It's dangerous but gets you out of this damned country. The Red Army is racing towards Greece and has taken Hungary. With luck, the Greek resistance will be fighting each other. One group wants to dominate this country after the war. I am sure they will attack, so you will travel during daylight. You will guard these trains with your lives."

"The resistance, sir. They are aware of the penalty if they wound or kill one of our soldiers."

"Colonel Becker. The more Greeks we dispose of the bigger the resistance becomes. I don't think our threat bothers them."

"General, sir. My orders are to remain here."

Karl lifted his head. "And my orders are you will be on the first train.

"Becker, your train will leave at nine.

"Koch will follow thirty minutes later.

"Zimmerman has the honour of the prize train, which will leave at ten. This time gap will continue until you reach Germany. There you will receive fresh orders. Dismissed."

The meeting was over and Karl returned to making more notes.

Becker and the majors saluted, turned, and left.

"Thirty minutes before we leave, sir," said Major Berg.

"I have a few things to do," said Becker. "I will join you in plenty of time." He walked away at a brisk pace.

"Suit yourself," muttered Berg. "The train goes at nine."

The three majors stood by the engine of train number one and watched as Becker arrived with suitcases and trunks in a small truck. They listened as he screamed orders at the soldiers to hurry and load his baggage into the one passenger carriage.

Berg shook hands with Koch and Zimmerman. "If I send up a red flare, we are under attack. It'll give you extra time to prepare."

"You worry too much," said Zimmerman.

"It's time," said Koch.

"Major," shouted the driver,

Berg turned, grabbed the handrail and pulled himself into the cab. The whistle squealed and steam exhausted from the engine. Wheels turned and the train edged ahead. Chains strained as within minutes the speed increased.

Both men gazed at the hundreds of armed soldiers crammed on the armoured or sand-bagged trucks.

"Our men at least can lie flat. Those poor buggers in the goods wagons are limited to standing room and one bucket in which to crap."

He nodded. "See you tonight," said Koch.

Zimmerman slapped him on the back. "I remember as a child wanting to work on the railways and now I have my own train."

Koch grinned, checked the time, and wandered across the rail yard.

Karl motioned to his aid. "Captain Spee, I want an update on those trains on the hour, starting at midday."

"I'll make the necessary arrangements, General."

"Spee, you will personally give me an update on where those trains are every hour."

"Yes, sir." Spee ran to the basement.

This entire level housed the main communications equipment for the SS. In the background the emergency generator vibrated the concrete floor. In front of their grey-green units, five uniformed corporals sat wearing headphones. Their task to transmit or receive signals from the many out-stations, He coughed as his lungs filled with cigarette smoke.

The communications officer, red-eyed, fought back a yawn. He lifted his head and took his time to stack the most important of signals. "What does he want now?"

"You are to contact the trains and note their position fifteen minutes before the hour and send one of your men with the information to me."

"Spee, can you read Morse code faster than you can talk?"

"No, sir."

"Well my team can and I will not waste their time running after you." He groped for his packet of cigarettes. "The Russians are not taking any prisoners. In a couple of weeks, we will be dead. I'll get the information and you can come and get it yourself?"

"Our magnificent army will force them back to Russia, the Fuhrer has decided."

"Spee, you're a bigger fool than I thought. Half our army is on its way to Germany. Now be a good boy and make sure you wipe the General's fat arse in the right direction. I have work to do, so bugger off."

Spee considered reporting the communications officer but decided to bide his time until the trains arrived in Germany. He sat at his desk and with pencil and ruler made a flow chart for each train.

At midday, Captain Spee presented his first report of the day. "General, sir, minor delays as a result of checking each bridge for explosives. The time difference between each train remains as ordered. Distance travelled seventy-five kilometres. No problems."

"Thank you, Spee." Karl continued on his plan for the defence of Thessalonica.

With the smartest of salutes, Spee returned to his desk.

Chapter Five

Major Berg stood on the left side of the engine cab. The driver kept a constant watch through the side and front windows at the track ahead. The fireman raked, riddled, and stoked the fire. On approaching a bridge, the driver sounded the whistle three times to warn the troops.

Once stopped the explosives team ran to the bridge, while anti-aircraft guns and howitzers rotated on their mountings. Sergeants scanned the vicinity with binoculars. Nervous soldiers released the safety catches on their weapons.

On finding nothing, the team returned. In minutes the train travelled at high speed. The constant stopping and starting drained the men and placed them on edge.

At the next bridge, Berg walked back to the carriage where the colonel enjoyed the comfort of a cushioned seat and drank coffee.

Colonel Becker placed his magazine on the table. "Problems?"

"Sir, sunset is at 2000. I suggest we decide where to stop for the night, rather than find ourselves surrounded by mountains."

"You have been reading my mind." He opened a large leather-bound folder. From this he removed a map. "Where do you suggest?"

Berg's finger followed the track before he glanced at his watch. "My choice would be this valley. Level ground exists in every direction and we should be safe with armed patrols at irregular intervals. To save time tomorrow, we send two squads to examine the next two bridges. I'd prefer three but the third is too distant."

Becker sounded calm as he replied. "I agree, we spend the night there." His finger pressed on the spot. "See to the arrangements."

The train shuddered and picked up speed.

"You may have a coffee, Major, and make me one while you're at it."

Berg cringed as he made two coffees but sat in a separate seat away from Becker. Exhausted he closed his eyes.

"Major," shouted Becker. "The train has stopped."

He glanced at the full cup of coffee, grabbed his cap and ran out.

Sergeant Brock leant out of the cab. "Another damned bridge, sir."

Berg laughed aloud.

"The fireman's making tea, sir, fancy a cup?"

He clambered into the cab, amazed he was so calm. "The best offer I've had all day."

Brock handed him a large chipped enamel mug. "Sorry about the mug but the good stuff doesn't survive for long on the footplate."

"It's hot and sweet, Sergeant. Out of interest, how did you manage to find sugar?"

"I'd rather not say, sir."

"It doesn't matter. Oh, we'll be stopping in a valley I've chosen, at dusk."

"Can you tell me where, sir?"

Berg took out his rail map and pointed. "In the centre of this valley."

"Can I make a suggestion, sir?"

"Of course."

"Stop at this end. If we have to leave in a hurry, it's downhill. I understand it's easier to hold the high ground."

Berg smiled. "I stand corrected. I should have spoken to you first. Who knows this line better than you?"

Brock tapped one of the steam gauges. "The team's coming back. Time to go." He pulled the levers and adjusted a few valve wheels. The squeal of metal on metal filled their ears as they picked up speed.

Three more bridges proved clear and they reached the hill overlooking the valley as the sun set.

Berg, his uniform and face covered in black dust, jumped from the cab and stretched. He glanced at his watch before walking to the first manned wagon. "Lieutenant."

A young, fresh-faced officer scrambled off the wagon, tugged his uniform jacket into shape, and saluted.

"Your men will take the first duty. Set up a perimeter guard at a thousand metres. Patrols are to consist of three armed soldiers. No lights and your men will be relieved in two hours. Spread the word to the next troop carrier until the night guard is covered. Send one of your men back along the track with a red lamp and stop the next train at a thousand metres." Berg glanced along the train. "Where's the sergeant in charge of the explosives team?"

"He and his men are sleeping, sir."

"Well don't stand there, go and wake them."

The lieutenant saluted, attempted to turn right but his feet slipped on the gravel.

Idiot, thought Berg, but thank God rank hath its privilege. At least I can wash and relax in the passenger car. He shouted at Brock who leant out of the cab. "We start again at sunrise."

"Yes, Major. The train will be ready. Potatoes are cooking on the fire. Do you want one?"

"How long before they're ready?"

"Twenty minutes."

"Save me one."

"Yes, Major."

"Sergeant Lubbock reporting as ordered, Major."

"Sergeant, you will split your team and with full packs march to the next bridge. One group will check for explosives and set watch overnight. Group two, will continue onto the next, and repeat the procedure. We will slow the train and pick you up as we pass in the morning."

The sergeant stood motionless as he accepted the order, saluted and strolled back to his men. "No fucking sleep," he muttered before bawling at his squad.

In the distance, Berg listened to the screech of brakes. The second train had arrived. At a brisk pace, he strode along the track.

In ten minutes, he relayed his orders to Major Zimmerman.

"And what is the Colonel doing?"

"Not a lot," Berg said. "We leave at dawn. See you tomorrow night."

Zimmerman walloped him on the back. "We will be closer to Germany. I look forward to seeing my children again."

The night remained uneventful. As the morning glow of the sun climbed over the mountains, Berg slapped the sergeant on the shoulder. "Time to go."

Sergeant Brock opened the throttle on the idling train and they sped into Macedonia. The prior examination of the first two bridges saved time as they raced north.

Captain Spee made his first report of the day to the general who nodded and waved him away.

"Sergeant, why are we slowing?"

"Sir," he waved his arms at the tree-covered slopes and the deep gorge to the right of the train "This line follows the contour of the mountain. If I travel at speed, I will not be able to brake if the line is blocked. This way I reverse, thus putting the train in a safer position for your men to fight."

Creases formed on Berg's brow. "What if we increased speed?"

"If the resistance remove one rail, it's over the edge."

"You make a good point. Stop the train. I need to speak to my men."

Brock eased back on the throttle and the train slowed to a halt. Berg jumped to the ground.

The young lieutenant from the first truck ordered his troop to standby.

"Lieutenant, pass the word we are approaching a forested and mountainous region. I promise you the resistance will be waiting. Be ready to expect the unexpected. If you see anything out of the ordinary, you have my permission to open fire. Do not leave the protection of your wagon. You have the firepower to destroy the enemy on the slopes. In the forest, he has the advantage. Understood?"

"Yes, Major."

"Very well. Make sure the officer on every armed truck understands."

"Yes, Major."

Berg clambered back into the cab. "God help us, Brock, they give me boys straight from school."

"They will not let you down, Major."

He shrugged. "If they do, I and everyone else will be dead."

Brock eased the train round every bend accelerating when and where he could.

"Brock, how much further until we're out of these mountains?"

"Five hours at best, Major."

Brock shouted and pointed ahead as he slammed the engine into reverse. Wheels spun and sparks flew. Carriages thumped carriages as the direction changed. Soldiers tumbled over each other.

No more than four hundred metres along the track lay several large boulders.

Berg leaned out of the window, his pulse raced as he removed his Lugar pistol. He scanned the forest but saw nothing.

"Stay in the cab, Major. The windows are bullet proof and it would take a cannon shell to puncture the armour."

"If we sit and do nothing we might as well shoot ourselves."

"Major, Major."

Berg could not help but smile. Colonel Becker stood alongside the cab.

"Sir."

"Is something wrong?"

"The track is blocked. I'll get my explosives team to blast the boulders and remove the debris. I suggest you return to the safety of your carriage."

"Where are these boulders?"

Berg pointed.

"Come, we will inspect the problem together."

Berg glanced at Brock, shrugged and jumped to the ground. "Sergeant, get your team and bring explosives. Lieutenant, ten men, now."

The group led by Becker followed, their eyes shifted left and right as they walked along the track. Berg positioned five soldiers on either side.

The boulders were taller and wider than an average man. Berg scanned the mountainsides. He saw nothing and shrugged. His thoughts raced, this was the perfect place for an ambush. "All yours, Sergeant. Don't waste time. Blast those rocks apart but leave the track in one piece."

The sergeant laughed. "This is why you pay me." He spoke in a soft voice to his men who removed explosives from their packs and placed them on the boulders. One man inserted the fuse and connected the wires.

"Back to the train," shouted the sergeant as he trailed a wire behind him. A hailstorm of bullets thudded into the sergeant.

"Shit," screamed Berg. "Run."

Becker hesitated and a wall of heavy calibre bullets sliced him in two.

The lethal deluge hit them from both sides of the gorge.

Berg dived under the engine as the throb of the anti-aircraft guns and the howitzers pounded the tree-covered slopes. He could hear the enemy but never saw them. A thunderous roar blasted the boulders. With haste he rolled from under the engine, grabbed the handrail and pulled open the steel door. Pain stabbed every inch of him. He dragged his body into the cab and gave the order. "Brock, shift this train." His head lolled to one side and he collapsed in a pool of blood on the footplate.

Brock operated the levers and opened the throttle. The train shuddered as it gathered momentum. Bullets struck the cab and ricocheted into the air. With its weight, those rocks scattered over the track fell to one side. Behind him, the big guns and machine guns blasted the slopes.

A few kilometres along the track, he turned to his fireman. "We might make it. What the..." He peered through the chipped armour-plated glass as the train entered a tunnel and the cab doors opened.

Two men wearing British army battle dress opened fire. One of the mercenaries clambered into the cab and opened the throttle wide before he leapt and joined his companion at the side of the track.

"They will have the ride of their lives," said Georgios as the carriages trundled on.

"We must wait for the next," said Savas.

"They will have heard the firing. It will not be so easy"

"How can we tell which train carries the artefacts?"

"On the next train, study the closed trucks. Prisoners have to relieve themselves and it shows. To be sure, we have a man posted in a hole under the track. He not only sees but is often covered."

A dull explosion rattled along the tunnel.

"They found the bottom of the gorge."

"Perfect place for the German bastards," said Georgios. "Let's get into position for the next train."

The ground beneath their feet trembled and dust floated in the air.

"What the hell?" asked Savas.

"The train. The vibrations take their time to travel through the rock."

***

Axel Koch listened to the boom of howitzers. "Driver. Stop the train." He jumped to the ground and ran to the first troop carrier. "Lieutenant, send one of your men. I want every officer here in ten minutes. Sergeant, you and two others release the prisoners and make them run. A few shots into the air will make sure."

"They're Italian, sir, good runners."

Koch shouted. "Get on with it."

The sergeant chose his men and raced to the first wagon. With a heave, the metal securing bar swung free and the double door slid back.

The odour of stale urine and faeces fouled the air. Exhausted men shielded their eyes from the bright sunlight.

The two soldiers grabbed those tottering by the door and threw them to the ground. "Go, go, go."

Confused, they went to help their comrades.

The sergeant fired his machine pistol into the air. "Go, go, go."

Those on the ground stared at their captors before they crawled away.

"Leave them. They'll soon get the message. Next wagon."

As they opened the doors to the last wagon the Italian prisoners ran, staggered, or crawled away from the train. Many glanced back expecting a bullet.

Major Koch faced his lieutenants. "You heard the gunfire. What they faced and whether they overcame the resistance we don't know. Their radio is not transmitting which means nothing. You will prepare your troops for an attack from either side. The signal to open fire and keep firing will be one long blast on the whistle. Whatever is there, the first train will have inflicted heavy casualties on the enemy. This train is not stopping."

"The prisoners, why release them?" asked a young officer.

"Weight. The lighter this train is the faster it runs. Dismissed."

The shrill sound of a train whistle forced Koch to turn away from the train and gaze up the track. Zimmerman's train slowed to a halt stopping metres from the last truck.

Koch met Zimmerman halfway and told him his plan.

"What choice do we have?"

"I'll give two long blasts of the whistle when we are clear of danger."

"It's a sound I'll be listening for but all the same, I'll have my men ready."

"Time we left." The two men shook hands.

Back in the cab the driver said, "Major Koch, with the ballast truck in front it's difficult to see the line. One, perhaps two men, checking the rails could make the difference."

"If I put men up there in the open they're as good as dead. Unhook the ballast car."

The driver descended the metal steps and strolled as if he had all the time in the world to the front of the engine. Five minutes elapsed before he returned. "It could help, Major."

Koch glanced along the train and turned to the driver. "Increase speed but whatever happens we do not stop."

The driver pulled the main lever and adjusted a few valves and with squeals and groans, the train rolled forward.

Koch bit his fingernails and stared ahead. "Sound the whistle, driver, one long blast." He glanced at the corpses of the colonel and the others at the side of the track. The chatter of small arms and the thunderclap of shells reverberated above the roar of the engine. Bullets ricocheted off the cab as adrenalin coursed through his veins. In minutes, the train rounded a curve and a sheer wall of rock replaced the slope on the left side. To the right, the gorge opened out to the distant foothills.

"Driver, two long blasts of the whistle."

He pulled the wire and the shrill of the whistle vibrated off the valley walls. "We made it, Major." His eyes caught a shift in direction of the ballast truck.

The engine chased the truck to the bottom of the gorge. The domino effect took over as one section tilted and followed the other.

Chapter Six

Major Lars Zimmerman's right hand gripped the black steel handrail and above the rattle and thump of the train, he heard two long blasts of a whistle. The explosion bothered him. He grimaced at the driver. "As fast as you can."

The driver adjusted the throttle lever and tweaked the controls. "It's the best I can do on this stretch, Major."

Zimmerman nodded and kept his eyes on the forested slopes. His mind mulled over the situation. If our radios worked, if something was wrong, I'd know.

Bullets struck the side of the cab in a continuous stream. Without thinking, Zimmerman, the driver and fireman, ducked.

"Reverse," shouted Zimmerman.

Astounded, the driver complied with the order.

Above the roar of the howitzer firing, metal screeched on metal as the brakes slowed the train and the engine wheels searched for grip to reverse. On rounding a long curve the torrent of small arms fire ceased.

"Stop the train," ordered Zimmerman. "I must check my men."

He jumped from the cab, lit a cigarette and strolled indifferently towards the first armed wagon. "Lieutenant."

A young second lieutenant scrambled from the wagon and saluted. "Steiner, sir."

"Send one of your men to gather my officers together. If these goat herders want a fight, I'll give them one."

"Yes, sir."

In minutes eleven officers stood protected by the engine and listened to the major's plan.

Zimmerman permitted himself a smile. "The SS do not cringe as cowards, we attack and destroy. Those," he pointed to the hillsides, "amateurs want us to run the gauntlet. From what I heard, I assume the second train exploded further along the track or in the gorge. We will change their plan. Our train will proceed at walking pace while our heavy weapons will pound both hillsides. Behind this bombardment, you as my officers will lead our troops and wipe out those who remain. The forest will give you cover. The last carriage is your marker. If the train stops, you stop. Any questions?"

"A brilliant strategy, Major."

"And you are?"

"Lieutenant Wagner, sir."

"Very well, Wagner, you will lead an arrowhead formation."

"An honour, sir."

"Make sure your men carry as much ammunition and grenades as they can. Lieutenant Steiner, your platoon will be the shaft of the arrow – follow Wagner, ten minutes behind. The wounded resistance fighters must be eliminated before they realise they have nothing to lose. A cornered rat will attack with unbelievable ferocity. You have ten minutes. Dismissed."

Eight minutes later eleven officers along with their platoons formed the arrowhead and vanished into the forest.

Zimmerman ordered each gun captain. "You will commence firing and not stop unless ordered by me." He pointed. "One blast of the train whistle and you begin. Remain under cover of your armour; I doubt they have any artillery."

Back in the cab, he gave the order, "Walking pace, and keep the doors and windows closed. A stray bullet will kill us bouncing around this cab."

The whistle blasted its shrill cry and the train shuffled ahead. The deluge of small arms fire began the second they rounded the bend. Moments later the howitzers and anti-aircraft guns commenced firing.

Pleased to be on the move, Zimmerman viewed the forest through his binoculars. The surprise thrust of his force overwhelmed the enemy. Grenades exploded across the hillside. He chuckled and turned to the driver. "They didn't expect an attack."

Lieutenant Wagner spaced his men three metres apart and led from the front similar to a scythe cutting corn.

The resistance, trained by the British, nestled deep in their trenches. Others further across the slope, behind their rock and earth fortifications, fired on the train but remained unprepared for an attack from their flank.

A grenade exploded in a dugout. Two of its occupants died from the initial blast. The blood from three others drained into the dry earth.

Through the smoke and debris of human flesh, Wagner fired from the hip, the noise of his machine pistol reassuring. His men left a trail of bodies lying in bizarre postures like broken dolls. Trees felled by the heavy guns toppled into a pot-marked hillside. The men in the rear of the arrowhead put the wounded resistance fighters out of their misery each with a single shot to the head, no quarter neither asked nor given. Fierce hand-to-hand clashes flared and died under the heavy barrage.

A soldier alongside Wagner collapsed, his face a bloody mask of flesh, blood, and bone. From below, smoke rose up the slope. Wagner signalled his men to stop as three more fell. In unison, they dropped to the ground. Progress continued with losses on both sides.

Zimmerman noticed the fall off in the barrage but remained unconcerned until it stopped. Angry, he jumped out of the cab and roared at the gun captains. "I ordered you to keep firing."

"Major, we are out of ammunition."

"Why didn't you load more?"

"We loaded what was available for our defence not offence."

Machine gun fire from the hillside rippled across the wagon. Thrown forward, Zimmerman spun. A confused look spread across his face as bullets distorted his chest to a mass of blood-torn flesh. With eyes wide, he tumbled to the ground, dead.

Leto, since the destruction of her village had become a resistance fighter. She dressed as a man and acted like one. With the stealth of a lioness, she crawled to a high point as her group rose up and charged headlong at the enemy. Leto nodded approval, but frustrated by the stubbornness of the enemy the attack failed. She spat on the ground, returned to her leader, and made a report.

Costas Petredes scorned the Germans as he stubbed out his cigarette. "They want a fight. These are my mountains. Many of our people will die today but I promise, not one enemy soldier will live to see the sunrise."

Leto scurried across the hillside and warned those in this section to prepare for uninvited guests.

Wagner crawled and the arrowhead progressed. A grenade detonated behind him. Men's screams were obliterated by the constant chatter of small arms fire. He glanced up as a man in a tree dropped a grenade inches from his face.

The resistance waited until the SS, weakened by their losses and blinded by smoke, arrived at the killing ground.

Murderous bursts of machine gun fire rattled across the cleared area cutting men apart. Bullets tore into the SS platoons as they scrambled for cover. The fire-fight ended with the detonation of explosive charges. Costas urged his men, now they had regained the upper hand, to press on and finish the job.

The SS, confused by the intensity of the counter attack, withdrew to discover they were under fire from another direction. Soldiers formed an impression of order as they dropped into vacated dugouts and held their positions. A squad of eight led by an officer scurried into foxholes, and hurled grenade after grenade until their supply exhausted. The line of fire did not falter.

From above, the resistance fired, advanced, stopped, and fired again.

The SS stood their ground but one by one they were injured or died.

Costas ordered his men and women to fall back. Three men positioned at strategic points prepared their equipment and waited for the signal.

Costas fired a red flare into the air and three American flame-throwers erupted into a wall of intense heat.

The SS continued firing into the flaming balls until the last man breathed the scorching fumes.

In a sweeping motion the three men advanced cremating all in their path. The stench of burnt corpses floated on the air; this fight was over.

Costas strolled towards the train and a barrage of fire struck the ground around him.

Sergeant Keifer plus a few stragglers, most of whom were wounded, and the gun crews made a stand. They moved forward in a tight well-disciplined unit.

Costas and his group hit the ground. It took him a second to gauge the situation. He turned his head to Nikolas, his second in command. "These are lunatics and know what they're doing. They'll throw their lives away and we'll pay the price. Get back and attack them from the tree line. I will hold them."

Nikolas crawled away, when far enough, he stood and ran. The sound of automatic weapons made him turn. From his vantage point, he saw the SS advancing, firing until their magazines emptied.

Costas and his team opened fire but were cautious when they raised their heads to aim.

The SS continued their advance and fought with knives and bayonets.

Dead or wounded surrounded Costas. Reinforcements arrived in time to save those still standing. He wiped blood from his face. "Where are our train drivers?"

Georgios and Savas swaggered along the edge of the track and stopped.

"What about the driver and fireman?" asked Savas.

"Promise them what you like, once clear of the train I'll shoot them." The threat in Costas' voice was genuine.

"I hear what you say." Georgios approached the engine and threw a rock at the cab. He held his hands high to show he was unarmed when a man peered through the glass. The cab door opened and the fireman, followed by the driver, dropped to the ground.

Georgios walked towards them, his hand held out ready to shake theirs.

Bemused, both men shook his hand and were surprised when he offered a cigarette. They took one and waited. Georgios gave them a light.

"Come," he said in a soft tone. "As engineers, we eat and enjoy the day."

They followed, smoking as they walked towards Costas.

Georgios stepped to the side as two shots rang out. With a hole in their heads, the fireman and driver tumbled to the ground.

"They died happy," said Costas. "Get the train into the tunnel and start unloading. We have a fortune to store for when this war is over."

Savas clambered into the cab and opened the throttle. Exhaust steam belched from the chimney as the engine shuffled into the dark of the tunnel and stopped. Behind, a gang of men removed the points, rails, and sleepers and tossed them into the gorge.

Inside the tunnel, men formed lines and carried dozens of boxes into a cavern lit by oil lamps.

Costas sat on a large wooden crate, stroked his black moustache and chain-smoked. Every so often, his section leaders reported casualties and the situation with the spreading fire on the hillside. He remained calm and told those not part of the unloading team to rest.

A long roaring tremor told Costas this was an earthquake. He grimaced as tracks buckled, steel wheels rattled, and everyone stopped. In the dimness of the tunnel people glanced at each other. A few crawled under the wagons, prayed and waited.

The ground shivered and the rough-cut walls shook. Fragments of rock dropped and shattered. Silence followed before someone shouted it was okay.

Blood flowed from a cut on Costas' head. He laughed and paraded the length of the train, his voice reassuring, "Hurry, we can eat, drink ouzo, make love and then sleep. Tomorrow we may have to fight another battle."

The rumble began deep in the mountains. It gathered momentum through the gorge. Rocks, boulders, and debris cascaded across steep slopes followed by a fog of dirt and dust. Those in the tunnel staggered and reached out for something to hold. Others tumbled to the ground and protected their heads. Oil lamps crashed to the floor, their flames casting macabre shadows on trembling walls.

Chapter Seven

Talos Vasco, a middle-aged man with his arm in a sling sat on the side of the mountain watched and waited. A stone struck the back of his head. He turned and saw the tree-covered slope buckle and twist. Terrified, he charged across the slope as the ground trembled. His eyes strayed for a moment at the wall of debris rising and falling. Adrenalin charged his pace as he took a diagonal path. He gasped for breath when he gained the shelter of an overhanging rock face. With one hand he clung to the rock and prayed. The dark enclosed him as the shifting mass slipped to the rail track and overflowed into the gorge. Fear gripped Talos; with his eyes caked in dust he slumped to the ground. From his pocket he pulled a clean rag, wiped his mouth, spat on it and cleaned his eyes.

With watery eyes, images came into focus. As his vision cleared he glanced left and right. The rail lines lay hidden under a broad expanse of trees and boulders the size of houses. With caution, he stepped onto the slope and made his way to the rail tracks. He searched for the tunnel exit but could find no trace. Believing the entrance might have survived he trudged along the track until the path became blocked with tons of rubble. Stunned, Talos understood nothing made sense after a quake. He made the decision to return to their camp high in the mountains.

As he clambered over rocks and forded streams, he realised only the women, old men and the children remained. The capture of the train required every man who could use a weapon. All had ended their lives sealed in an unknown tunnel.

He continued along narrow rock-covered goat tracks surrounded by dense foliage until exhausted, he tumbled to the ground and slept. As the night sky brightened, Talos awoke, stretched one arm and sat on a rock. He glanced around, aware his camp remained a day's walk. A small stream provided a face wash and drinking water. His muscles ached as he started walking but before long he entered the high forest. Hours later, he arrived in a narrow valley masked by pine trees. The path twisted and turned on the course of a stream.

A woman's voice rang out. "Stop or I'll shoot."

Talos shouted, "Joanna, it's Talos."

From behind a boulder a young woman, wearing men's clothing and holding a single shot rifle, appeared. "You are the first to return. Was the attack successful?"

He stared at her and whispered, "Everyone's dead. The earthquake closed the tunnel."

"There may still be a chance. Come and tell the old man what happened."

Talos grabbed Joanna's arm. "I searched, the tunnel's gone. Even if a hundred strong men were available, we could not shift the rock fall. Some are taller than a house."

She grabbed his hand and together they walked into the makeshift village. Women with babies in their arms watched.

"Where's my husband?" one shouted.

"My two sons?" screamed another.

A child ran to them. "When's mama and papa coming home?"

With his one good arm, he grabbed the child to him. The boy understood and cried. He pulled away and wiped his eyes before running back to his house.

Misery surrounded Talos. The expressions on the women's faces said everything; he didn't have to tell them. The man with one good arm had survived.

At the old man's dwelling, they stopped and waited until he came out.

The folds of skin on his face almost hid two bright eyes. He pointed to a chair. "You have carried a heavy burden. Rest before you tell us what happened."

Tears flowed from his eyes as he described the attacks on the trains. His voice dropped as he told of the quake. How rocks, trees and the earth descended as water into the gorge covering everything in its path. He gave the sign of the cross. "God saved me."

"We must gather our tools and go back. Some may be alive," barked an old woman.

"No one is alive," roared Talos. "Do you believe if there had been a chance I would have returned? The mountain buried them and you need explosives and heavy lifting equipment and we have neither."

The old man's expression changed, his eyes watered and his lips trembled. "This war is coming to an end but I fear another soon to start. Here we have food and water. The Germans set fire to our villages and murdered those they found. Here we are safe." He looked at those standing in front of him. "Go, mourn your losses. Tomorrow we start again. Come, Talos we must talk."

The next morning two unmarried women and Talos began the trek back to confirm no survivors. With sufficient provisions, he led them along the narrow paths. They rested for the night and continued as the sun rose.

In the early afternoon the three of them searched for an opening or a sign their friends or family might have survived. While she clambered over a huge boulder, one of the women, Kiki, slipped, Talos grabbed her hand and saved her.

Exhausted they collapsed and slept in the open.

On their return to the village, not a word passed between them. The old man waited outside his hut. "I see from your faces no one escaped. Talos, you are the man of the village. When this war is ended, you must go to Thessalonica and inform the authorities. They will know what to do."

***

In *Gradisca's* engine-room, the chief sat in a deckchair between the two triple expansion steam engines as they thundered and rattled every nut, bolt and steel plate.

Klinger fixed his Italian-made binoculars on the dark line, which separated the sea from the night sky. In an hour, the sun would blast light over the area, once again making them a target for allied aircraft, submarines and surface vessels.

"Bruno, go and wake our guests. I want them on this bridge in their uniforms, ready for inspection, in five minutes."

"With pleasure, sir." Bruno scampered away.

"Quartermaster, how long have we known each other?"

"A few years, sir."

"If I gave you an order you considered wrong, would you obey me?"

The quartermaster gave him a confused look. "You're the Captain."

Klinger's eyes narrowed. "In a few minutes I'll know your answer."

The sergeant screamed at his men and formed them into a line across the bridge. He gave the SS salute. "My men are ready for your inspection, sir."

Klinger nodded to Bruno. "Take the wheel. Quartermaster, relieve these men of their weapons and ammunition. I need to see how fit they are."

Klinger stepped back as the SS handed over their machine pistols and ammunition. "Sergeant, with you leading, your men are to run at the double from the bow to the stern three times."

The sergeant glanced questioningly at Klinger and shrugged. "At the double," he bawled.

"Quartermaster, those weapons," said Klinger pointing. "Toss them over the side."

Feet pounded along the metal deck. The sergeant charged onto the bridge.

Klinger sensed his change of attitude.

"You bastard. You ordered our weapons be tossed over the side."

In a calm voice, Klinger said, "I could have you shot for insulting a senior officer." He lifted his Knight's Cross with oak leaves and swords. "I was awarded this for valour not for murdering men carrying out their duty. Sergeant, I'll have a boat lowered, give you water, provisions and a compass, or, you operate the guns on the aft deck and die a hero's death with the rest of us. You have a choice, make it the right one."

The sergeant licked his lips. "May I talk to my men?"

"You have five minutes."

"Crete at Green one zero, sir."

"Thank you, Bruno."

The sergeant reappeared followed by his men. He saluted as a soldier not the SS. "We fight and die as soldiers, sir."

"Good decision. Go and prepare the guns for action. We may have made Crete but the Atlantic remains a dream."

Klinger stared at the tree-covered mountains, which stretched from one end of the island to the other.

Two hours later, they entered Souda Bay, Crete, and tied up alongside the coaling barge.

Klinger contacted the chief engineer. "You have until dusk to fill the bunkers. Then it's non-stop to Germany."

"I'll bear that in mind, sir."

"Bruno, I'm going for a shower."

"Do we have any air support, sir?"

Klinger shook his head. "We're on our own." He smiled. "Maybe no one will bother sinking this heap of rust or perhaps a storm in the Bay of Biscay will save them the trouble. Whatever, we will sail and head home. The crew deserve a dash of hope."

***

It seemed Klinger's head had just touched the pillow when the bang on his cabin door woke him with a jolt. He gripped the side of his bunk. "Come in."

"Cup of coffee, sir," said Bruno, whose dark-rimmed eyes gave clear evidence of little sleep. "Like you, I needed to catch up on my beauty sleep. The chief tells me he's emptied the coal barge."

He sipped his hot coffee. "Have we enough?"

Bruno lowered his gaze. "No, sir, but the chief believes if we travel at eight knots, there's enough wood built into this ship to make up the difference."

He glanced at his watch. "Time we left. Get the ropes singled up. And no lights."

"The Chief and his stokers are having a shower. Can we let them have ten-minutes?"

Klinger looked at him. "If this was a destroyer I'd scream abuse at the mere suggestion, but it's not and I can bend the rules." Tiredness he knew was another of his enemies. It forced good men to make stupid mistakes. We sail in two hours."

"Thank you, sir."

As Bruno left the cabin, a German Brigadier General, his eyes fatigued and his right arm in a sling, strutted into the cabin. "Are you the captain of this vessel?"

Surprised, Klinger stood. "I am, sir."

"Sit. The islanders know the war is over. My troops are disillusioned, as am I. How many of my men can you take?"

"I could take five hundred but have barely enough provisions for my small crew. This vessel is on a mission that has every chance of failure. You and your men are better staying where they are and when the British arrive, surrender."

"A hospital ship with no crew and little food?"

Klinger leaned back in his chair. "It's not what you think. I'm ordered to make the passage to Germany. Those in command believe if this old boat appears to be a hospital ship there's a chance."

"And what do you believe, Captain?"

"What I believe is of no consequence. Like you, General, I do as I'm ordered and want to see my family."

The general let his eyes wander around the sparse cabin. "You are correct. Better to surrender than drown."

Klinger walked with him back out and into the sunlight, his mind wondering if he should sail and continue the war or give up. He saluted as the general left.

"Good luck, Captain. You will need it and pray it's dark when you sail close to Malta."

Klinger saw Bruno wiping the sweat from his face, waiting. "Problems?"

"No, sir. The Chief tells me he's ready."

"Get the crew and the SS soldiers into the officers' mess. I want to talk to them."

Klinger entered the mess where his crew of fifteen and the soldiers waited. He sensed their unease. "Make yourselves comfortable and relax. I need your help. The war is going badly for the Fatherland and my orders are to take this vessel and its cargo to any port in Germany. On the island, the army are waiting for the British to arrive and they will surrender. You may wonder what's the point in continuing this voyage when we can remain safe and in harbour. I can see the sense in staying. We can relax, become prisoners of war and at some time in the future go home. It's against any regulation I know of but I leave the decision to you. If it is a draw I'll cast the deciding vote." He glanced at the men's faces.

Bruno took charge. "Those for staying, hands in the air."

Not one hand moved.

"I'd better get you home," said Klinger.

One by one, the men left the room. Each smiled and nodded to Klinger.

"Let's go, Bruno. It's time."

***

Klinger tossed his cap into a corner of the bridge and stepped out onto the port bridge wing.

"Helmsman. Ring on stand-by."

He turned to Bruno. "Cast off forward."

"All clear forward, sir."

"Slow ahead port. Slow astern starboard. Rudder amidships. Let go aft."

"All clear aft, sir."

Klinger peered forward and aft. "Slow ahead starboard. Rudder fifteen degrees to starboard."

He watched as the aged vessel turned towards the open sea. "Wheel amidships. Half ahead both. Steer two- seven-zero."

Gradisca nosed her way through the unmanned submarine boom that stretched from one side of the bay to the other, into the open sea.

The sun was getting low as he raised his binoculars and scanned the sea to port and starboard. It appeared empty, his ship the lone resident of the infinite expanse of sea. "Bruno have one of the men bring me a cup of coffee and then get some sleep. Relieve me at midnight."

"Yes, sir."

"Helmsman. Keep your eyes open and your course straight."

Sunset arrived, followed by the dark, and the Royal Navy patrolled elsewhere.

***

At dawn, Klinger strolled onto the bridge and swung his binoculars across the sharp horizon. He grinned after finding it clear. "The war's elsewhere, well at least for now."

"I'll believe in miracles when we dock in Hamburg," said Bruno.

"In time this war will find us."

"If you say so, sir. Permission to leave the bridge."

"I'll have a coffee and toast," said Klinger.

"On its way, sir."

As the day progressed, watches changed and men grabbed sleep. At any other time a passage through the Mediterranean in October might have been welcomed. The weather was perfect and they had not sighted another vessel. The elderly ship steamed at eight and a half knots into another night across the calm sea leaving a straight wake.

The dawn arrived as Klinger and Bruno repeated the same words as they had the morning before.

Klinger scanned the sea praying it remained empty and safe. "Not a vessel in sight."

"Long may it stay that way, sir."

"What the..." But the blip on the horizon vanished. "I saw something. I know I did."

"On the horizon. Smoke. Red, one zero, sir," the helmsman shouted.

Klinger searched the position. "Shit." One puff of smoke. A ship directly ahead on the same course. "Bruno, have your breakfast but make sure the army readies those guns for action and make my coffee strong."

Klinger scrutinized the sea ahead, left and right in a constant motion. On each occasion he stopped it was to place a dead reckoning position on the chart. Hour after hour and the sea appeared to have been swept clean.

"Ship. Green, four- five, sir."

Klinger examined the vessel and flipped the pages of his recognition book to confirm. "Destroyer CA class. More guns than a porcupine has needles and they never operate alone."

"Ship. Red, two- zero, sir. Lead ship is flashing."

Klinger grabbed the wheel. "Go. Wake the First Mate."

The lead ship constantly signalled by flashing light as Klinger steered a straight course.

"Captain," said Bruno.

The helmsman took the wheel.

Klinger ran to the bridge wing and flashed, 'Wait. Wait. Wait.' When he was ready, he signalled. 'SS *Gradisca* on passage for Algiers."

"Bruno, fall aft with the soldiers and be ready to open fire on my command."

"I gather we go down fighting," said Bruno.

"We might win," said Klinger. He gave a wild laugh.

A flash from the destroyer's forward 4.5 inch gun. The shell fell short. A waterspout shot up, its spray drenching the bow.

He contacted the engine room. "Chief."

"I hear you, sir."

"We've reached the end of the road. Open the throttles wide and get out of there and don't bother to close the hatches."

The decks vibrated as the speed increased.

The signal lamp on the destroyer flashed. "Stop and stand by to receive boarding party."

"Helmsman, steer towards the first destroyer. They won't expect that." He wandered onto the port bridge wing and waved to Bruno.

The white painted structure collapsed and one gun fired. A brilliant flash lit up the side of the destroyer. The second shot found the bridge.

The vessel veered away to port as its aft guns fired and straddled *Gradisca*. The next salvo struck like a giant hammer. The bridge superstructure buckled sending lethal splinters through the air.

"Zig zag," said Klinger as two more shells burst near. "Sixty seconds and change. Why make it easy?"

The second destroyer fired each of its four guns. Shells exploded, damaging more of the superstructure.

"Torpedoes, sir."

"Hard to port."

"Rudder not responding, sir."

Klinger lifted the lid on a steel box secured to the front of the bridge, and pressed the button. Four explosions blasted through the hull, shredding metal. The sea flooded the holds pressurising the air under the hatch covers until they burst. Two torpedoes added to the destruction. He flashed a message to the destroyer. 'I am abandoning ship.'

"Into the boat, helmsman." He sounded the ship's steam whistle six times before retreating to his cabin. From his desk he withdrew a bottle of Schnapps, filled a glass, sat in his chair and downed it in one gulp.

With the glass refilled, he returned to the bridge. Waves rolled across the forward deck.

"Captain," shouted Bruno. "We're waiting."

Klinger turned. "I have my orders and cannot leave. Good luck. The British will look after you, even if you did singe their paintwork."

The ship shuddered.

"Give my love to Hamburg. Now go before you join me."

Bruno hesitated, ran to his captain and hugged him.

"Good bye, sir." He turned and fled to the lifeboat.

An intense pain surged through his left shoulder, blood drained down his arm.

In ten minutes, the sea covered the decks from forward to aft. He stepped out and with his good arm waved, as the lifeboat with his crew drew away towards the waiting destroyer.

Gradisca listed to port. Klinger leant against the bridge bulkhead and sipped his drink.

On the lifeboat, Bruno stared as she rolled into the sea and disappeared beneath average swells in a flurry of foam.

Those in the lifeboat waited for one of the destroyers to drag them alongside a scrabbling net.

"Your war is over," shouted a sailor as he helped Bruno inboard.

He placed his right hand on the man's shoulder. "I'll be pleased when this stupid war ends. Take me to your captain."

The pale-faced sub-lieutenant standing close said, "Sir, this man is an officer and has asked to see the boss."

"Sir," said the sub, "My German is poor." He beckoned. "Come, follow me."

"My English has a Manchester twang," said Bruno. "Before this damned war, I studied at the university for five years."

Chapter Eight

November 15th 1944

Aware food would be difficult to find, Talos Dallaras placed a fishing line and spare hooks into the pouch on the front of his rucksack. Three candles along with half a box of matches in a sealed tin in another pouch. A round tin with a tight top contained his firelighters, cotton strips soaked in olive oil. To the top, he secured an oiled canvas sheet and one coarse blanket. Fastened to his leather belt, a neat canvas pouch containing an old map and compass, two water canisters and a sharp bayonet. With no car Talos and Kiki, his wife, carried one rucksack apiece, as they began their journey from their village to Thessalonica.

With little money or food they walked avoiding Russian troops along forgotten paths during the day. Before dusk arrived, Talos kept his eyes open for a good location with a natural windbreak. With the skills obtained in the resistance, he quickly constructed a rough shelter and filled it with any dry materials he could find.

Talos fished whenever possible and set snares before going to sleep. With the small animals caught and roots from untended fields they ate well. As they walked Kiki searched bushes for wild fruit. The roots became soup for lunch and the berries, breakfast. Throughout their journey their nightly ritual became routine but as they neared the city food of any description became scarce.

Ten days later, they entered a dirty and uncared for city. Russian troops, acting in a similar manner to their Nazi counterparts, stood on street corners stopping and checking the papers of those who ventured out, their actions threatening. Two soldiers stood in Talos' and Kiki's path and demanded to see their papers. While one gave them a cursory glance, the other stroked Kiki's hair. She shuddered as his rough hand touched her cheek.

Talos grabbed their papers and pulled her away.

The soldiers laughed and said something in Russian. He noted as they walked that most shops were empty of food and customers. As they made their way to his uncle's home, a scuffle broke out in a baker's shop. The police dragged a woman dressed in rags into the street, removed the half loaf she held to her chest and beat her.

Twenty minutes later, they weary couple stopped. "This is my uncle's house." He rapped on the door and waited.

The wrinkled face of an old woman leant out of a ground floor window from the next building and peered at them. "What do you want?"

Talos walked towards her. "This is the house of my uncle, my father's brother, Konstantinos Dalaras. We have travelled from the mountains to talk to him."

"You can't talk to the dead. He and his wife starved to death during the occupation. Wait, I have a key." The window shut and minutes later the woman dressed in black left her home and tottered towards him. "The key. The house is as they left it and so is the bed they died in. There's no food but I have some potatoes and mixed with wild herbs they make a tasty soup. You are welcome, come this evening."

Talos blinked slowly. A trace of sadness entered his voice. "We are from the mountains where we know death. I will tell my father his brother has died. Before we leave I will honour his name. Where are they buried?"

The woman shrugged. "I do not know. One day they were there, the next gone. When the Germans were here it was best not to ask."

For a moment there was silence. "I understand," said Talos. Your offer of soup is welcome. Thank you. You're very kind but where do I find the mayor?"

The woman smiled, her large grey eyes sparkled as she played with a small wooden cross. "Do you know George Seremetis?"

"My uncle was a clerk to a lawyer who knew him."

"A good man who has helped many of the resistance to escape. He has an office in the municipal building but he is a busy man."

"I have important information."

"Go with your wife and rest. Wash, relax, tomorrow will be here soon enough. Your information can wait."

The lock turned and they entered the dark and musty house filled with shadows, the floor covered by threadbare carpet.

The shutters creaked as Kiki opened them to let light into the rooms.

With logs from the back garden, Talos lit a fire. The flames gave cheer to an empty room.

When the water boiled in the kettle resting in the embers, she added fresh lemon juice. In silence, they relaxed and sipped the liquid.

The old woman banged on the door and shouted, "My soup is ready."

The potato soup gave warmth but little sustenance.

"Delicious and thank you," said Talos. "You must excuse us, it's been a long and tiring day."

On entering his uncle's house they climbed the stairs. The bed was as the woman described. In a chest of drawers, Kiki found clean sheets and remade it. Huddled together to keep warm they slept until the daylight woke them.

With no food in the house, Talos and Kiki left and walked hand in hand to the municipal offices. The aged building was drab and in poor condition but a uniformed man at the entrance vetted everyone before allowing admission. "Why are you here?" he asked.

"We have important business with Mayor Seremetis," said Talos.

"You can wait outside his office. When he returns he might, if he has time, talk to you. He's inspecting the harbour facilities this morning. Ships filled with food are anchored in the bay. With luck some of us might eat tonight, providing the Germans didn't booby trap the quays."

Talos and Kiki found the mayor's office and sat on the long wooden bench outside. The chill of the unheated stone building crept into their bones. For a while, they chatted but exhausted from their journey, they leant against each other and slept.

"They've been waiting for you, Mr Seremetis," said the security guard.

"How long?"

"All day."

He held up a hand. "They're in luck. I came back to retrieve files for another meeting tomorrow. I'll see them in my office."

Talos stirred as someone shook him. He snapped open his eyes and realised where he was. "What's the time?" He nudged Kiki.

"Time you were at home. The Mayor is waiting to see you. Don't waste his time, he's had a long and busy day."

Confused, they followed the man into an office where desks covered in files filled most of the space.

Seremetis leant back in his chair and steepled his fingers. "You waited the whole day to see me. Please sit and tell me why."

Talos described the attack on the trains and the avalanche in detail.

Seremetis shook his head and yawned at the same time. "I apologise but sleep is a luxury these days. It's out of my jurisdiction. What do you think I can do?"

"Supply men and heavy lifting equipment to open up the tunnel."

The mayor's sharp eyes settled on Talos. "I can't help you."

"You answer without thinking. Men who died for our country are entombed inside a mountain and you won't help."

"I can't help because I don't have the resources. You live in the mountains and it's difficult. You must realise the hard facts of life at this time. When was the last time you ate meat?"

Talos looked at him quizzically. "We ate rabbit two nights ago. Why do you ask?"

"I had one mouthful of goat, one month ago. The Germans took the food and left the people nothing. Three hundred thousand died in Athens from starvation and many more from German brutality."

The mayor looked uncomfortable. "I want to help. My conscience tells me I should, but I can't. You're concerned for the dead. I'm worried about the living. This country's on the brink of civil war and my jail is full of Nazi collaborators. Your request, if it were possible, would be the last thing on my list."

Weary, Kiki shrugged and placed her hand over Talos'. "Come, husband, we're finished here. The Mayor has explained why and I understand. Maybe one day our families will be remembered."

Talos stood and held out his hand. The mayor came round from behind his desk and with a firm grip shook it. "I'm sorry. Go back to the mountains and take care of your wife. I see she is pregnant."

Blushing, she grabbed her husband's hand, and dragged him from the office.

Hungry and cold, they returned to the house and went to bed.

The following morning they began their journey home.

Part Two

Chapter One

London England - June 2013

The high temperatures and blue skies started on the previous Friday and miraculously continued throughout the weekend. Petros Kyriades checked the forecast on his iphone; outlook wall-to-wall sunshine.

He pushed his helmet visor down and straddled his BMW. The engine started on the turn of the key. It idled for a few moments before he engaged gear. The traffic remained light until the outskirts of the city.

At the rear of Andreas' Bistro, he stopped, dismounted, removed his helmet and entered by the main door.

The lunchtime rush remained an hour away as Andreas polished the glass counter. "The accounts are on the table by the window. Coffee?"

Petros smiled at his property manager. "I don't know why I check these." He pointed at the ledgers. "You account for every transaction to the nearest penny."

He shrugged. "Because once a year, you have to present them to your accountant."

Petros grabbed the mug of black coffee and sat by the window. One by one, he flipped the pages, making notes on his pad as he sipped his coffee. Finished, he closed the books. "I'm bored out of my skull."

The entrance slammed open and two youths charged in. "Give me the fucking money," shouted the taller of the two as he wielded a long-bladed kitchen knife.

The other glanced at Petros. "Stay where you are or you're fucking dead."

Petros stood and fixed his eyes on the thug. "Leave while you can still walk."

The smaller laughed. "Hark at this geezer, Jimmy."

Jimmy screamed. "I told you not to use my name, arsehole."

In an instant Petros stooped, lifted the ledger, and hurled it as a Frisbee.

Spinning, it struck Jimmy on the back of the head. Stunned, he raised the hand with the knife, staggered and tumbled to the floor.

"What did you say, arsehole? Move and I'm dead." Petros charged forward.

Arsehole turned. Andreas struck him in the face with a cast iron saucepan. With blood pouring from his nose, he fell back, hit his head on the wall and collapsed.

Petros noticed Jimmy attempting to slither away and stamped hard on his right knee. "What do you want to do with these reprobates?"

For good measure, Andreas kicked both hard in the balls. "Chuck them out with the rubbish and forget they were ever here."

"Do you fancy having fun?"

"Now I know you're bored," Andreas said.

"Strip them and toss them in the dock. They could do with a wash."

Andreas checked no one was around and with Petros, dragged the naked semi-conscious thugs to the edge of the quay.

"Anything you want to say?" said Petros.

"You broke my fucking leg."

"Me, I saw you slip when you went for a swim and I have a witness."

"One, two, three," said Andreas. With a boot in the centre of their backs, Jimmy and his mate tumbled into the cold, dirty water.

Petros contacted the police on his mobile but kept his eyes on the floundering pair.

"I can't swim," shouted Jimmy.

"I can't hear you," said Petros, "I'm deaf."

The police arrived in a launch and with the dexterous use of a boat hook, they dragged the hapless creatures inboard.

On returning to the bistro, Petros lifted and dumped the thugs' clothes into a refuse bin. "They won't be back."

Andreas chuckled. "The joke's on them." He pressed a button on the electronic till and the drawer opened. "Ten pounds in loose change. When my lunchtime customers arrive, they bring the correct money. Saves so much time when you have one hour away from your desk. If those two idiots came this afternoon they would have taken hundreds."

"Two short planks have more brain power. Good job Bear wasn't here."

"Oh. Before I forget. Do you remember at my wedding chatting to a relative of mine?"

"Things got a bit hazy. Something about he'd lost a train. I gave him my card and told him to contact me."

"Not quite. It's a village tale from nineteen-forty-four, just before the Russian army liberated Greece. I grew up with the story. Anyway, he Skyped and asked if I could have a word. He believes a train full of stolen artefacts is inside the mountains. What I know to be true is, in the late sixties, the Greek authorities retrieved two German steam engines from a gorge a two-day walk from my village. Human bones littered the area. No one knows if they were Greek, German, or Italian. The engines, although badly damaged, were returned to Germany for restoration."

"So what is your uncle asking?"

Andreas lowered his head. "It's my fault. I exaggerated your escapades in China and Libya and he believes you and Bear are the men to find the train, his last chance so to speak. If you went to my village, carried out a cursory search, and found nothing, that would be the end. I'll pay whatever it costs."

Petros stood and walked to the large map of Greece on the far wall. "Where's your village?"

Andreas joined him and pointed. "There's a valley in the mountains where the resistance lived during the war. The Germans destroyed many communities including ours. When the Russian army liberated my country, the decision to stay where we were was unanimous. The government built roads and connected power lines. As a child I loved it."

Petros shrugged. "Let me have a chat with Maria. She wasn't happy when Bear stuck his head in the way of a bullet. If she says I can go, I'll talk to Bear but I know his answer. Because I'm bored, you get five days on the house, after, it's one thousand a day plus costs. If what you say is correct I'll be finished in three."

"When will you know?"

"I'll ring you later."

Petros turned his head as a uniformed police officer entered the bistro. Tall, with an athletic build, he placed both hands on the counter and smiled at Andreas. "I believe a couple of young men gave you some trouble this morning."

"You mean those two who went for a swim. You'd better get them to a hospital for jabs. There're dead rats and dogs floating in there."

The officer's eyes lit up. "Their statement says you and a blond-haired customer beat them up, stripped and threw them in the water."

"Why would they lie?" asked Petros.

A smile formed on his lips. "I've no idea, sir, but as information decides what we might charge them with, I thought I'd better visit and check it out. Those two need putting away."

"It's a warm day. Maybe they thought it a good idea," said Petros.

"You might be right, sir. Oh, the rubbish bin outside, I suggest you shift it elsewhere. My colleagues will be visiting to take a statement later."

***

Petros sipped his coffee and studied Maria as she piled one brick on top of another for Alysa who took great pleasure in knocking them over.

His coffee finished, he placed the mug in the sink. "How would a few weeks in Cyprus suit you, Alysa, and mama?"

Before she had a chance to answer Alysa repeated, "name, name, name."

Maria rearranged the bricks to spell ALYSA.

She pointed to Charlie. "My name."

Charlie, a full grown Alsatian, glanced at her, barked and rested his head on his cushion.

Alysa grabbed the five bricks, sat on the floor in front of Charlie and proceeded to spell out her name. When she finished she shouted, "Name"

"She's growing; next year she'll be going to school," said Maria.

"You haven't answered my question."

"If it's a collection the answer's no."

"It's more of a favour to Andreas. We could all fly to Larnaca. I need at most three days. After, we can do the family bit."

"Tell me more and I'll think about it."

Petros reiterated the story as told by Andreas. "Maria, I love you and Alysa but my property business is managed by Andreas. My father and my brothers complete repairs almost before the tenant puts the phone down. I've cruised from Teddington lock up to the shallow end of the Thames half a dozen times. I need something more."

"What you're saying is your family is not enough."

A look of shock filled his face. "No I'm not, and if it were true I wouldn't be asking, I'd have gone."

She pulled him close. "Twenty-four-seven is not easy. I realise you need more in your life but collecting is what you do. I knew your business when I met and married you but as this is a good deed for Andreas, you can go but you'll visit the family in Cyprus when you return from Greece. How many days did you say?"

"I promised five but reckon three at most."

"Are you taking Bear?"

"I'd like to but..."

"I'll have a word with Jocelyn."

"I knew I married you for a reason." He kissed her full on the lips.

"Papa. Name," said Alysa.

He selected six bricks and placed them in order between Alysa and Charlie. "My name."

She brushed them away. "Not Alysa."

"Dog, fancy a walk along the river?"

"Not Dog, Yarlie. Me walk along the river with Yarlie."

Petros turned to Maria. "Want to come?"

"Might as well. The fresh air may tire madam."

Alysa stood on a stool and opened the main door. "There's a first," said Maria.

Charlie and Alysa raced across the garden to the water's edge. Hand in hand, Petros and Maria followed.

***

At eleven the next morning, Petros pressed Bear's bell push. The door opened and Bear's frame almost filled the narrow hallway as he leant against the wall.

"You're late. I expected you an hour ago. You don't have to worry, Maria phoned Jocelyn and explained your trip to Greece when you left this morning"

"I need your help. It's a favour for Andreas. He wants us to put a ghost to bed."

Bear took a deep breath. "Come in. Coffee?"

"Please."

Bear filled two cups from the bubbling percolator and placed them on the kitchen table.

"How can I help?"

"The same as you always do. Be there to pull me out of the shit."

Bear leaned forwards, his elbows on the table. "I know you better than you know yourself. You're bored and stubborn enough to go it alone. I gather we might be clambering over mountains. We'll need the proper gear."

"A map of the area would be useful. Climbing equipment, we'll buy in Thessalonica. You don't happen to have blonde Bob's phone number?"

"That rascal's flying helicopters for the oil and gas rigs."

"Make contact. We might need a pilot in a rush."

"When are we leaving?"

"I'm giving a talk to the sixth form at my old school next week but I'll let you know soonest."

"In truth, I'm bored to death doing nothing. At least this is something."

"You and me both." He stood. "Stay where you are. I'll let myself out."

Bear followed to the door. "Blue skies for a week, must be summer."

Petros gazed at the clear sky, excited by the prospect locating a missing train. As a favour to Andreas, Maria's approval would drag him out of a rut. He strolled towards Tower Hill underground station with a spring in his step.

He checked the time. With the sun on his face, he chose to walk the three miles to Stanfords Map Shop in Covent Garden. Maps of Greece seemed plentiful but in the end, he required an assistant to find a detailed map showing the topography of northern Greece.

On the train home, he studied the location pointed out by Andreas. The absence of a railway line surprised him but he noted the many roads.

***

"Bear phoned," said Maria as he closed the main door. "He wants you to call him back."

He punched a memory button on his mobile.

"Blonde Bob's not flying for the next couple of weeks, maybe more. The air safety people have grounded their machines. Something to do with gearbox problems."

"That's good news for us. Contact Charles Haskell and ask if he can arrange a chopper from Thessalonica. We'll supply the pilot."

"It'll be an arm and a leg job."

"I know but it means we can be in and out in a couple of days. I'll charge it to expenses. My accountant can make it tax deductable or something. Whatever, it's better than walking for four days with a pack on your back."

"You're getting old."

"Older and wiser. I have the money; why not use it to our advantage."

"Can't disagree. Oh, blonde Bob says whatever the job, seven-fifty a day plus expenses. I said I'd be in touch."

***

Petros arrived at his old school and parked his ancient BMW in the playground, pausing as he did to study the once familiar scene. A sign in bold black letters directed him to the administration office.

Mary White stopped staring at the screen of her word processor and lifted her gaze. She smiled. "Petros Kyriades, the headmaster's in the library with the sixth form. You'd better hurry, in two minutes you'll be late."

He chuckled before saying as he walked away. "Don't

think I'll get detention."

Wearing blue jeans, a white shirt with no tie and an Armani black blazer, he opened the door to the library and strolled in. "Good morning, Headmaster, Ladies and Gentlemen."

Headmaster Georgiadis Stamati stood. "May I introduce Mr Petros Kyriades, a former pupil of our school. As an entrepreneur, I invited him to speak on the problems of running and operating a property empire."

"Thank you, Headmaster." He took the one empty chair, turned it round, sat and leant on the back. "To begin with my advice to you all is simple. Other than hard work, planning and living a balanced life, ignore everything adults tell you. The world I lived in is not the same as the one you are about to enter and so the lessons are different. What I will do is answer any questions you wish to ask."

For a few seconds the room became silent.

A young man with cropped black hair stood. "Mr Kyriades, can you explain how you entered the property business?"

Petros grinned. "I had a stroke of luck, made some money and invested it in a couple of apartments. From that day, any money I made I put into property."

A young curvaceous girl wearing a tight white blouse, short skirt, stood and smiled. "Mr Kyriades, rumour has it you were thrown out of the army and became a mercenary. Is it true?"

Georgiadis jumped from his chair. "Miss Biros, your question will not be answered by our guest."

"I have no problem with the question, Headmaster. Young lady, it's no secret I was once in the regular army. I made a mistake, resigned my commission to save any embarrassment. I loved the excitement of army life and believed the same existed as a mercenary. I was wrong, it's tough and the pension plan is lousy. My first and only mission became a total disaster but one good thing came out of it, I met my best friend and sort of adopted a baby girl."

Another boy, his face covered in acne stood. "Mr Kyriades, why was the mission a disaster?"

Petros turned to Georgiadis. "I'm happy to tell the story, Headmaster."

Georgiadis nodded.

"I'll keep it short. At the end of our patrol, we, that is, the officers and troops, expected to return to base in the comfort of a Hercules. Unfortunately, we walked straight into a trap planned by the guerrillas whose political objective was to overthrow the government.

"I rested my men in the shade of a dry ravine a good distance from the runway. This actually saved our lives. The guerrillas attacked the rest of the force, but we were far enough away to evade capture. When the assault ended, my men decided enough was enough and chose to return to their own villages. On checking our map, my sergeant and I needed to walk four hundred miles to reach safety."

A hand shot in the air.

"You have a question?"

"Sir, what happened to the survivors of the attack at the airstrip?"

"There weren't any. With the Angolan border four hundred miles away all we had to do was stroll through forests, swamps and negotiate a few hills at night."

"Sir," said a fair-haired, overweight boy. "Why at night?"

"Think about it." He paused for a few moments. "Walking in the sun will dehydrate you fast. Unless you drink plenty of water, you'll die. All we had between us was two water bottles, so we rested during the heat of the day and searched for water holes at dawn and dusk along with the animals.

"The baby I mentioned we found alongside her dead mother. Now you have to imagine two grown men and a baby with no food in the middle of nowhere. The next few hundred miles were not funny but we managed to feed the child and keep ourselves alive.

"We named her Lucy which is lucky spelt badly and left her with a priest. From that moment, our luck turned. In a Luanda hotel, a farmer exiled from Zimbabwe offered us a job to collect some items from his farm. The money I made from this I invested in property and my second company, where I have a fifty percent share, The Collectors, came into being. Before you ask, my friend, Bear Morris, the sergeant, has similar holdings. He is also a man I'd trust with my life. Out of interest, those with ten friends or more raise your hands."

He grinned as everyone raised their hands. "I'll not say any of you are wrong but most of your friends will not be around after you've left school. If later in life you have five good friends, you can count yourself fortunate."

A dark-skinned girl stood and waited for Petros to finish.

He smiled at her. "You have a question?"

"Your business partner is Mr William Morris and I understand his parents were from the Caribbean. Does the colour of his skin cause you any difficulties?"

"Not that I'm aware of or is there something I don't know? I have never judged a person by the colour of their skin or background. Bear Morris is everything a man could want in a friend. As I stated previously, I trust him with not only my life but those of my wife and daughter."

The questions continued for another thirty minutes before

Georgiades called a halt. "Thank you, Petros. I can't say it's what I imagined this session would be but I believe my students found it interesting from the normal career discussion they have attended during the last year."

"My pleasure, Headmaster." He turned to the students. "Thank you for the questions and for listening."

Chapter Two

Ten days later Bear and Jocelyn, Petros, Maria, Alysa and his mother Zena, arrived at Larnaca airport. Photis spotted them and hurried through the arriving horde. Even though now aged over eighty, he appeared a fit man. His head of grey hair was combed straight back from his forehead.

He grabbed Alysa and kissed her, hugged and kissed Zena, Maria and Jocelyn before greeting Petros and Bear.

Alysa struggled in his arms. "I'm a big girl. I walk on my own."

Photis laughed. "Would you like to hold my hand?"

She peered up at him. "Mama says you are uncle Photis."

"I am and you'll be living in my house for a few weeks while your papa is away working."

"Will aunt Eleni be there?"

He took her hand. "She's waiting to see you."

Photis turned to the others. "Eleni is not well but looking forward to your visit."

They strolled to the car park where a dark blue Mitsubishi pick-up waited. No longer did it shine as new. Layers of dust covered every part.

"Petros, will you drive? I tire easily these days."

"No problem."

The women along with Alysa sat in the rear while Bear secured their cases.

Petros slid behind the wheel and turned the ignition. Photis and Bear jumped in the front passenger seat.

"When we're near Limassol directions might be handy, Photis."

"He's asleep," said Maria. "Don't worry, I know the way. If you want I'll drive."

"It's okay," said Petros, "I'll be fine once I'm on the Troodos road."

Two missed turnings and an hour later Petros turned off the ignition and helped Photis to the ground.

Alysa jumped out and studied everything before she noticed Eleni sat in the shade of the many vines. The others watched as she skipped towards her.

"Are you aunt Eleni?"

"I am."

"Are you old?"

"I was old when you were born. Do you know who this is?"

Alysa looked intently at a photograph before pointing. "That's mama and papa with me in the middle, when I was a baby. I'm nearly five."

Zena and Maria stood at Eleni's side, bent and kissed her on the cheek.

"Shall I make some coffee?" said Zena.

Eleni grabbed her hand. "Please, Photis has to look after me these days. It will be nice to have women in the house and of course you, Alysa."

"I'm a girl," said Alysa.

"And don't we know it," said Petros.

"Papa wouldn't bring Yarlie."

"And who is Yarlie?" said Eleni.

"He's a full grown Alsatian who dotes on her. She can do no wrong. He's better off at home with my brother taking care of him. It's too hot in Cyprus."

Eleni held Alysa's hand. "Your papa is right about Yarlie. And anyway, he will be waiting when you get home."

Bear and Petros carried their luggage inside and up the stairs. Both noticed the once pristine house although clean was not up to Eleni's standards.

"We get old," said Bear.

"With mama, Maria and Jocelyn here it'll soon be as it was. I'll have a word with Maria and see if we can arrange for a live-in housekeeper."

They dumped their suitcases in what appeared to be the correct rooms and returned to the courtyard.

Maria handed out the mugs of coffee and lemonade for Alysa.

"Aunt Eleni, did Photis tell you Bear and I are leaving tomorrow to visit Thessalonica for a few days? Our flight's at six in the morning, so we'll get a taxi to the airport."

She smiled and nodded.

"Zena, Maria," said Photis, "I have enough food in the kitchen for our meal tonight."

Zena moved towards him and held his arm. "While I am here, leave everything to me. You look after aunt Eleni."

He leant back on the wall of the fountain in the courtyard and sipped his coffee. "That will be good for Eleni."

Exhausted, everyone retired early.

Chapter Three

With the minimum of luggage, Petros and Bear flew out of Larnaca to Thessalonica at six in the morning. Bear slept until Athens where a change of aircraft was necessary.

In the arrivals area Zane Vasco checked the time and held up a placard with the name Petros Kyriades.

Clear of customs and immigration, Bear and Petros strolled through the barrier.

"There's our man," said Petros as they strode across the concourse.

"Thank you, thank you for helping an old man and his dream. I have a car waiting to take you to my village."

"Our pleasure," said Petros. "Your English is good but I speak Greek."

"Your friend doesn't. To be polite we will speak English."

"It'll be a lot easier. Back to this train of yours, will we need climbing equipment?"

Zane paused. "If it is necessary there's plenty in Florina the next village."

"How come?" asked Bear.

"Tourists. In the winter they find it difficult in the mountains and we have a rescue team."

"You wouldn't have a helicopter handy?" said Petros.

Zane frowned. "Why would you need a helicopter?"

"It saves walking," said Bear.

"I believe there are many private helicopters at the airport."

Petros turned to Bear. "Call blonde Bob, the job's on."

"Do I agree the price?"

"Zane can a helicopter land in your village?"

77

"On the football field there's plenty of room. Why?"

"One will be landing tomorrow morning."

Zane rubbed his chin. "Not a good idea. I suggest the helipad in Florina. It's not in use this time of year and you can refuel."

"Makes sense," said Bear.

"Make the call to Bob, Bear. Ask her to be in Florina as near to ten o'clock as is possible. I'll arrange a fuel tanker."

They arrived at a black Mercedes saloon. A tall man with an angular face and dark-brown hair waited.

"My brother-in-law's son, Laith."

Laith extended his right hand. Bear grasped it and noted the strong grip.

Petros chose to squeeze until the other's grip loosened.

Laith grinned. "I like you. You're not city wimps out to con an old man."

Petros looked him square in the eye. "We're not out to con anyone. We promised Andreas we would help. No charge was mentioned."

The young man inclined his body towards Zane. "My uncle drives us mad talking about this damned train. In some ways, I hope you find it, if only to shut him up. Don't get me wrong, in our village we love him but two unknowns from London. What were we to think?"

"And one is black," said Bear.

"The colour of a man's skin is not important. It's what's in his heart. Jump in, it's a long drive and it'll be dark when we get there." Laith opened the driver's door and sat behind the wheel.

Bear leant on the car. "I hate to mention this but we missed out on breakfast and an aircraft snack wouldn't sustain a mouse. I suggest as it's a long journey we eat."

Zane turned to Laith. "Anywhere local?"

"Jump in, I know a place."

Twenty minutes later Laith stopped on the gravel parking area outside a traditional roadside taverna. "Their speciality is chicken kebabs. I recommend them."

The four men entered the stone building and a small bearded man wearing thick-framed glasses welcomed them. "I'm Stavros. Welcome. You are on holiday?"

"We're from the mountains in the north," said Zane. "I'm told your chicken kebabs are good."

"My food is cooked fresh There is none better." He directed them to a table set for four. "Something to drink?"

Zane ordered sketos. Laith, metrios, Bear, nescafe, and Petros, a fresh orange juice.

"And a dozen chicken kebabs with your chilli sauce," said Laith.

In Greek Petros added, "Make that eighteen, my friend eats well."

Stavros left them chatting and returned with their drinks, fresh bread rolls and a bowl of salad. "My wife is preparing your kebabs."

Bear grabbed a roll and crammed it full with salad. "Rabbit food."

Twenty minutes later Stavros deposited a large platter covered in kebabs and a bowl containing an overpowering red liquid on the table. "Enjoy."

Bear dipped a piece of roll into the sauce and stuffed it into his mouth. "That is fantastic."

Zane and Laith stared at him.

"If Bear says it's good, it is," said Petros.

With the platter empty and Bear's hunger pangs satisfied, Petros paid Stavros and they continued their journey.

***

The wide road wound through mountains and wooded areas. Bear slept and Petros studied his map. "Zane, not many railway lines in this area."

He turned his head towards him. "Not economical. In the early twentieth century, steam locomotives serviced one town in every area. During the war, the Italians utilised the rail network to its full potential and the Germans capitalised on their efforts. You could catch a train in Athens and alight in Berlin.

"Today the car is king. The upkeep of tracks in the mountains is not cost effective. Roads are cheaper."

The others slept while Laith drove through the night until they reached the town of Florina close to the border with Macedonia. He stopped the car outside a house, which appeared freshly white-washed, and jumped out. "Zane will drive from here to his village. I'm going to bed."

Zane, Petros and Bear alighted, stretched and walked back and forth along the road.

Bear glanced at his watch. "Anywhere a man can find something to eat?"

"When we reach my village you will have a feast for breakfast," said Zane.

"If I survive," said Bear.

"I'll drive," said Petros, "Just give me directions."

Petros slid behind the wheel, adjusted the seat and started the engine.

"Straight ahead, turn right at the third crossroads."

The road from Florina remained good and wide until the turn off for Zane's village. At some time a concrete slab existed but combined with a lack of money and winter rain it now resembled a farm track.

"How far?" asked Petros.

"Twenty kilometres but the higher we go the better it gets."

"I believe you."

At seven kilometres, the road became asphalt single track with sections cut out of the rock for passing places.

"Before they cut the road the donkey remained our only form of transport," said Zane.

Surprised at what he saw, Petros drove into a modern village complete with cobbled square and a taverna.

"Completely rebuilt," said Zane. "During the war our latrines were holes in the ground at the far end and our home one large room where we lived. In case of a surprise attack we slept in tents dotted across the hillsides. We lived to fight and survive. A permanent roof over your head, luxury." He pointed. "Stop the car outside Sophie's Taverna."

Sophie's was the largest two storey building in the square, built in the Greek style and painted white with blue shutters. Other buildings formed terraces or were large houses in their own plots.

Petros' eyes scanned the square. "I like this place."

"Sophie speaks good English. She studied as a girl in London. I've booked two rooms and breakfast will be ready when you want."

Bear's stomach rumbled for all to hear. "Now would be good."

Zane chuckled and entered the main room of the taverna. "Sophie, my friends are here. Is their breakfast ready?"

A well-proportioned woman strolled into the main room with a plate filled with bread and pastries. "Hot. Fresh from my oven." She pointed to a table. "Cheese, yoghurt, cold cuts of meat, olives, boiled eggs, spinach pies, cereals and I'll make tea or coffee for you in a minute."

"Should silence your stomach until lunch time," said Zane.

Bear pulled up a chair and began with the hot bread and cheese. "PK, this bread is delicious and the cheese a present from the gods."

"I'll wash my hands and rinse my face first and then eat. Give me your bag." Petros lifted the bags and traipsed after Sophie to the rear of the house.

"Two rooms, clean and large bed for your friend."

"Thank you," said Petros

Sophie smiled. "You speak English with a touch of Greek."

"My mother's Cypriot and I was born there."

"Unusual, a blond-haired Cypriot." She opened a door. "Bathroom."

"Tell my friend to leave me some food. I'll be down in a minute."

"Don't worry, there's plenty more in my kitchen."

***

Bear grabbed a paper serviette, wiped his mouth and hands. He turned to Petros who nibbled on a roll. "Now my body's replenished, what's next? Where's this train?"

Petros gazed at him across the table. "Zane told me it's a day and a half stroll through the mountains."

"Why can't we drive?"

"No roads."

Bear checked his iphone for messages. "Blonde Bob will be in Florina at ten thirty. Fuel is ordered for her arrival."

"It's the best way," said Petros.

Bear belched. "Somehow I don't think Zane would make it if we took a stroll through the mountains."

"Charming. When he returns we drive back to Florina and hire some climbing equipment."

Chapter Four

Blonde Bob checked the controls one more time before operating the collective and the craft lifted into clear sky. With a quick glance at her note-book she adjusted her course and speed, levelling out at one thousand feet.

***

Showered and changed into clothes more suited to travel in the rugged landscape, Petros and Bear enjoyed another cup of coffee while they waited.

Bear glanced out the window overlooking the main street. "Here he comes and bloody hell, he's driving what looks like a world war two jeep."

Petros stood. "Let's go." They strolled out into the street.

Bear side-stepped out of the way as Zane stopped the vehicle. "Where on earth did you find that?"

"Seventy years ago these marvellous machines littered the landscape. No one came to collect them so along with others we retrieve many." He stopped and thought for a moment. "We salvaged twenty-five, give or take."

"Collectors of world war two vehicles would give an arm and a leg for one."

Zane shrugged. "Maybe they would but they're not for sale. Jump in."

"Full speed to the helipad in Florina," said Petros. "A friend of ours is arriving soon and we'll need climbing equipment."

"We can borrow the rescue gear; they have rucksacks ready to go. Their team leader's a friend." He rubbed his chin. "Of course a suitable donation might help."

"How suitable?" said Petros.

"A few hundred Euros."

"Good as done. Bear, how much cash are you carrying?"

Bear shook his head with a smile on his face. "Enough."

The jeep, unlike the car, traversed the road to Florina with little difficulty. A dry-stone wall enclosed the helipad field and a large sign stated '**No Unauthorised Admittance**'.

Zane stopped the jeep as the rattle of helicopter rotors filled the air. Each man stared into the sky as a Eurocopter 120 swooped across the field, hovered and landed in the centre of the pad. The engine noise wound down, the rotors stopped and the pilot, helmet in hand, slid out of the seat to the ground.

Blonde Bob's blue denim outfit fitted the curves of her slender but firm body to perfection. In her late thirties, she was tall, with the face of an angel framed by long blonde hair. Swinging her helmet, she strode towards them. She shook her head. "Bear, long time no see. Give me a kiss."

Bear hugged and kissed her on the lips.

"The passion's missing, you must be shagging someone." She glanced sidelong at Petros with her blue-grey-eyes. "I've heard a lot about you but you're married."

Petros shrugged. "They tell me you can fly a chopper." He pointed to the mountains.

Blonde Bob grinned, revealing a mouthful of perfect teeth. "I can fly through the gates of hell, put the fire out and shag the devil before he realises. Good enough?"

The roar of a heavy diesel engine ended the conversation. "My fuel," said Bob with a smile on her lips.

Bob supervised the refuelling of the helicopter personally and only when satisfied did she nod to Petros. "Pay him. Who's this old man?"

While Petros handed over a wad of Euros, Bear

introduced her to Zane.

"Any young men in your village?"

"Behave," said Bear.

"Don't worry, I'll be a good girl. But you know me, when I'm good I'm very, very, good and when I'm bad, I'm even better."

"Don't go there," said Bear.

"When can we leave?" asked Petros.

She smiled sweetly. "Five minutes. I need a pee. Where's the loo?"

"Behind the wall," said Bear.

"No problem but no peeking. You can wait in the chopper."

As she wandered away, the three men sauntered across to the Eurocopter.

"How good is she?"

"None better," said Bear.

They fell silent. Bob secured her safety straps. "Everyone tied in? These things can get bumpy. Where to, granddad?"

Zane frowned." This is my first time."

She laughed. "I remember my first time. The prat didn't have a good fuck in him."

Zane said nothing, but a large grin covered his face.

With the checks complete, she started the engine and waited. Her eyes moved methodically across the instrument panel as the chopper rose into the air.

Through the intercom system, Zane spoke and pointed towards the mountains. "Head towards the flat top. From there I should see the old track."

She nodded as the craft lifted. The tops of trees metres below folded as they hurtled across. A forest of tall pines covered the landscape. "Keep talking to me, old man, you know where we're going."

Zane nodded and pointed ahead. "Why do they call you Bob?"

There was a brief uneasy silence. "My dad wanted a boy and named me Roberta. I hated it and when I joined the army someone called me Blonde Bob and it stuck."

"You were in the army?"

"Don't sound so surprised, old man. One of their top pilots until I fucked up in Iraq. They gave me a choice, courts marshal or resign my commission."

Zane nodded his understanding. "We all make mistakes and have to live with the consequences."

"I didn't make a mistake but some high ranking wanker fucked up and dropped me in the shit. Keep me on target, old man."

"You're going in the right direction but I have never seen the location from the air." His voice revealed a hint of uncertainty.

"Bear, I fly this thing for two hours in one direction then I return for fuel. What are we supposed to be looking for?"

"A seventy year old rail track concealed by a ton of foliage."

"Descend," shouted Zane.

"Do you want me to land or simply fly at ground level?"

"Land and let me get my bearings."

"Anywhere in particular?"

Zane pointed to the remains of an abandoned stone farmhouse. "At the front of that building or as near as you can get."

"Bear, you're my eyes. I intend to land on the hunk of grey stone to the right of the ruin."

Bob checked the wind direction and with Bear giving

instructions settled the chopper on top of the boulder.

Zane peered left and right. "We are close to the gorge, I'm certain." He pointed. "Fly towards those trees."

The noise of the engine increased and they lifted into the air.

"There's the gorge," shouted Zane. "The old track wound around the mountains. There should be what remains of a bridge to our left."

Bob banked the chopper and followed the contour of the mountain.

"One bent and twisted bridge, old man."

"Now go in the other direction and look for a suitable landing site."

"Trees and more trees," said Bob.

"To the right," said Petros.

"Hey, hawk eye's right." The Eurocopter flew straight towards the mountain and hovered over a blackened area. "Should be okay. Bear, Petros, keep your eyes open for anything. I'm going to land."

Both men positioned themselves and studied the ground beneath them.

"Looks good," said Bear.

"I second that," said Petros.

With faultless control Bob descended until her eyes told her all was clear. The wheels touched, she breathed deeply, switched the engine off and jumped out. With long strides she orbited the craft, tripped, and fell to the ground. She stood, brushed the rubbish from her clothes, and beckoned to Petros and Bear. She pointed to a pair of rust-covered tracks. "Found your railway."

Zane joined them. "Now we walk."

"You walk," said Bob. "I'm staying with the chopper."

Petros nodded. "Zane, how far?"

He hesitated before speaking. "It's many years since I was here. I'll be honest, I don't know."

Petros scanned the way ahead. "Bob." She stopped what she was doing.

"I intend to return one hour before sunset. If we're not back, you fly to Florina and collect us in the morning."

"I can fly in the dark."

"Never said you couldn't but a double bed is better than sleeping rough. You could even get lucky."

Bob gave out a dirty laugh. "Good thinking."

Bear handed Petros one rucksack and shouldered the other. "We're wasting time. Zane, you lead and we'll follow."

They walked in line through long dead grass and trees. The surface of the old railway track and the remnants of metal ties and plates gave assurance.

Three hours later Zane stopped. Petros and Bear joined him.

Bear placed his hand on Zane's shoulder. "You okay?"

He pointed. "Up there is where my grandfather waited when the earthquake struck. I recognise the overhang where he sheltered."

Bear dropped his rucksack, walked a short distance and returned. "Makes sense, we have a gorge over there, flat surface and a mountain. Ahead the slope into the gorge indicates a shift of earth and rocks. Under there might be a train and a tunnel. The odds aren't high that anything survived."

"Suggestions?" said Petros.

"Let Zane rest, while we complete a recon."

Without their rucksacks, Petros and Bear clambered up the shallow incline checking as they went. An hour elapsed before they stopped and rested.

"Nothing," said Bear

"Ditto. This, from what Zane described, was the exit from the tunnel. How about we climb to the top, drop down, and find the entrance?"

Bear's eyes wandered over the steep hillside. "Might as well give it a try, providing this lot doesn't move."

"The weather, grass and tree roots should have tied it together. Come on, shift your fat arse."

With caution, they tested every foot and handhold before they ascended. They rested in an area of sparse variation.

"This hasn't moved in donkeys'," said Bear. "The fault line and slide are over there. If it didn't collapse, the tunnel's under our feet"

"Might as well find where the entrance should be before we go back."

"Seeing as we're here, why not? Then you can tell Zane the truth; his tunnel's gone."

"One step at a time. I'd rather not fall into any large holes."

"Small ones will twist or break an ankle," said Bear.

"Thanks a bunch, I didn't know that."

"Just watch your step."

The shrubbery as they descended a slight slope changed to woodland along with a vast canopy, which filtered the sunlight.

"Shit," shouted Bear as his foot caught on a root and he tumbled headlong. Thorny bushes tore at his clothes and face as he rolled into a narrow channel.

"Where are you?" shouted Petros.

"Follow my voice but mind those damned roots."

In the middle of a mass of long grass and scrub he found him. "Sat on your fat arse as usual."

"Okay, smarty knickers. Take a gander at this." He pointed to a crevasse. "Another metre or so and goodbye cruel world."

"Are you thinking the same as me?"

"Yeah, but not today. We need the proper gear before we enter this black hole."

Petros shook his head. "Naturally, but we need a marker."

"A pile of stones to identify the spot."

They rummaged around and built a tall cairn. Bear stripped a long branch and shoved it in the centre.

"Small piles marking our return route will make it easier tomorrow," said Bear.

As they descended to the old track insignificant piles of stones indicated their route.

The rattle of stones woke Zane from his sleep. "Did you find anything?"

"Not Sure," said Petros. "We discovered a large crack in the rock. Tomorrow and with the right gear we'll check it out."

They picked up their rucksacks and returned to where Bob waited.

"Any luck?"

"Maybe," said Bear. "We wasted six hours today walking. Can you get this chopper any closer?"

"Let's have a look." With the pre-flight checks completed she started the engine. "I'll fly along the ravine and you lot can scan the area for an empty parking spot. I'll tell you if it's feasible."

Bob lifted the chopper, drifted into the centre of the gorge and hovered. "As far as I can see, far too many trees."

"There's the landslip," said Bear. He chuckled. "It took us three hours to walk and fifteen minutes to fly. Bob, go higher there's a flat area further up."

With a gentle caress of the controls, the craft rose up the side of the mountain. "I can see where you mean. I'll take a gander."

The Eurocopter hovered at twenty metres and in stages descended. The two inboard wheels touched the grass and stone-covered slope.

"I prefer to land on the level. Bear, Petros, jump out and position large rocks under my outboard wheels. If I'm happy I land, if not, tomorrow you jump and I'll return later."

The two men opened the door and slid to the ground. With their heads low they scrambled clear from the down draught and began to lift and tumble largish rocks. On finding what appeared suitable, they lifted and placed one slab in position. Finding and locating the second took time.

Both men stood at a safe distance and noticed the pure concentration on Bob's face as the craft hovered. Zane pointed when Bear gave the thumbs up.

The wheels touched earth, the inboard nestled into the ground and the outboard on solid rock.

The searchlight flashed and Zane motioned to Bear and Petros to return.

Heads low they were inside the craft in seconds.

"What do you reckon?" asked Petros.

"I can drop you and any gear but the ground's unstable. Get yourselves a radio to contact me when you want me to pick you up."

"Let's go home," said Bear, "I'm starving."

"You haven't changed." The chopper rose into the sky, climbing so fast that Petros gripped the armrests and closed his eyes. It banked unexpectedly and headed for Florina.

Chapter Five

"What's the plan?" asked Bear as he shovelled a forkful of toast and scrambled egg into his mouth. After removing a few crumbs from his lips with a paper napkin, he belched.

Petros sipped his fresh orange juice. "Do you have to do that?"

"Sign of good food."

"If you say so. Anyway, Zane's in town borrowing two search and rescue radios. Bob, I hope, is refuelling the chopper. You and I wait until they arrive and then we return to the crevasse."

"I reckon the tunnel will be there but not a lot else. After seventy years, whoever died in there will have decomposed. A few brittle bones and bits of clothing but not a lot more."

"Trains rust and rot," said Petros. "With luck the artefacts will have been well wrapped and in crates."

Bear smothered a fresh roll with butter and marmalade. "What remains isn't our problem. Zane informs the authorities and we return to Cyprus."

"I hear Bob."

Bear devoured his roll, grabbed four meat pies, enclosed them in a napkin, and shoved the package into his rucksack. "Behind you."

They ran at the double to the end of town where Bob and Zane waited. Heads low they clambered into the rear seats of the Eurocopter. As their safety belts clicked, they were on the move. Bob activated the sat-nav control and flew directly to the drop-off point.

"Much better than walking," said Bear.

"Uses less fuel," said Bob. "Arm and a leg job to top this thing up."

Petros grimaced. "I don't want to know."

Over the intercom Bob spoke. "Don't forget the radio check."

"No problem," said Bear. "I've no intention of walking for three hours."

Within thirty minutes, the chopper descended and hovered one metre over the ground.

"I pray you find something," said Zane.

With their rucksacks slung over their arms, Petros and Bear jumped.

Bob waved, climbed to a hundred metres and flew back along the ravine while completing a radio check. "Hear you loud and clear. Don't get into trouble. See you later."

"Out," said Bear as they climbed to the crevasse.

Petros scanned the locale. "We need a couple of solid anchors."

Bear looked around. "Those trees will do. I'll use two with a safety line to a third."

Petros peered into the dark of the crevasse. "What are your thoughts on the rock formations?"

"A mixture of limestone, granite, and soft sandstone. With luck, we can descend and return without too much hassle. Better take the gear, just in case. These search and rescue teams use great rope, this is Mamut Infinitive, expensive."

Bear secured three lines while Petros prepared the ropes with a figure of eight, a piece of polished steel, with two rings at either end. Finished, he tossed coils of rope into the hole.

Both men stared into the void, nodded and with Bear first, began a controlled descent. The daylight from above gave sufficient light.

"It's narrowing," said Bear.

Petros dropped a stone and mentally timed its descent.

"Three seconds plus, twenty five metres, give or take."

Bear shone his headlamp and dropped through the more spacious fissure until he bellowed, "I'm entering a cavern. Going in. Hey, PK, Zane was right. There is a train."

"Bear, how's the air?"

"I'm still breathing."

Petros dropped to the ground seconds later.

The beams from their twin headlamps penetrated the dark, strange eerie space. They strolled on, their lights illuminating the bones of those trapped by the avalanche. The remains of ragged clothing clung to the dead. Bear stepped back and a brittle skeleton turned to powder under his foot.

"I'll try and be careful where I step but there're so many."

"I stopped counting at one hundred," said Petros. "I can't imagine what it was like to choke to death in a dust storm."

"If any survived, their prospects of being rescued were zero. I see the engine and goods wagons are intact."

"One wagon's empty." Petros turned and a beam of light shone on the entrance to another cave. "Might as well take a look."

Wary of where they stepped, both men stopped at the entrance of a huge chamber. Dust-covered wooden crates from large to small littered the floor.

"Our job's done but might as well take something for Zane as proof," said Petros.

Bear rummaged in the dust and pulled out a steel crow. "Made to measure. Something small will do."

Petros lifted a smallish crate onto another.

Bear eased the thin edge of the crow and levered the top free. "It's full of rocks."

Petros removed and inspected the stones. "Let's open one

of the larger ones."

Bear forced the top off until he could see inside. "More rocks."

"Let's open two from each goods wagon."

An hour later they sat on the edge of one wagon and ate the pies Bear had taken.

"Zane won't believe us, you know that," said Bear. "A dream for all those years but he was right about the train."

"I wonder how many died to steal this train load of stones?"

"As in all wars," said Bear, "Too many."

"Might as well get back."

"Ready when you are."

They prepared their lines for the ascent into the crevasse but once there, free climbed to the surface.

"Great to be in the open," said Petros. "That cavern should be left as a tomb in memory to those who died."

"I agree but who will believe there isn't any treasure."

"Well, they can go and check for themselves. Not our problem," said Petros as he contacted Bob. "Ready and waiting."

"On my way in ten. Out."

Both men coiled up the ropes and returned each piece of gear to its proper place. Twenty-five minutes later Bob arrived.

The moment both men secured their belts in the Eurocopter, Zane asked, "Is the train there?"

Petros turned to Bear and back to Zane. "Yes, it is and considering the years it's been there, in rather good condition. The bad news is, every crate we opened contained rocks. We can't state each crate is the same but we believe this train was a phony made to divert resistance forces."

Zane's shoulders slumped. "So the train was inside the mountain. You have found what remains, which is wonderful.

My grandfather told me three trains departed from Thessalonica. Two with Italian and Greek prisoners and one filled with priceless Greek artefacts. That is what he truly believed."

"He believed," said Petros. "Intelligence or an informer might also have understood the train carried loot. The resistance did the job successfully and died in the process. I must admit I'm intrigued why the German SS went to so much trouble."

"I agree it doesn't make any sense. So what's our next move?" asked Bear. "Remember Maria expects us back in a couple of days."

"Tomorrow Bob flies us back to Thessalonica. I'm going to search the archives in the library."

Zane looked at him quizzically. "May I ask why?"

"Something happened during the month of July 1944. I think we can say the trains were a decoy. So what did the Germans want so much they were prepared to sacrifice their crack troops?"

"And what will I be doing? I can't read or speak Greek," said Bear.

Bob interrupted. "We're home boys. I leave at 0800 prompt, which means you pay for two days. Any later you'll pay for three."

"Message received and understood. We'll be there."

The three men waved and kept their heads low as they strolled away from the downdraft. The Eurocopter lifted off and roared across the village before banking towards Florina.

They mounted the worn stone steps, entered the taverna and sat at a table.

At that moment, Sophie arrived with a large pot of coffee and three mugs. "I heard the helicopter. If you are hungry, I can start your dinner now." She studied their faces. "Maybe you like to shower and rest first."

"Give us an hour," said Petros. "The trains, Zane. Have you any information remotely connected to them?"

Bear took a long drink of coffee. He raised his eyes. "And I thought we'd finished."

"Three trains destined to be attacked intrigues me," said Petros. "As I said earlier, a day searching the archives might reveal what was going on."

"I can tell you many of the German army hierarchy were shot by the resistance during the liberation of Thessalonica. Much of the documentation they destroyed but the central library holds some."

"I'll start there," said Petros. "Bear, arrange a hotel for the night and we'll head for Cyprus on the next available flight."

He nodded. "Maria will not be a happy bunny if she finds out."

"Whose going to tell her?"

"Not me but we've been in this position before and arrived home two weeks later. I'm off for a shower. Thanks, Zane. Maybe we'll meet again."

"I hope so but I'm not a young man."

"The way I feel in the morning, that makes two of us." They shook hands and Bear lumbered to his room.

"You are lucky to have him as a friend," said Zane.

"I know, but don't tell him." Petros stood. "If I discover anything of importance I'll tell Andreas."

"Thank you for listening to an old man." With a hug, they said goodbye.

Zane left to make his way home and for a few minutes, Petros gave thought to the next day.

Bear returned and grabbed a chair. "What's on your mind?"

"My next move. Are you for or against some research?"

"Do you really believe you'll find anything in the public records?"

"The local papers of 1944 might reveal something of interest. Remember Greece went from war with Italy to war with Germany and then into a civil war with itself."

"What remains will be sparse."

"Chance, luck, opportunities, these are what we survive on and I have a gut feeling we can locate the missing treasure, or whatever a ton of people died for."

Bear rubbed his chin. "A long shot."

Petros stifled a yawn. "I agree."

"Can I make a suggestion?" said Bear.

Petros nodded.

"You shower, we eat, and sleep in that order. Tomorrow you can search the archives. Whatever you find, we still return to Cyprus."

"Agreed."

Both men stood and went to their rooms.

Chapter Six

The Eurocopter's rotors turned, ready for takeoff when Petros and Bear arrived.

Blonde Bob motioned for them to jump in and buckle up. As their belts clicked, the power increased and they lifted.

"I'd almost given you up," said Bob.

"You said eight. We arrived at three minutes to," said Bear.

She laughed and set a course for Thessalonica. "When we land, I'll check the craft with their ground staff. You wait in the office and get your deposit."

"Good idea," said Petros. "What's next on your agenda?"

"Check in with my boss and see if the company's back in operation. If we're not, I'll take a flight to Rome and visit a few friends."

"Male or female?" asked Bear.

She grinned. "None of your business."

Blonde Bob contacted the airport control and requested permission to land. Ten minutes later, the craft descended into the hire company's heliport.

Petros paid Bob, who counted every note.

"Anytime, anywhere," she said. "Bear, give us a kiss for old times." They hugged and she kissed him with passion. "Still cold. Hope she's worth it. Take care you two." With a wave, she grabbed her bag and disappeared towards the main airport's departure point.

"Did you two once have something going?" asked Petros.

"Long time ago and best forgotten."

"Forgotten already."

A taxi drew up outside the office and a man in a business suit, carrying a brief case, alighted. Bear and Petros jumped into the rear seats.

"Thessalonica Municipal Library," said Petros in Greek, "and take my friend to a four, five star hotel."

With a rapid change of gears, the Mercedes departed the airport and headed into town. The driver screeched to a stop, pointed and shouted, "library."

"Text me when you've found a hotel," said Petros.

"Have fun."

Petros shut the car door a millisecond before it raced back into the steady stream of traffic. He turned and stared at the multi-storey building in front of him. The modern concierge guided him to the reference section where a flock of female assistants sat and waited.

A dark-haired, bespectacled girl, behind the light wooden counter smiled and in English asked, "Can I help you, sir."

Petros gave his best smile. "Newspapers 1944."

"Please follow me."

As the girl left her position, another stepped into her place.

"The originals are in controlled storage but we have every page on computer. It'll give you the advantage of key words rather than checking every page." She opened a door to a large well-lit room with keypads and flat screen monitors attached to polished tables. She pointed. "Notepads, pens and printing facilities are available. You pay as you leave." She pressed a few keys and the front page of a Greek newspaper dated 1st, January 1944 filled the screen. "Any problems understanding Greek, press the button on the table and one of us will attend and assist."

"That's fine but I can read Greek and German. Thank you."

Methodically, he downloaded articles from October 1944

daily newspapers in Greek and German. He perused every page, rummaging for a clue or incident, any meaningless detail, which might direct his search or solve the mystery of the trains. Given the vastness of the task, he flipped October's pages reading anything of interest.

The departure of the hospital ship *Gradisca* filled with wounded prisoners, captured by British warship *HMS Kimberley* and escorted to Alexandria in Egypt, grabbed his attention. The article stated that the International Red Cross attempted to intervene. Even so, one thousand of the wounded ended the war in a British POW camp.

He keyed in trains and Thessalonica. The war timetable came on the screen. His finger hovered over the down arrow as he noticed one week in July 1944 not a single train appeared to operate. He quickly scribbled the dates on his pad and entered them into the library's search engine. The screen went white before it detailed a few headings. Whatever happened during those seven days remained unrecorded in Greek or German.

The *Gradisca* showed as having sailed one evening from Thessalonica bound for Crete. Why would she sail for an island where the war was over? It didn't add up.

Petros flipped back to the other page, which mentioned *Gradisca*. It didn't make sense. The *Gradisca* sailed from Thessalonica at the beginning of October 1944 and sailed again later in the month. He took a deep breath, and grasped the thought.

From his jacket pocket, he removed his mobile, while checking the prohibited sign. In several languages notices stated the use of mobile phones was forbidden. He pressed the call button for assistance and in a few seconds a bright-eyed girl sauntered into the room, cancelled his call and wandered across.

"Can I help?"

Petros whispered. "Where can I use my phone?"

"Come with me." They walked in silence to the other end of the room where several booths with the sign of a telephone stood. "Sound proof," she said. "Your notes will be safe until you return."

"Thank you." Petros entered the circular booth and closed the door, cancelling any external noise. He punched in the number for the Imperial War Museum, London, and waited.

"Good morning. How can I help?"

"Is it possible to speak to Mrs Susan Masters?" asked Petros.

"Who shall I say is calling?"

"Tell her Petros Kyriades."

"One moment, sir."

"Susan Masters. Are you still writing your book, Mr Kyriades?"

He chuckled. "I finished volume one a year ago. I'm in Greece undertaking research into the hospital ship *Gradisca*. She appears to have been in two places at the same time. As I know you have access to multiple archives, could you have a check on her movements during October 1944?"

"It'll cost you dinner for four at the Covent Garden Kitchen."

"Bribery and corruption will get you everywhere. It's a done deal. If you don't mind, who are you taking?"

"You, your wife and my husband."

"Look forward to it. I'll ring you when I get home and you can make the arrangements."

"I'll start my search and give you a bell."

"Can you text me. They don't allow mobiles in this library."

"Will do. Ring off and let me do some checking. Bye."

The line went dead.

Petros continued his research but found nothing referring to the trains. The *Gradisca*, worn out, ended the war laid up in Venice, decommissioned, and transferred to the shipping company Lloyd Trestino, after which it went aground then scrapped in 1950.

His mobile vibrated. A text from Susan. *Interesting that the Royal Navy sunk a vessel named Gradisca in October 1944. Ring me on my direct line.* She gave the number.

He rang her and she answered. "Petros, thanks for calling back. Two ships in the Med with the same name just don't happen. I checked with the Royal Navy archives and came across the incident where another vessel disguised as a hospital ship and named *Gradisca* opened fire on *HMS Cavalier* and *Cassandra* resulting in damage to *Cassandra*.

"*HMS Cavalier* recovered the crew from a lifeboat. There's a detailed report on the questioning of the crew but tells us nothing except the ship was a wreck and ready for the scrapyard. If a cargo existed, it went to the bottom when the captain blew holes in the hull.

"The other *Gradisca* was a hospital ship and at the time was on its way from Alexandria in Egypt to Algiers, an almost identical course one day or so behind. In Egypt a British control commission searched the entire ship, checked the medical staff and removed one thousand prisoners for internment in a POW camp."

"They say the truth is stranger than fiction and here we have it," remarked Petros. "Verifiable facts, where two and two don't make four. The ship, which sank, do we have a position?"

"I'll check.... Here it is, 15.10 East and 34.50 North."

Petros took a deep breath. "You don't happen to know the depth of water?"

She laughed. "Not a chance but I can find out. Why, are you into deep sea diving these days?"

"No way. I owe you, Susan, and more than a meal. I'll let you know how this works out."

"What are you searching for?"

"To be honest it could be something valuable or absolutely nothing. The question is, the Germans used three trains as decoys and one rogue ship, why? What were they trying to hide? Thanks, Susan. I'll be in touch."

He shuffled his notes together, folded, shoved them into his pocket and shut down the computer.

At the exit desk, the young assistant said in a formal manner, "Twelve Euros."

Petros paid and strolled out into the afternoon sun, sat on a concrete bollard and waited for a text from Bear.

The text came, *El-Greco. Room 324.*

Petros flagged a taxi and in less than five minutes strolled into reception. "Room 324 please. My friend booked the room."

The middle-aged man gave Petros' passport a fleeting look as he handed over the key. "Breakfast six until ten in the main dining room." He raised his hand and pointed. "The lift is over there unless you wish to use the stairs."

In the comfortable room, Petros found Bear stretched out on one of the beds asleep, snoring. He sat on the edge of the other bed and began to read his notes. No trains, two ships with the same name and Germany's last chance to strip Greece of its valuables.

The other bed creaked as Bear rolled over. "Find anything interesting?"

"Yes and no. No mention of the trains but two ships with an identical name. One departed the same day as the trains"

"Simple," said Bear, "The Germans shipped the gold out

but it's now at the bottom of the sea."

"But why the trains?"

"I sometimes think you have shit for brains. How you finished Sandhurst I'll never know."

"I worked harder at school."

"The only thing you worked harder at was behind the bike shed. Anyway, the SS were into heavy diversionary tactics. The whole of Thessalonica knew about three trains being prepared. The different resistance groups for once cooperated to stop the trains and recover whatever. A ship sailed late into the night and no one gave it a second glance."

"The trouble with your fantasy is you might be right."

Bear rested his back against the padded headboard. "I have my moments but what's next on the agenda?"

"We return to Cyprus as planned."

"What no deep sea diving?"

"It's a little deeper than I want to go."

"How deep is deep?"

"You'd need a manned submersible. But there are other factors to consider before we even go along that road."

Bear shifted his feet to the floor and stood. "We don't do salvage. This is out of our league."

"I know and we require permission from the Greek government to investigate the wreck."

"Why," said Bear. "Whatever it is, it's been underwater for seventy years and they haven't bothered their arses. As far as I'm concerned, it's finders, keepers."

"I don't think they know where the ship is."

"And you're going to tell them?"

"No choice. We could spend a fortune salvaging whatever might be there and they can take it and not give us a penny."

"That can't be right."

"You'd better believe it. Do you remember the forty-three million in gold bars recovered from *HMS Edinburgh*? The then conservative government returned fifty-five percent of their value to the Soviet Union and forty-five percent to the salvage company and made them pay fifteen percent VAT on their share. Get this wrong and you're out of pocket. What we need is a lawyer who understands the law of salvage."

"So the plan is?"

"When we get back, find the best lawyer available."

Bear checked the time. "I'm off for a dump, shave, and shower. When you're ready we find somewhere for dinner. I'm starving."

"As plans go, that's the best today. What time's our flight to Larnaca?"

"Nine in the morning, it's an early start. I've booked an alarm call for six, breakfast for six-thirty and a cab for seven-thirty."

Petros lay on the bed and closed his eyes. "I wonder if there's any treasure?"

"From past experience the more you think the more problems you create. At the moment I couldn't give a toss," said Bear as he closed the bathroom door.

Chapter Seven

Maria and Jocelyn arrived at Larnaca airport ten minutes after Petros' and Bear's flight from Thessalonica landed.

"Back in less than a week," said Maria.

"Makes a change," said Jocelyn. "Those two men seem to forget time when they're together."

"At least they take care of each other. On their own, I hate to think. There they are."

The two women waited until clear of the crowd before hugging and kissing their men.

Jocelyn checked Bear's face and head. "Makes a change, no cuts or bruises."

In a line of four they strolled to the dark blue pick-up.

"Did you find the train?" said Maria.

"We did and plenty of skeletons," said Petros.

"Dare I ask what was on this train?"

"Rocks, boxes filled with rocks. Hundreds of Greek resistance and German SS died for boxes filled with rocks," said Bear.

Jocelyn frowned. "Why did the SS guard rocks?"

"It's a long story and we'll tell you when we arrive at Eleni's."

Maria gave her husband a sidelong look. "You're planning a collection."

Petros smiled. "For once I'm not sure. It depends on other people and if it's worthwhile."

With Maria driving they soon arrived at Eleni's.

Alysa, on seeing her papa, jumped from Eleni's lap and ran to him. He lifted her high in the air and held her close.

"Where did you go?" asked Alysa.

"Papa and Bear have to work."

"Why?"

To earn money."

"Why?"

"Alysa will you stop saying why."

"Why?"

"Because it drives your papa mad," said Maria. "What were you doing with Eleni?"

"Looking at pictures of you as a baby."

"How do you know they were of me?"

"Because Eleni told me, silly."

"No flies on that one," said Bear. He checked the time. "A cup of coffee and a few sandwiches might be good."

Eleni chuckled. "Bear, don't ever change. You can make the coffee and the sandwiches are in the fridge."

***

In the cool of the courtyard, Bear and Petros described their search.

"And of course smarty pants here," said Bear, "had to check a few facts that bothered his tiny mind. To be fair he might have discovered something. The Germans prior to leaving Greece robbed the country blind. We know Nazi Germany charged Greece an occupation tax. Whoever thought of using three trains as a diversion knew what they were doing. While everyone focused their attention in the wrong direction, the gold left in an aged tramp steamer disguised to appear as a hospital ship. The irony is this ship ran into the Royal Navy. But when discovered those in charge planned her sinking. Why this ship was forgotten might be due to an accumulation of events or those who knew died at the hands of a Greek firing squad. The actual truth we'll never know. This ship is another overlooked seventy year old wreck on the sea bed with a cargo of gold."

"We cannot be sure she carried gold," said Petros. "My guess is if it wasn't gold, it was something of significant value. There are certain procedures we must follow before we consider searching for the wreck."

"Who would know?" asked Photis.

"If we started any salvage operation half the world. First, I talk to the Greek embassy in London. If they're not interested, I obtain an official letter giving me permission to salvage. The owners of the ship are for the moment unknown. As a rule, non-historic shipwrecks are fair game for salvage."

Bear held up his hand. "At the moment it's guesswork and a load of big ifs. If we receive permission to retrieve the cargo from the wreck, we have to find it first. The Navy plotted its position but I don't suppose they bothered to check if it happened to be a mile or so out. And that covers a large area of the seabed." He checked his watch. "Soon be dinner time."

"Bear, I've known you for far too many years and still can't understand how you can eat so much, remain fit and active."

"Simple, my metabolic rate is so high it demands feeding, so I oblige. Actually I like my food."

Everyone laughed.

***

The following morning, Bear rose early and went to the kitchen, made two cups of coffee and returned to the bedroom. "Are you awake, Jocelyn?"

She sat up and took the steaming cup of coffee. "If I wasn't I am now."

"Fancy a day out? I'll ask Photis for the loan of his pick-up. Have lunch at a beach taverna."

She placed her cup on the bedside table. "What are you after?"

He grinned. "Nothing I haven't had already."

"You cook breakfast and we leave when we've eaten. I'll have three slices of toast."

He bowed. "Your wish is my command."

She tossed a pillow at him and missed.

Bear was in the kitchen cooking bacon, eggs, tomatoes, and mushrooms when Jocelyn descended the stairs.

"Smells great but where's my toast?"

"On the table with a pot of Eleni's homemade strawberry jam." He spooned coffee granules into two cups and added freshly boiled water. "Coffee, madam."

***

The time was passing nine when Bear and Jocelyn departed the house and headed for Paphos. At half ten they stopped at Aphrodite's Rock and strolled through the underpass to the stone-covered beach.

Bear stared at the blue sea and perfect horizon. "Nice and peaceful. We don't have many moments like this, do we? Either you're working or I'm away collecting."

She grabbed his hand and they sat. "Is something bothering you?"

"Yes and no. Thanks to teaming up with Petros I'm worth a few quid and it causes me one big headache."

"Can't think why."

"When I die the government takes the cream from everything I've worked for and no doubt my ex will try to grab her share."

She shrugged. "So what's the problem?"

Bear put his right arm around her shoulders and pulled her close. "Will you marry me?"

She stared at him, surprised. "Can I have time to think about it?"

"No."

"This is rather sudden. But after the years we've lived together we might as well."

"I suppose I'd better buy you an engagement ring."

"A large solitaire diamond," she replied enthusiastically.

"You're only marrying me for my money."

She grinned. "Is there any other reason?"

"What about my good looks, charm, and appealing nature?"

"Shut up." She pushed him back onto the stones and kissed his lips hard. "And of course, I love you." She leant on one elbow and stared at him. When shall we get married?

"You choose."

"I'd like to be a June bride. Don't ask me why."

"Go for it."

"I'll hire a wedding planner."

"Not a bad idea, save all the hassle."

"I'll ask Maria to help."

"Trust me she'll jump at the chance having done a brilliant job for Andreas." He stood and pulled her to her feet. "Come on, let's go buy you a ring and make it official. Then I can have lunch with a clear conscience"

"You love food more than me."

"No chance." He playfully slapped her backside.

***

Maria spotted Jocelyn's ring as she entered the house and embraced her. "So, she's making an honest man of you."

"I'm as pure as the driven snow," said Bear, "but I had a strange moment and asked the question. To my surprise she said yes."

"Bear's asked Jocelyn to marry him," said Maria as Petros strolled into the house,

He slapped Bear on the back. "About time. When's the wedding?"

"We haven't decided on a date but it will be a small affair."

"Smallish," said Jocelyn.

"I stand corrected."

"You're a good man but she's a better woman," said Eleni as she descended the stairs. "Before you leave we'll have a celebration."

"Not necessary," said Jocelyn.

"My house makes it my decision. It's a long time since we had our friends around."

Bear and Jocelyn turned and faced each other. "We'd better do as we're told," said Jocelyn.

Eleni sat in her chair. "Of course you and Maria will have to make all the arrangements. I'm getting far too old."

Photis entered and everything was repeated.

***

The following week became a blur of organisation with Eleni giving her approval or not. Two days before they were due to leave, the guests arrived, danced, and feasted into the early hours.

Outside in the courtyard Bear and Jocelyn stood by the

old well.

Bear hugged her. "I do love you."

"I love you too but after my first attempt at marriage you were the problem I didn't want."

He laughed. "And now?"

"Your problem I can't live without."

"Glad to hear it. As guests of honour, we had better go back inside."

"Listen to them. They're having a great time. I bet they don't even know we've gone."

Maria opened the door and strolled towards them holding a bag. "A taxi will arrive in a few minutes. You have a suite booked at the Four Seasons for two days, all-inclusive. I've packed a few things for Jocelyn. Bear, whatever you want you'll have to buy."

"Why?" asked Bear.

Marie handed him the bag and kissed him.

"Men," said Jocelyn.

Chapter Eight

Their flight to London was straight forward; an unusual tailwind reduced the journey time to four hours. Alysa amused the other passengers by singing nursery rhymes as she strolled back and forth along the central aisle.

On exiting the airport Bear and Jocelyn jumped in a taxi while Petros, Maria and Alysa wandered to the short stay car park where Jack, Petros' stepfather, waited. In less than an hour, they were home.

Alysa screamed with delight when Charlie, sliding on the polished floor, collided into her.

"Stupid dog will never learn," said Petros.

"Yarlie not stupid," said Alysa. "My dog."

Petros ruffled the animal's coat. "Okay, not stupid, just dumb."

"I love my aunt," said Maria, "but it's always great to be back in our own home."

"Couldn't agree more. I'll take the suitcases upstairs and dump the washing in the laundry basket. Then I'll have a shower."

***

At breakfast Petros sat at the table eating a piece of toast while Alysa deviously dropped spoonfuls of porridge to the floor where Charlie waited.

Petros lifted his head from The Times and said, "Stop feeding Dog,"

"Yarlie hungry."

Maria arrived with her arms full of washing. "Eat, young lady."

Alysa shoved an overflowing spoon into her mouth as her eyes met her mother's.

"I'll be in my office," said Petros. He stood, winked at his daughter, strolled to room used as his office and sat in front of the computer screen. His fingers tapped the keyboard and the screen filled with information on the Greek Embassy in London. He scanned the information from consular affairs to general enquiries. Again he checked the fields for booking an appointment with an official. With a shift of the cursor he brought up the details on the ambassador. His credentials fitted; graduated in law, served in the navy and studied shipping law. He closed the enquiry and returned to the kitchen.

Petros poked his head into the utility room. "I need to go into town. With a bit of luck I'll talk to an official at the Greek embassy."

"Don't be home late," said Maria. "Your parents are coming for dinner."

"I'll be here in plenty of time. Must change." Ten minutes later wearing a navy blue blazer, grey trousers, white shirt, tie, and polished black shoes, he kissed Maria and Alysa goodbye.

***

At the entrance to the Greek embassy, Petros showed his passport. Security gave him a scan and body search before allowing him through the electronic entrance.

"Can I help you?" asked a young man wearing a light blue suit with matching tie.

"A quick chat with the ambassador would be wonderful."

The man's expression remained reserved. "May I ask why?"

Petros smiled. "A ship full of Greek gold."

"An interesting subject. How do you know it's Greek gold?"

"I don't but if it's not yours its mine."

The man hesitated. "I may be overstepping my authority. Your name, please?"

"Petros Kyriades, I'm Cypriot by birth."

"Almost Greek. Please follow me."

"Where are we going?"

"To talk to the ambassador's secretary. I know he's in his office and she might be able to persuade him to see you. I must add there are no guarantees."

"Such is life."

They entered a space that from its bland decor and a pile of ancient periodicals, was a waiting room.

"Take a seat. I'll be a few minutes."

In less than a minute, the man appeared followed by a tall woman with short blonde hair wearing a medium length black skirt and open-necked white blouse. In her slender arms she carried a red folder.

"Mr Kyriades. I've spoken to the ambassador and you have fuelled his interest. He can let you have ten minutes. This way please."

Petros turned to the young man. "Thank you."

The ambassador sat behind his large mahogany desk, stood and offered his hand. "Mr Kyriades." He pointed to a chair. "Please, make yourself comfortable." He returned to his seat and steepled his fingers. "Tell me about this ship full of gold. My country could certainly use it at the moment."

Petros reiterated from beginning to end the tale of the trains and the other *Gradisca.*

"You are aware of my qualifications?" said the

ambassador.

"I am. You understand why I'm here. Who is the owner of the second Gradisca? My own thoughts are it was a German freighter destined for the scrap yard, not part of any Greek shipping line, and the original owner is long gone and the ship forgotten. Under international maritime law anyone who finds an unknown wreck can file a salvage claim and place a lien on the vessel."

The ambassador rubbed his chin. "You have done your research and perhaps I should not say this, Finders Keepers works but only if you are first. Place your claim. I will have the ownership investigated and if it is Greek advise the owner or their beneficiaries. You have not told me its position?"

"At the bottom of the Mediterranean."

There was a pause before the ambassador said, "Very wise but I can assure you I am not in the business to defraud you out of what might legally be yours. Thank you for bringing this to my attention. Please leave your address and telephone number with my secretary. As soon as I know anything of importance, I'll get her to contact you. Remember, process that claim form. Without it, you have wasted your time."

Petros realised the meeting was over, stood and held out his hand. "Thank you for your time, Ambassador, and I'll file my claim today."

"It's a question of priorities. If the vessel is Greek, your information is worth a tidy sum. I will vouch for you. At least you will recover your expenses and more. One way or the other, you will make a profit. I will contact Athens sometime tomorrow."

"An honest lawyer, not many of them around these days."

"More than you might think, Mr Kyriades. Goodbye."

As if on cue the blonde-haired secretary opened the door,

waited for Petros to stroll through and closed it behind him.

"For our records. Your full name, address, telephone and mobile numbers, please."

She entered them into her computer. "Thank you, Mr Kyriades. I'll escort you to the main entrance."

"I can find my own way."

She frowned creating crow's feet at the corners of her eyes. "We do not allow anyone to wander around the embassy on their own. Security is paramount these days."

"You have a point." Petros hurried after her. She opened the door and he followed to the main entrance.

"Goodbye, Mr Kyriades."

As he turned to say goodbye, the door closed.

***

Petros took the tube to Aldgate East and from there walked to the red brick Victorian building in the shadow of the Gherkin. A brass plaque to the right of the main entrance stated the offices of Newton and Newton, Family Solicitors, third floor. On entering, he raced up the stairs and entered the reception.

The receptionist, a middle-aged woman, seated behind her desk, peered over her spectacles. "Have you an appointment?"

"I haven't, but if he's free, I have important business to discuss with Mr Derek Newton, the senior partner."

"Your name please?"

A door opened to his right. "Petros Kyriades, what are you doing here?" said the silver-haired Derek Newton as he held out his hand.

They shook hands. "If you can spare some time I need a chat."

"Is it important?"

"Could be."

"Sybil, would you mind, tea for me and black coffee for my friend. Have we any of those chocolate biscuits left?"

She nodded. "Of course, Mr Newton."

"Come," said Derek.

Petros strolled into a room of conservative sophistication and peace. On a modern desk in an alcove stood a high spec computer.

Derek sat in the leather chair behind his polished oak desk and motioned towards a well-worn leather armchair.

Petros made himself comfortable.

A knock on the door signalled the entrance of Sybil, carrying a silver tray with two cups and saucers and plate overflowing with chocolate biscuits. "Will there be anything else, Mr Newton?"

"No thank you, Sybil. Can you deal with any calls? If they're important I'll call back."

She almost curtsied as she backed out the door.

"Sybil's like me, we have respect for the old ways, they were slower and happier. Peter, my son, has his modern plastic and stainless steel office filled with all sorts of high tech equipment. Me, I have Sybil. How can I help you?"

Petros sipped his coffee. "Salvage."

Derek stared at Petros blankly for a few seconds, his tea untouched. "I know nothing regarding the law of salvage."

"That makes two of us but you'll know who to talk to and protect my interests."

He sipped his tea. "And what are these interests?"

"A gut feeling. I know the location of a ton of gold. It's in the bowels of a forgotten ship at the bottom of the sea. There's a ruling under Finders Keepers providing the owner of the vessel cannot be found and it's not in territorial waters. What I need is to file a salvage claim today on an unknown vessel."

Derek brushed biscuit crumbs to the floor from his tailored blue suit. "You're here for my advice. Allow me to call James Eden. He's dealt with an assortment of claims with regard to shipping. Groundings, fires and cargo salvage. Would you like another coffee?"

"No thank you."

He lifted the handset on his desk and pressed each number deliberately.

"Good afternoon. This is Derek Newton, a friend of James Eden. Is he in? If so, remind him he still owes me a bottle of vintage port."

The line appeared to go dead until, "Hi, Derek, I was just thinking about you."

"If I believe you, a pink elephant is flying past my office window."

"There we are then. I believe a flock were reported headed in your direction."

"Point taken. James, I need you to talk to a client and friend of mine with regards to marine salvage."

"I haven't heard of this one. The latest salvage deal is the Italian passenger ship. Its captain's being charged as we speak. Is this kosher or a scam?"

"A ton of kosher gold and I know my client."

"This sounds comparable to the *SS Gairsoppa*. Silver bullion by the ton."

"Interested?"

"More than interested, old man. Business is a tad quiet. Might have to sell the Lamborghini."

"I need you here like this morning."

"On my way. Coffee, black with fresh cream and you pay

125

the cab."

The line went dead.

James, dressed as if about to attend court, bounced into the office, slammed his briefcase on Derek's desk.

Sybil entered with a cup of coffee laced with cream. "I've taken the taxi fare out of petty cash."

"Thank you," said Derek. "Thanks for your rapidity in this matter. Petros Kyriades, James Eden."

"The man who believes he's found a ton of gold." James remained standing, opened his case, removed a two-page document, and handed it to Petros. "Fill it in as best as you can. We need to move fast. I have tickets for the opera tonight. You just don't know how difficult it is to obtain tickets for the opening night. Right, someone tell me a story and I'll make a decision."

Again, Petros told the story as James drank his coffee and listened.

"Do you know where this vessel is?"

"Within a mile or so," said Petros.

"You say the Royal Navy sunk this, for the moment, unnamed vessel. The position will be on record so, like you, anyone with half a brain could find it. But it is rather an interesting situation. The world of communication has changed and we must use it to our advantage. This has the makings of a huge fortune or I borrow the bus fare home. I'll register your claim with the UK Receiver of Wrecks when I return to my office. Before you say a word, I appreciate this wreck is not in UK territorial waters but we are in the EU so your claim will be accepted. If you start a salvage operation, I charge a thousand a day plus a handling fee of one percent on everything you recover. Don't cringe," He waved his arm and laughed. "I'm a lawyer and screw people but I'll keep you on the straight and narrow. I've never undertaken anything crooked, it plays havoc with one's reputation. Your word will suffice for the moment and anyway, Derek is my witness." From his top pocket, he removed a card. "For you. Keep in touch. Okay. We must have dinner one evening." James left the office at the same speed he entered.

"Bit of a character," said Petros.

"A maverick, a know-it-all, but your claim will be signed and sealed before the receiver of wrecks goes home tonight."

"I thought they only applied to the UK twelve mile limit."

He will have worldwide rights flagged on your wreck. At a thousand a day he keeps you out of the mire."

"There you go." On his way out he thanked Sybil for the coffee."

He contacted Bear.

***

At the same time in Starbucks, Mark Antonio, the embassy messenger, elaborated on the story of a ship full of gold to his friends as they drank coffee.

With his back adjacent to Mark's, Miles Johnston listened, excited by every word. He peered at the grey-painted ceiling and proclaimed to himself, "Discover the correct blend of greed and idiocy and you can make millions."

Mark checked his watch and said farewell.

Miles followed him at a discreet distance along the street, through the underground to his home in Hampstead.

From a distance, he noted the address. Still living with mummy and daddy he assumed. A few pounds might give me more information. As he made his way to his house in

Knightsbridge, he gave this germ of an idea much thought. He shuddered, failure to pay his debts remained unthinkable.

Chapter Nine

The Greek ambassador sat across his desk from Petros. "Mr Kyriades, my government has searched its records. You'll be pleased to know your vessel does not appear to be owned by any Greek or shipping consortium. In fact, no one knows if it existed and the idea of such a fraud is hard to believe. It may be the harbour officer on duty wrote the wrong name in the register. Salvage rights are yours and I would advise the Law of Finds possibly applies. Greece has no interest."

"In simple language can you explain?"

"It is a law that assumes that the property involved was never owned or was abandoned and the ancient principle of Finders Keepers applies. I would say after sixty plus years this ship and its cargo has been abandoned.

"And if or when I recover the treasure?"

The ambassador handed over a letter. "This absolves you completely. It states you have informed my government of your suspicions and your story investigated. Furthermore, the vessel does not belong to Greece, etc, etc. I have countersigned it as a Graduate of Private Shipping Law and International Law. What do you propose?"

"Not sure, I need further proof before committing a substantial sum of money to find nothing but a heap of scrap metal."

"In my opinion you're wasting your time and money but I am intrigued at the thought. An update on your progress to my private email would be of interest."

"If I can, I will." Petros folded the letter and pushed it into his inside jacket pocket. "For my lawyer."

The ambassador smiled. "In salvage every 'I' must be dotted and 'T' crossed. Good luck."

Petros stood and shook hands. "I might need it. Thank you for your time."

***

Petros checked the address on James Eden's card. He peered through the glass entrance doors and waited for them to open. A man pulled one side of the double door inwards. Petros grabbed the glass, entered and strolled to the VDU located in the centre of reception. He pressed the keys for James Eden and it displayed the firm's name, floor, office number and whether the occupier was in or out. He was in luck. The lift sped to the fourteenth floor. He smiled as he noted the thirteenth floor as in many tall buildings was missing.

A young buxom woman wearing a short black skirt, a purple blouse, with matching streaks in her blonde hair, looked up as he entered.

"Petros Kyriades to see James Eden."

Her eyelids fluttered as she busied herself arranging different coloured folders into four piles "You don't have an appointment."

"I know but I need to see him."

With a flicker of the lashes, she smiled, displaying two rows of dentist-white teeth. "Take a seat. I'll let him know."

While waiting, he noticed her jotter was a mass of pencilled doodles. Cubes, squares and rectangles drawn while on the phone. He wondered what an analyst might make of them.

The internal door opened. "Petros, you have news? Come into my parlour."

"Said the spider to the fly."

"Unlike the fly you have a choice," said James as he sat in a real leather upholstered office chair. "Grab a pew."

Petros lifted a stainless steel chair and placed it in front of the glass desk. He removed the letter from his pocket. "Greece does not want to know. All I have to do is find the wreck."

James leant back in his chair, placed his thumbs behind his red braces, and pushed them in and out. "What you need to help find the wreck is a small boat equipped with preferably two side scan sonar outfits and a suitable ROV."

"Couldn't agree more, if I knew what you're talking about."

James held up his perfectly manicured soft hands. "I can advise on every aspect of salvage; who, what, where, and when. Sign my contract and off we jolly well go."

"I sign and you receive a thousand a day until?"

James stood. "Until we recover whatever or prove it isn't there." He handed Petros his gold Parker fountain pen.

"Three months and we renegotiate," said Petros. "You collect ninety-thousand in monthly instalments."

James inserted a three-month clause into the standard contract and printed two new copies. "Carole, my secretary, can be one witness and I'll grab someone from the next door office."

In less than ten minutes, the contract was signed and witnessed.

"Carole, I need the original for my bank security box."

"Why?" asked Petros.

"Just in case."

"What's side scan sonar?" asked Petros.

"Palermo, Sicily, Alfredo Abruzzi has a reasonable sized boat with excellent equipment. Side scan is your underwater eyes. If it can see it you can salvage. He's not cheap but honest. I can contact him and make all the arrangements or you can do it yourself."

"I'm paying, so start earning."

"I've a ton of work to do. I'll give you a bell tomorrow."

***

The late afternoon sun cast long shadows on the pavement as Petros strolled from Tower-Hill underground station to where Bear lived with Jocelyn. He pressed the doorbell and waited.

Bear opened the door, beckoned Petros inside and strolled to the kitchen. "What brings you round this way?"

He grinned at the selection of wedding magazines that littered the table. "Bedtime reading?"

"A present from the wedding planner. He and Jocelyn are in discussion on how to spend as much money as possible."

"You didn't have to ask the question. Now you pay the price."

"She can have whatever she wants but you didn't come here to talk over my wedding."

"I've hired a salvage expert to help me discover the other *Gradisca*."

Bear frowned. "When you have a bee in your bonnet you're a pain in the arse. Why don't you let this one go? You don't need it." He held up his hand to stop Petros. "But you'll do what you have to do and anything I say won't stop you."

"I thought you might like to join me. No bad guys with guns. A nice sea cruise where you have nothing to do."

"Boats, you know how I feel about boats. Every time you and I are on one, we're in deep shit. I'll give this one a miss. You don't really know where the wreck is. When you find it I'll reconsider."

"Who's going to watch my back?"

"Amadou's a good man. Give him a ring."

"I have to pay him."

"Big deal. You can afford it."

"It won't be the same."

"PK, I'm fast approaching my sell-by-date. If you want me to sort out logistics I will but trouble finds you and I'm tired of ducking and diving."

"Okay, it's a deal. You're my logistics officer. Tomorrow, I'll introduce you to James Eden, a lawyer who knows everything there is to know about salvage. I'll be happier with you working with him. He's a bit of a wild card."

"Now what happens?"

"I ring Amadou."

***

The white transit van slowed and stopped ten metres in front of Miles Johnston as he strolled along Cable Street towards his office in Cannon Street Road. The passenger window lowered and a hand beckoned.

The rear doors opened and one man wearing a dark grey suit fell in step alongside Miles. "Mr Johnston, Roly wants a word. You have two options, you get in the back of the van or I break your legs with a baseball bat."

Miles grimaced, returned to the van, and both men jumped into the rear. "You might as well kill me. I don't have the money."

The good-looking blond-haired man chuckled. "If we kill you we don't get the money but if we threaten to kill your wife that's different."

Miles shook. The hostility of his response came as a shock. "You wouldn't."

"Not our decision," said the other man as he twirled the bat in his hands.

They drove to Mile End Park, a quiet tree-lined avenue in the east end.

"This way," said the blond man, "Roly's feeding the squirrels. He's fond of wild life."

A dozen grey squirrels scampered around a man in his early sixties, dark weather-beaten complexion, wearing an olive green suit. He tossed the last of the nuts onto the grass, stood, and faced Miles with a frown. "Some people say they're vermin but see how they have adapted to city life. A good example to us all. We have a problem, Miles, in that you owe me one-hundred-thousand pounds and I want my money."

Terror filled Miles' eyes. "I don't have it."

Roly's eyes, devoid of any compassion, responded. "You have a nice house, take out a second mortgage or after a week your wife has an accident."

Roly and the blond man started to walk away.

"What if I can lead you to more gold than you ever dreamed of," shouted Miles.

Roly stopped, turned and beckoned to Miles. "I run casinos and make more than enough to meet my needs. This gold, tell me more?"

"At the bottom of the sea."

"And you expect me to believe this cock and bull story. Just remember I use people and then dump them when they're of no further use. Time's running out. One-hundred-thousand and the clock's ticking."

"Give me a few days and I'll discover its location."

Roly pondered his answer for a moment. "Get me the information and I might choose to let your wife live a little longer after my men have enjoyed her company. You never know, she might relish being humped by real men."

Miles shuddered at the thought. "I need time."

"Two days. Now fuck off before I change my mind."

***

Miles checked the time as he entered his office. Eleven o'clock. He dumped his briefcase on his desk, sat, slumped forward and placed his head in his hands.

He finished work early and returned to Starbucks. To his relief, the young man was there with his friends. Miles waited and again followed Mark. This time he caught him up further along the street.

"Hi, I overheard you telling a story about a ship full of gold the other day. The way you imparted it sounded convincing."

Mark stopped and scrutinised this man for a moment. "Do I know you?"

"Miles Johnston," he held out his hand. "Venture Capitalist." He saw the bemused look on Mark's face. "I make money available for new projects, start ups and the like. Whoever discovered this gold will require someone like me to help with investments and of course, you could receive a substantial finder's fee."

Mark's eyes brightened. "Mark Antoni. How much?"

Miles turned his head left and right. "I'd rather not talk in the street. Are you hungry?"

"I fancy a Big Mac."

"I prefer more substantial food but MacDonald's will do for a preliminary chat and to set out the ground rules."

Mark nodded as they set off along the street. Inside MacDonald's, Mark ordered two Big Macs with fries and two cokes.

Miles paid and joined him at a table near the plate glass

window. "My card with my work, home, mobile numbers and email address."

Mark gave it a glance and shoved it in his pocket. "What do you want to know?"

"Keep your voice down. We don't want half the world listening. I need to know the name, address and contact number of who discovered the gold. Can you give that to me now or can you get it?"

With a mouthful of burger, Mark said, "Cash, up front."

Miles glanced over the top of his plastic cup as he sipped his coke. "Whatever you say. How about one hundred now and the same again once I verify your information?" From his wallet he removed two crisp fifty pound notes and slid them across the table.

"I could take your money and do nothing."

"You could but then that's a risk I take every day. Stay for the long run and you might possibly earn a few thousand or more."

"Same time tomorrow evening, in here and a double Big Mac ready and waiting. I'll get you the information. Have the money."

"I'll be here, make sure you are. You can finish your meal in peace." Miles stood, frowned as Mark stuffed his mouth full.

Chapter Ten

James Eden, dressed in his bespoke pin-striped suit, slid out of his Lamborghini and strolled to the lift. He looked pleased with himself. A new day and a contract worth ninety thousand pounds. Once in his office he browsed through the morning's mail tossing most of it in the bin. His mobile played Land of Hope and Glory. "Alfredo, on time to the second. I have a client who is looking for a world war two wreck to the south of Malta, interested?"

"My friend, if your client has the money, I am interested."

"He has the money for side scan sonar and you'll need an ROV, I suggest, for deep water usage."

"This equipment I have. When will your client arrive?"

"Two days."

"I will be ready. Can I have a name?"

"Petros Kyriades. He's Cypriot but speaks English as his first language. A good man."

"Normal rates will apply if he pays in cash."

"You're a rascal, Alfredo. He'll have the money in American dollars. Ten thousand for one week all inclusive."

"These are difficult times my friend, but I agree."

"Do this and there might be more, so don't let me down." James ended the call and contacted Petros giving him the details."

***

Petros went to the kitchen, made a cup of coffee and strolled into the garden. Here he contacted Amadou in Libya.

In seconds the phone was answered. "Amadou."

"It's Petros."

"Long time."

"Since the revolution. Are you busy?"

"Yes and no. The radicals are fighting each other so I sell weapons to both sides but it's small stuff. Do you need my assistance?"

"If you can spare a week or two I need someone to watch my back who I can trust. You I trust."

"When and where?"

"We meet at the harbour in Palermo in two days."

"Are we taking a trip?"

"I'm searching for something. When we meet, I'll fill in the blanks. Bring ZZ, he's useful."

"He's changed since you last saw him. Taller and an expert with small arms and like his late friend, Akeem, deadly with a knife. Women tend to be his failing. One glance from a beautiful woman and he's like a love-sick puppy."

"No problem. No women on this trip. See you and ZZ Thursday morning. Give me a buzz if you're going to be late."

"We haven't discussed a fee."

"Same as last time."

"Done. See you Thursday." He broke the connection.

***

Miles Johnston sat at a centre table in MacDonald's reading The Times, and sipping his coffee while he waited. He scowled as Mark sauntered in fifteen minutes late. "I've finished this muck they call coffee and I'm ready to leave."

"Where's my Big Mac?"

Miles handed him a white envelope. "Information."

He handed over one sheet of embassy paper. "This is all

there is." He moved to grab the envelope.

Miles read the limited information and then allowed him to take his money. "Get your own Big Mac. You work for me not the other way round. Are you sure this is everything?"

"I copied the file."

Miles stood and placed the paper in his brief case.

"What's next?" asked Mark.

"I'll be in touch."

"Might as well have my supper."

"I don't know how you can eat those burgers." With that Miles left as Mark joined the queue.

In MacDonald's car park, he texted Roly with the information. His mobile rang.

"Where's the boy and how is he dressed?"

"Inside MacDonald's eating. Light blue suit, white shirt, white and blue embassy tie. Why do you ask?"

"Interest only." Roly severed the connection.

***

Mark counted the money twice while he ate his two Big Macs. Tired and thinking of what he could buy, he strolled outside, his mind elsewhere. At this time in the evening, the traffic remained heavy so he waited for the lights to change before crossing the road.

At speed, a white transit mounted the pavement. Mark heard the van before he saw it. He raced for cover but the nearside wing struck him hard catapulting his body into the air. Confused, he tried to rise as a white blur reversed and hurtled towards him. The rear wheels crushed his rib cage.

With a roar, the van drove away, returned to the road, collided with a car, reversed, shot forward and vanished into a side street.

Drivers halted their vehicles and went to Mark's assistance. A woman checked for a pulse but shook her head at the others.

The police arrived fifteen minutes later and took charge of the accident scene.

***

Satisfied at his stay of execution, Miles arrived home in a happy frame of mind. As he stepped out of his garage, he experienced excruciating pain and slumped to the ground.

A tall dark-haired man dressed in white overalls searched Miles' pockets. In his briefcase he discovered the sheet of embassy paper and a mobile. With help, the body ended up in the passenger seat. With his companion following in another car, he drove to an abandoned factory. He shifted Miles' body into the driver's seat and fastened the seat belt. From the other car, the driver removed two five litre red plastic containers and emptied their contents over Miles and the interior of the car.

A Zippo lighter flared and one of the men tossed it onto the rear seat. In an instant, the interior erupted in flames. He slammed the door and strolled casually to the waiting vehicle.

The driver, using Miles' mobile, texted his home number. *"Am negotiating major contract. Working late will stay in hotel tonight. See you tomorrow."*
He wiped it clean and tossed it out of the window. "Fancy a pint?"

"Why not?"

"Okay. We dump and torch this and take a black cab to the pub. You can always guarantee a lock-in at The Nag's Head.

***

In the lounge of his Victorian home, Roland Wallace sat with Don Mercer and Peter Fox, all respectably dressed and wearing ties. Roly removed his glasses, cleaned and replaced them. He glanced at a single sheet of paper. "From the scant information I have, a man named Petros Kyriades may have stumbled upon a fortune in gold. I want it but at this early stage I'm prepared to let him do the work and at the right time relieve him of such an onerous task."

Don lit a cigarette. "Bit out of our league, isn't it?"

"Right up our street." He stood, turned and stared through the window at his ornamental garden before facing the others. "This is my retirement fund. With what we could make we can enjoy the rest of our lives. Peter, talk to your telecommunications guys and tap into the Greek's telephone line. I need to know what he's planning. The ship he's searching for is a Finders Keepers claim. My lawyer tells me a James Eden is the best man in London when it comes to salvage rights."

"What can I do?" said Don.

"Bide your time. I'm going to get Edwards, my lawyer, to talk to this salvage expert."

Don stubbed out his cigarette. "No problem. Roly. This ain't gonna happen overnight. When you need me, I'll be available."

Don and Peter left the house. Moments later the roar from two Lotus sports cars charging along the drive, vibrated the windows as they departed.

Roly leant back in his chair and closed his eyes.

Chapter Eleven

The wall phone in the kitchen gave its shrill ring tone. Petros lifted the handset. "Petros Kyriades."

"Good morning, Mr Kyriades. This is Fiona at A A Travel. Your ticket for Palermo is ready. I have arranged a car to pick you up and another to take you from the airport to the harbour."

"Thank you. I'll be there in twenty minutes." He replaced the handset. "Dog, we're going for a run."

Charlie bounded into the kitchen and sat.

"Give me a chance to change."

Dressed in his navy blue tracksuit, Petros and Charlie raced up the hill towards the local travel agent.

From the fair-haired Fiona he collected an envelope. "Mr Kyriades, you could have booked your ticket on line."

He smiled. "I might press the wrong keys. You never do. Plus, you can order cars."

Outside Charlie waited. "Time to see who's the fastest. Ready, steady, go."

Charlie showed the way home but waited for Petros before racing to the river's edge where he poked around in the shrubs.

Petros strolled into the house, made himself a coffee and sat watching the news on television until interrupted by the doorbell.

"Good Morning, Mr Kyriades."

His eyes scanned the two men wearing BT engineers' overalls. "Is there a problem?"

"Water, sir," said a tall, willowy man with red curly hair. "Mains burst and the lines are contaminated. If it's convenient, can we check your connections? My apologies." He removed an identity card from the top pocket of his overall. "My ID, sir. If you have any doubts, please telephone for confirmation."

"How long will you be?"

He turned to his partner, a short, heavily-built man with a scar the full length of his right cheek. "What do you reckon, Alf?"

"Ten minutes at most."

"Follow me. The main box is under the stairs." Petros opened the half door, turned on the light and pointed.

"Thank you, sir. Shouldn't be long."

Petros watched as he removed the cover and began poking probes onto the connections. "I'll leave you to it." He returned to the kitchen and finished his coffee.

"We've finished, sir. Secured a couple of your terminals for good measure. Have you a bin where I can dump the ends?"

"Give them to me; I'll get rid of them."

"Thank you, sir. We'll let ourselves out."

"Let me," said Petros. "If Dog sees you without me you'll be in trouble."

As the door opened Petros shouted, "Dog."

Charlie loped across the lawn and the drive but stopped and barred his teeth at the two men.

"He dislikes strangers," said Petros.

The two men stepped out and once inside their van, drove away.

Petros stroked Charlie's head. "You sensed something, Dog. Let's go and see what they were up to."

Under the stairs, he removed the BT cover and laughed when he saw the chip tucked behind the main connections. "I wonder who they work for? No problem. You want to listen, be my guest."

Still chuckling he strolled into his den and picked up his

mobile.

"Yes."

"Hi, Bear. Two men arrived and placed a bug on my telephone line. Have you the number of an engineer?"

"I'll contact a friend of mine. I guess you'd prefer privacy?"

"I'd like it fixed."

"I'll ring back if he can't make it in the next hour or so."

"Thanks, talk later."

Less than half a mile away two men listened to a call from Maria to Petros.

"Maria, hang up. This line's bugged."

"What on earth do you mean?"

"Maria, don't argue. Hang up." Petros ended the call.

"We've been rumbled. The Greek's no fool."

"What are we going to tell the boss?" said the other.

"The truth. He might not like it but never ever lie to him or he'll have your balls for dinner."

***

Todd Aitkin, a professional communications expert and an associate of Bear's, arrived at Petros' house and checked the bug. "Not exactly top of the range but it works. Do you want me to disconnect or fuck with their reception?"

"Your choice."

"I choose The Rolling Stones and 'I Can't Get No Satisfaction.'"

"Classic."

For a time Todd added a few chips of his own to the circuitry. "All systems go. Every time you make a call my little bug starts broadcasting The Rolling Stones to whoever they are if they listen. Bit of fun really but it lets them know not to bother. I suggest you draw your curtains at night. It dampens infra red listening devices."

"What do I owe you?"

"Cash, one hundred. Cheque, one-twenty-five as it has to go through the system."

From his back pocket, Petros removed his wallet and handed over five twenty pound notes. "Thank you for being so prompt."

"Bear told me it was urgent. Any problems give me a bell."

Charlie stirred as Todd made to leave. He barked, settled into his basket and closed his eyes.

"Great dog," said Todd.

"Only if he likes you."

***

After dropping Alysa at her nursery Maria drove a few miles to JG's Karate school and parked her silver Audi saloon. Dressed in a dark blue tracksuit she entered the white painted building and charged up the stairs to the large practice room.

A soft voice with a Glasgow accent said for the rest of the class to hear, "You're late and therefore first on the mat."

JG, as everyone knew him, stood with his arms folded in the centre of the room, around him, a circle of women aged between twenty to fifty.

In his white outfit with a black belt tying the jacket together and ready for anything, JG addressed the group. "Ladies, most men believe women are easy targets. You are here to prove them wrong. As you know from the sign at the entrance I teach martial arts and my students are well trained but that can take years of practice. In the next few weeks if you're attacked and I hope it never happens, I intend to teach you how to defend yourself. Sales pitch over." He pointed to Maria. "In the centre and bring one of my handbags with you."

Some of the women laughed.

"The thug will grab your bag and do a runner. The last thing he wants is a fight. Show me your hands."

Maria held out her hands.

"Perfect, lovely long fingernails to scratch, claw and poke in his eyes. Use what you have. In most cases, the bastard will run but unfortunately, with great looking women like you, some may have rape on their minds. A kick in the balls usually ends that thought and gives you enough time to scream and run. Now, kick me in the balls."

Maria hesitated but lashed out with her right leg, which JG deflected.

He grabbed her and pulled her close. "Come on darling, be nice to me. Give us a kiss."

She twisted and turned but he held her.

"What did I just tell you to do? You're up close and he's getting personal. This position is perfect for you to knee him in the crutch. Go for it."

Embarrassed at her own helplessness, she lifted her knee with all the strength she could muster.

He grinned and let her go. "Don't worry, I'm wearing protection. Ladies, what is her problem? I'll tell you, she's frightened and these bastards love the fear they create. It's a game you can't afford to lose. Think positive, after all, he's only a man who can't get it up. Use that fear to hurt him."

One by one, he practiced the move on each woman. "Time for coffee. Then we start all over again until it becomes instinctive."

At the end of the session, JG gathered them together. "Next week we'll learn more dirty tricks. Take care and drive carefully."

Together the class descended the stairs. Some went to a nearby coffee shop while others jumped in their cars and drove away.

Maria returned to the nursery and waited for Alysa to finish her finger painting.

***

James Eden listened patiently as Paul Edward gave him the details of a wreck south of the Scottish Isle of Mull on which he wished to dive and salvage. "Mull, you say. I'll check my wreck library." His fingers flitted across the keyboard.

He looked up. "They're three wrecks listed. Two you cannot touch as they belong to the Royal Navy and therefore the government, and the third has a salvage claim by the owner. Touch them and you break the law."

Paul ran his fingers through his hair before he gazed at his wristwatch. "You live and learn. Shipwrecks are what they are and it was my understanding they were fair game."

James swivelled in his chair. "Now you know. Sorry, can't help."

Paul stood and prepared to leave. "One more question, what does Finders Keepers mean in regard to salvage?"

James shook his head. "Why do you ask? I've told you the wreck you're interested in is a no-dive location."

"I read an article where a ship full of silver was recovered and the salvage team made a fortune."

"It's straight forward. Under international maritime law if you can prove the owner of the vessel has lost all claim to the cargo you can file a salvage claim. The opposite would be the wreck of HMS Edinburgh. Designated a war grave it carried a consignment of gold bullion intended as payment for supplies to Russia.

"The government offered the salvage rights to a British company but returned fifty-five percent of the recovered bullion to Russia. The divers were rather upset when the government at the time charged them VAT. So you see even if you find a vessel you can salvage, be careful it doesn't cost you more than you can make."

"Interesting. Must dash, have a client in half an hour."

James managed a top-quality smile. "Sorry I couldn't help. You know the way out." He did not stand or offer his hand. At speed he inserted Paul Edward's name into the Google search engine and read all he needed to know.

James pulled a file from a drawer and placed it on his desk. "Two Finder Keepers in one week. Not a chance in hell and Edward was fishing."

Carole, dressed in a long woollen pullover, distressed light blue jeans, knee length black boots, ruffled her cropped-blonde hair as she knocked and opened the office door. "Petros Kyriades and a William Morris are waiting."

He opened his desk drawer and from the petty cash box took a twenty-pound note. "Ask my friends what type of coffee they prefer, I'll have my usual and whatever you want. Keep the change."

She smiled at him and gave a shrug. "When did you last buy coffee?"

"Why?"

"Thirty will get you large coffees. Twenty, small."

"He fumbled in the cash box and gave her another ten pound note."

"You can go in when you tell me what's your coffee preference," said Carole.

"Hot, black and sweet," said Bear.

"Hot and black for me," said Petros.

Petros, strolled smiling into James' office followed by Bear.

"Some secretary," said Bear.

James chuckled. "She's actually brilliant and we work well together. You should see her when she has a mood change and wears her Japanese gothic Lolita look. She appears stunning but innocent, butter wouldn't melt and all that. Anyway, enough about my secretary.

"Petros, *Tuna Turner*, your search vessel, is tied up, ready and waiting in Palermo Harbour. When you first see her you'll think it's a stern trawler. She once was but her conversion to search and salvage is first class. I've briefed the captain on your requirements. Any problems tell me sooner rather than later."

"I'm flying by easy Jet tomorrow morning," said Petros. "I also have two colleagues joining me."

The office door opened and Carole returned with three polystyrene containers filled with coffee and placed them on the desk. "I bought a slice of carrot cake with the change."

"Thank you," said James.

She did a curtsy, turned and skipped out the door, closing it behind her.

"She has a first class honours in law."

"And a nice arse," said Bear.

"Agreed," said James. "I gather Mr Morris will be the coordinator. If extras are required he can approve the additional expenditure."

"If we find the wreck we'll both need him, " said Petros.

"Out of interest, has anyone been asking questions?"

"Strange you should ask. Before you arrived a lawyer who often assists the criminal fraternity in their defence, sat right there asking questions on the Finders Keepers salvage regulations."

Petros raised his eyebrows. "What did you tell him?"

"I spouted the standard spiel. Client confidentiality rates high on my agenda. Without it, I'm out of business. What made you ask?"

"Two clowns attempted to bug my telephone lines."

"From your tone, I gather they failed."

"No they fixed their device and I had someone add a little extra."

James scribbled a mobile phone number onto a card. "This is a pay-as-you-go and your direct line to me. Anything which concerns you and it doesn't matter how large or small, contact me. I earn my money. I expect no problems with Alfredo Abruzzi. You can speak to him but be careful who might be listening. Sicily is the home of the Cosa Nostra or as they like to be known, Men of Honour."

"They have a reputation to be feared. I'll stay out of their way."

James stood and held out his hand. "Have a good trip and I hope you find what you're searching for."

Petros shook his hand. "I'll keep in touch."

"So will I," said Bear. "Let me know the next time Carole turns Japanese."

"Your brains are in your trousers," said Petros as he grabbed his arm and dragged him out of the office.

Carole smiled and gave a cute wave.

"Even you must admit it's tempting," said Bear.

"I enjoy living," said Petros.

Bear chuckled. "What a way to go."

***

Petros paused as he ambled from his garage to the main door. A full moon lit the sky and for once in a long while, he saw the milky-way. The thought of finding the gold stimulated his mind. As he entered the kitchen, he kissed Maria.

Charlie and Alysa greeted him. "I teach Yarlie game."
"What sort of game?"
"I show you. Bang."
The full-grown Alsatian rolled on his side.
"Yarlie dead."
"I don't think so."
She smiled at her father. "Pretend dead. Biscuit, Yarlie."
The animal leapt and caught it.
Alysa rummaged in a cupboard and tossed Charlie more biscuits into the air. "Yarlie catch."
"How was the self-defence class?" asked Petros.
"I enjoyed it. When I've finished this course I'd like to try a martial art, maybe Judo."
"Why not? What did you learn today?"
She giggled. "Where to hurt a man."
Petros gave a fatigued smile. "What you mean is how to bring tears to his eyes."

Chapter Twelve

Petros gripped the armrests and closed his eyes as the Airbus climbed rapidly.

The whine of the engine settled as he peeked out of the window at a layer of unbroken dark cloud in every direction. The sense of being sealed in a metal container unable to control his life gripped him. He closed the blind, nestled into his seat and dozed until the attractive brown-haired cabin attendant shook his arm and reminded him to fasten his seat belt.

The aircraft landed with a thump on the runway at Palermo. Petros glanced at his watch; they were on time. Followed by a line of holidaymakers he strolled, holding his cabin bag and his blazer draped over his shoulder, towards the airport buildings. Once through customs and immigration he wandered to the main entrance. A young man dressed in blue jeans and a white shirt held a card with his name.

He stopped. "I'm Petros Kyriades."

He smiled. "Tommaso Giovanni, your driver. My uncle is Alfredo Abruzzi and I'm a deckhand on his boat."

"Jack of all trades," said Petros.

Five minutes later they travelled along a busy road towards Palermo harbour. Petros pressed a memory button on his mobile.

"Good morning, PK."

"Amadou, where are you?"

"I'm eating my breakfast in Panini's, opposite a large car-park close to a sandy beach. Lots of yachts and ships in the harbour."

"Tommaso, my two friends are at Panini's."

"I will stop and they can travel with us, unless you want to eat. Panini's excellent."

"We'll see if they've finished before making a decision."

Tommaso drove into the car park opposite the cafe and stopped.

A warm, gentle breeze blew from the sea as waves lapped the sloping beach. The area buzzed; three cruise liners berthed in the harbour acted like mother hens, their chicks, passengers arriving and departing. The beachfront sported a continuous line of cafes, bars, souvenir shops and restaurants.

Fishing boats having returned from a night at sea unloaded their catch, winches clanked, men shouted and lorries trundled across the jetty. The old and new mixed in a haphazard fashion adding to its appeal. Petros' eyes scanned the area before he found Panini's, and Amadou with ZZ under a large white sunshade.

He waved and strolled with Tommaso to the cafe. "You both look well," said Petros as he hugged the two men. "Have you eaten?"

"Yes, we are ready," said ZZ. He drew Petros to one side. "But without my knives I am naked, unarmed."

Petros turned to Tommaso and in a quiet voice asked, "Is there a shop which specialises in knives?"

He nodded. "I'll take you but we walk."

The three men followed Tommaso along narrow lanes into the heart of old Palermo. They stopped outside a closed general hardware shop.

"Wait," said Tommaso as he pressed the doorbell.

The little window located in the centre of the heavy wooden door opened. "Uncle, I have a customer."

They listened as bolts rattled back and the door opened. Tommaso entered and in minutes returned. "Come. Meet my uncle Enrico. He produces the best blades in Sicily."

Enrico was small and rotund, dressed in a dark suit with a

white open-necked shirt. His eyes were bright and his manner alert. He beckoned and they followed into a spacious courtyard and stopped at a lean-to shed, its rear fastened against a natural stonewall. From his jacket pocket he removed a key and unlocked the heavy steel padlock from the door. Inside shelves loaded with tins of emulsion paint went from floor to roof. With his foot, he kicked the tattered rug on the floor to reveal a small hatch. This he opened, pulled a metal lever and a door in the rear wall containing the tins of paint opened.

"Everything the Cosa Nostra requires is here."

"You sell guns to them?" asked Amadou.

"No, this is their armoury. For this, I have free protection. This is Sicily. Everyone understands that if you wish to stay in business you pay protection. Nothing has changed since the old days."

From a cupboard at the far end, he removed three thin leather pouches and placed them on a wooden bench in front of ZZ. "Excellent blades."

ZZ let his gaze travel over the three sets of double-edged knives. He turned to Enrico. "May I?"

He nodded.

ZZ removed one from each pouch, weighed it in his hand, and threw it at a roof support.

He removed, cleaned, and replaced each blade into its pouch. Lifted one and asked, "How much?"

"One-hundred euro the set, cash."

Petros removed two fifty euro notes from his wallet and handed them to Enrico.

"Is that everything?" asked Tommaso.

"For the moment," Petros said. "Right, back to the car and then the ship."

Tommaso led them back through the courtyard and along

the labyrinth of narrow streets to the where he parked the car.

Fifteen minutes later they alighted. A black and white trawler nestled against the concrete quay, its name *Tuna Turner* in polished brass.

Petros' eyes commenced a bow to stern circuit of the ship. He turned to Amadou. "It was once a fishing boat until converted. Those hydraulic davits on the stern look as if they could lift a ton or two."

"So long as it has a good bed and doesn't bounce too much I'm happy."

Alfredo, a small, lean, muscular man with a shaven head waved at his nephew. His angular face creased from years of salt spray and sun. "Any problems?"

"No, uncle."

Petros boarded first. "Petros Kyriades and these are my friends, Amadou and ZZ."

"Welcome. Tommaso will show you to your cabins. There is a single and a double, and both have en-suite facilities. When you have unpacked, we need to talk."

"Of course." Petros turned to Amadou. "The single is mine."

Amadou shrugged. "A bed is a bed and ZZ lives in my house when he's not with a girl."

ZZ grinned. "Is it my fault I'm so handsome?"

"Please," said Tommaso, "follow me."

Five minutes later Petros found his way to the bridge where Alfredo was sorting through his charts.

"Where is this wreck of yours?"

Petros removed his wallet and handed over a sheet of paper. "As plotted by the Royal Navy at the time she sank."

Alfredo read and found the appropriate chart and marked the location. "The sea is one hell of a large place. Do you know how difficult it is to find a wreck? You can miss it by metres and never know. We must pray it's in the shallower water."

"Apart from the depth, any other reason?"

"The cost of hiring deep sea equipment rises with the depth."

Petros studied the chart. "We have to find it first."

"With side scan sonar, if it's there we will find it."

"I'm familiar with the basics of sonar but side scan I've never worked with."

"It's the best equipment the scientists have produced for underwater exploration. We can search large areas fast and produce detailed pictures when we want them. Best of all, it gives a GPS position so we can find the same location every time. With the equipment I have we cover the larger area first. When we locate the possible target, we increase the search frequency and produce high res images for analysis. Think of it as an underwater television camera."

Petros nodded. "I love technology when it works. How long until we're over the wreck?"

Alfredo removed a pair of compasses from a draw, set them to a distance equating to twelve knots, and marked fine pencil lines on the chart. "Three-hundred and fifty miles at twelve knots." He lifted his head and faced Petros. "Give or take thirty hours we will be on site. We can leave when you wish."

"When you're ready."

"One hour. I must go and say goodbye to my wife. It's a custom I dare not miss, although she tells me I love my boat more than her. I'll have Marco the cook prepare lunch. We dine in the crew's mess."

Petros liked Alfredo. He appeared a calm man who respected his wife and the sea. "I better unpack. See you in an hour."

***

Tommaso drove Alfredo home and fifty minutes later returned.

Alfredo ran up the ladder to the bridge and prepared the instrumentation for sea. Satisfied all was in good working order, he contacted the engine-room. "Davide, start the engines."

The hull vibrated as the two diesel engines roared into life.

Alfredo waited until his engineer switched the control of the engines to the bridge.

Tommaso took the helm, while Marco the cook and Simone readied the ropes for slipping.

Alfredo took one final look around before ordering, "Wheel amidships. Let go forward and aft." He operated the throttles and manoeuvred the *Tuna Turner* off the harbour wall until she faced the entrance. He set the throttles to three knots. "Take her out, Tommaso."

***

Petros, Amadou and ZZ sat in chairs on the stern and waved to those on the shore or on other vessels.

"Relax and enjoy," said Petros.

"Why are we here?" asked ZZ.

"Just in case," said Amadou. "We watch PK's back."

"So we get paid for doing nothing." ZZ grinned.

Petros laughed. "I hope so but things can change and I need good men to support me.

***

The *Tuna Turner* weaved its course through the craft anchored or manoeuvring. When clear of the harbour, Alfredo set 080 on the automatic pilot and entered numerous coordinates into the bridge computer before setting to operate. For five minutes, he watched the rudder indicator shift to port and starboard. With the course steady, he pushed the throttle levers down so they produced twelve knots

When in the open sea and steady on its course, he turned to Tommaso. "Keep your eyes open. Call me if you have a problem."

Tommaso grinned. "You always tell me to call you. My certificate is the same as yours."

"I know but I am the captain."

He saluted as his uncle left the bridge.

***

Marco the cook shouted along the central passage. "Food's ready. Come and get it."

Alfredo headed the queue, his four crewmen behind him with Petros and his team at the end.

Alfredo, his plate full, stopped as he came to Petros. "Do not worry, Marco makes more food than we can eat. You will not go hungry on my boat."

"What are we eating?" asked ZZ.

"Spaghetti Bolognaise," said Amadou. "You'll like it. Tomato sauce with meat and pasta."

Marco filled ZZ's plate. "Good Italian cooking."

Every man sat at the one table bolted to the floor in the crew's mess, Alfredo at the head. He gestured with his left hand. "Petros, my crew. Tommaso is on the bridge, he is my second in command. Davide with the sparkling blue eyes, is my engineer. He fixes everything if it breaks. Marco my cook is my wife's sister's boy. He's a good cook, used to work in a posh restaurant in Rome. He was homesick and asked me for a job; cook and deck hand. Last, but you'll never meet a seaman like him, is Simone De Luca. His father is an important man in Palermo."

Petros went to stand but Alfredo motioned for him to remain seated. "Petros Kyriades, like you, an islander by birth. My friends are Libyan but speak English. None of us are familiar with Italian. We hope to find a vessel sunk during the war. With luck we might find something else. If we do you'll be on a bonus."

"We are all family," said Alfredo. "Marco, we drink red wine to toast the success of our search."

Marco left the mess room and returned with eight half-filled plastic tumblers on a tray. With care he poured the dark red wine.

Alfredo lifted his glass. "Success." They all drank.

"I've had a long day so it's an early night for me," said Petros.

Amadou and ZZ nodded in agreement.

Chapter Thirteen

The *Tuna Turner* maintained a steady ten knots and ploughed through the moderate swell. Alfredo held onto the stainless steel rail that circled the bridge. Long curving waves lifted the bow allowing it to slide into the next.

He studied the chart, fixed the position of his vessel and checked the time. In an hour he planned to alter course and transit the Straights of Messina.

Aft, Petros, Amadou and ZZ sat on the deck and chatted.

"This is boring," said ZZ. "I have more excitement with my right hand in bed."

"Get used to it," said Petros. "We have another day before we start our search."

Petros slapped him on the back. "ZZ, set up a target and we'll have a knife-throwing competition."

Simone supplied a few planks of wood, secured them to a beam and painted a rough target.

"I'll go first as knife throwing isn't something I do well," said Petros.

ZZ handed him three of his blades. "It's the same as firing a rifle."

"I believe you," said Petros. He drew his right arm back and flicked the knife. All three points struck the wood.

Amadou hit the target but only just.

ZZ balanced each blade in his right hand, concentrated and the blade hit the target centre. The other two struck within a few millimetres of the first.

"You'll have to teach me," said Petros.

"It is easy. Come let me show you."

Amadou leant on the side of the ship and watched Sicily go by.

By lunchtime, Petros managed to strike the target.

"You need to practice," said ZZ.

"Lunch," shouted Marco.

ZZ oiled his blades before returning them to their pouch.

Once through the Straits of Messina the surface swell came from the west and a warm breeze from the African coast wafted across the deck. Alfredo checked the radar for other shipping in the vicinity. Satisfied, he took a final glance around and left the bridge.

Lunch consisted of smoked ham, freshly baked bread and fresh fruit.

As Petros carved a slice of the ham he counted the men in the mess room. "Alfredo, who's on the bridge?"

"I am but I eat like you. There is not another vessel for thirty miles. I do not worry, why should you?"

"It's something I'm not used to. When I drive my boat I live on the bridge and stay in harbour at night."

"Really," said Alfredo. "You have certificates?"

"Ocean skipper with celestial navigation."

"Tommaso and I are qualified but for long trips Simone takes a turn on the bridge during daylight hours. This afternoon I intend to test the side-scan sonar equipment ready for tomorrow. Usually Tommaso keeps the watch until midnight. If you could help out it would leave him fresh for tomorrow. It is your decision."

"Love to but can I observe the sonar in operation?"

"Certainly, you can assist Tommaso while I operate the monitors and depth sounders."

The afternoon vanished in a haze of activity as with the ship's speed reduced to five knots, two bright yellow tow-fish were prepared and lowered into the sea, their depth controlled by Alfredo in the small control room.

Petros and Amadou entered the control room and watched the picture on the screen change from virtually nothing to a detailed black and white picture of the seabed.

"I use low frequency for long range and high for a detailed search," said Alfredo. "Colour is available but for most scans black and white is perfect."

"What's the black line?" asked Amadou.

"Imagine you are a passenger in a light aircraft. You can see the ground left and right but you cannot see the ground directly beneath. That is the black line."

"I don't believe it," said Petros.

Alfredo changed the frequency until the object was well defined. "It's a man's bicycle, you can see the cross bar."

"It's so clear."

"If your wreck is where you think it is you'll be surprised at what we can see. Do you know what happens when a ship sinks?"

For a moment he remained silent. "Never gave it any thought."

"Let me explain," said Alfredo. "A process of change begins as it adapts to new surroundings. In other words, it begins to rot but the process is dependent on many factors. What the vessel made of? Oxygen in the water? Chemicals, and marine life? Eventually it becomes a part of the seabed and because of the lack of oxygen, the whole process slows or stops. The vessel is in a state of preservation."

"Interesting," said Petros as he gazed at the screen.

"The equipment is working," said Alfredo. "I'll go and take over from Simone and he can help Tommaso. See you at four."

"We might as well give a hand. Amadou, where's ZZ?"

"On his bunk reading a book in English."

On the aft deck, Tommaso operated the winch while Simone guided the wire. Petros and Amadou manhandled the tow-fish into its stowage.

"Anything else?" asked Petros.

"Not at the moment. Thanks for your help. I've a few checks to make before I secure the tow-fish," said Tommaso. "See you at supper."

As Petros and Amadou strolled back to their cabins Amadou asked, "Do you believe we'll find your wreck?"

"I do and I'm convinced whatever the Germans placed in the hold is valuable. If it's not I'm out of pocket a few thousand pounds. Anyway, a quick shower and I'm on the bridge until midnight."

"You'll be down for supper?"

"I'll come and get it but eat on the bridge."

"Your decision. I'll come up and chat."

Chapter Fourteen

The *Tuna Turner* rolled in the slight swell. Two men studied the chart in front of them. "We are at the location you gave me, Petros. I intend to complete a grid search at a low frequency and see if anything of interest is on the sea bed."

"You're the captain," said Petros. "I'll stay on the bridge and keep watch. Simone can relieve me if you spot anything of interest."

Alfredo chuckled. "As a paying guest, you are a bonus. I see with my eyes a leader and men follow you but you do not hide the truth." He slapped Petros on the back and descended the bridge deck ladder.

Alfredo's eyes never faltered as at three knots they navigated each leg of the grid marked on the chart. Lunch came and went but no trace of a wreck appeared on the screen. With tired eyes, he demanded one more leg of the grid before he rested for the night.

Tommaso and Simone took turns to sleep while the other checked the tow-fish cable.

Ready to finish, Alfredo glanced from the screen and sipped his tenth cup of cold coffee. Something clipped the farthest edge of the monitor.

"Tommaso," he shouted.

"What's the matter?"

"We may have something. Go tell Petros. Run boy."

Alfredo switched to high frequency, his eyes consuming every detail on the screen. He felt the ship turn. The outline of a vessel on its side began to show. He pressed the printer to automatic, as every three seconds a frame from the screen shuffled into the out tray. Was this the wreck? "Tommaso, go, relieve Petros. I want him to see this."

The ship continued to circle.

Petros arrived and stared over Alfredo's shoulder. "It's so well defined. I can see the starboard anchor still in its hawse pipe. When will we find out if it's my vessel?"

"Tomorrow, Isabella will sit in the wreck's belly."

"And Isabella is?"

"The name of my wife and the ROV on the main deck. Both are nosey."

"Remote operating vehicle," said Petros.

"My Isabella will get up close and personal. Her ability to uncover the truth will amaze you. How did you discover this ship?"

"I was searching for a train," said Petros.

Alfredo leant back in his chair and clasped his hands behind his head, his eyes never leaving the screen. "You look for a train and find a sunken vessel. How?"

Petros explained.

A confused look spread over Alfredo's face. "Quite a story. I just hope you are right or you will have wasted a lot of money."

"The ship's there. The gold or whatever may not exist."

Alfredo shrugged and made sure the sat-nav fixed the position before shutting down all the equipment. "Petros, go tell whoever is keeping an eye on the cable to heave in the tow-fish. My eyes are tired. Enough is enough."

"I hope it's my ship."

"So do I," said Alfredo, "or we start again. I have told you the seabed is a big place when you are searching for something. Please tell Marco to start the evening meal."

"I'll keep watch until midnight," said Petros.

"Tonight we save fuel and shut down the engines. Have Tommaso and Simone prepare the sea anchor. We can let the waves rock us to sleep."

"How well do those things work?" asked Petros.

"They reduce drifting by sixty percent which means we will not be far off target in the morning. It also allows me to place Marco on the bridge."

"But he's the cook."

"A cook with a good pair of eyes. He will wake me if he sees another vessel and anyway, we will have every deck light on and not under command lights. Other vessels will stay well clear."

"You're right. I'll get up to the bridge. Shout when you're finished with the engines."

***

At supper, Amadou turned to Alfredo. "ZZ and I will keep watch through the night. I can work radar but am unfamiliar with the controls on this model. Will someone show me how to set the range finder?"

"Four eyes will be better than two, but you do not have to do this."

"Today you, Petros and your crew worked long hours while we lay on our bunks reading. It is fair we help and tomorrow you will be refreshed and find our ship."

"It's teamwork," said Petros, "and no I didn't ask them. I have trusted these men with my life. So long as they can brew coffee they'll be happy."

Alfredo glanced around the table at his crew. "I thank you. Come, I will give you instruction on the radar and how to contact me in a hurry. The rest of you get some sleep."

***

The sky in the east brightened. Amadou yawned and glanced at his watch. "Two more hours, ZZ, and we can go to bed."

"I'm ready for my bed. When do we wake the cook?"

"Soon. The captain wants an early start."

"Could it be the wrong ship?"

"The desert as you know is full of wild camels. You lose one and try to find it. You could see a thousand in a day but you will not know which is yours until you can actually see it up close. During the war hundreds of ships ended their working lives on the sea bed. If this is not our ship the captain starts his search until we find it or we give up."

Amadou sent ZZ to wake the cook and make two cups of coffee.

They sipped their drinks and watched the sun climb into the clear blue sky. From below came the rattle of pans and the aroma of breakfast.

Tommaso arrived with a roll filled with cooked ham. "I'll take over. Davide and Simone are winching the sea anchor in. As soon as they're finished I'll start the engines. The boss wants us over the wreck and ready."

"If you find anything interesting wake me," said Amadou.

Tommaso turned his head. "Get some sleep. Whatever we find will not be going anywhere before you wake."

"I will come and see later," said ZZ as he slid on the companionway handrail to the deck below.

Amadou descended the steel steps one at a time.

Tommaso stared aft waiting for the signal to indicate the sea anchor was clear of the water. Davide gave a thumb up and raced to the engine room. Two minutes later the engines roared into life. With the wreck's coordinates in the computer-assisted pilot, the ship turned and headed at ten knots to the exact location.

Petros and Alfredo strolled onto the open deck aft with their cups of coffee.

"How far will we have drifted?" asked Petros.

"The tidal currant is weak in the Med. A few miles perhaps. We will lower the tow-fish and check before the ROV goes exploring."

"I do hope we have the right ship."

"It is close to your position but we will see."

Petros let out a sigh. "You have another busy day in front of you."

"You pay me to do a job. You recommend me if I do it well."

"I'm sure James keeps you busy."

He shrugged. "I make a living. The days of shallow water salvage are over. Come help me prepare Isabella for her swim."

"In position," shouted Tommaso.

Alfredo nodded to Simone as he readied the tow-fish before entering his compact control room. Within thirty minutes, he found the wreck.

Petros' eyes never left the VDU as the stern of a vessel appeared. "The detail's incredible. You can see every rise and fall in the sea bed."

Alfredo sighed as he shook his head. "This is not your vessel."

"How can you tell?"

"She is an iron-clad and in three pieces. Sail and steam. The deck, mast stumps, and to the left, part of her funnel. Quite large, maybe seventy to eighty metres."

Disappointed, Alfredo programmed a new search pattern. The hours ticked by and the seabed remained empty.

Marco delivered coffee and filled rolls to everyone. "Captain, when shall I start supper?"

Alfredo turned to Petros. "We have a few more hours of daylight remaining. It is your call."

"I reckon we keep going until dusk or finish one more leg of the grid, whichever arrives first."

"You never know your luck," said Alfredo.

The daylight began to fade when Alfredo shouted, "I have a large contact."

"How large?" asked Petros.

Their mood of expectancy rose as the screen showed a vessel on its side.

"What do you think?"

"Isabella will tell us tomorrow. The wreck is a mile from the position you gave at a depth of two hundred and sixty metres on a sloping seabed. The thing is we started our search to the right, if we had chosen left." He shrugged. "I am hungry and if we work any longer mistakes will be made."

Petros took himself to the bridge while all hands recovered the tow-fish and secured it for the night.

As a repeat of the previous night, Amadou and ZZ stood watch while the crew slept and the ship drifted.

Chapter Fifteen

ZZ roused the cook and crew at first light. Breakfast consisted of buttered toast and coffee. A clear blue sky greeted the day as they proceeded to the previous night's sat nav position. One hour later, Tommaso and Simone wandered aft and prepared the ROV for launch.

Alfredo, with his third cup of coffee in his hand, strolled along the deck, gave the order, and waited until Isabella with her umbilical cord attached, descended.

Petros' eyes never left the screen as Alfredo operated the joystick. It remained blank for some time until at twenty metres above the seabed the four-halogen searchlights operated. The illuminated hull of a ship, its port side covered in silt, showed clearly on the monitor.

"From the naval report, neither warship damaged her enough to sink her. Can you check the hull?" said Petros.

Alfredo manipulated Isabella to the bow, turned, and traversed the length of the ship. "Someone blew holes in the hull four times but from what I can see, left the forward hold untouched" The image on the screen changed to the aft deck. "Two guns with a steel framework over them."

"Could have been an armed merchantman," said Petros.

"One way to find out."

"How can we be sure?"

"Paint lasts a long time underwater. Do you know the grey paint on the Bismarck is still in good condition? We need to find a large red cross amidships."

Isabella travelled to the central section and with the thrust from her main propellers cleared the layer of silt from the superstructure. Back and forth, she manoeuvred until at last a dull white became visible.

"Liners are white, not tramps," said Alfredo, "and this was never a passenger ship. There is your red cross, or at least a part of it. We have your ship. Now for the hard part. We have to enter without snagging the umbilical."

"Maybe the hatch covers came off when she sank."

"Let us take a look."

Isabella, with both motors at full power, surged through the clear water to the other side. On the screen could be seen twisted metal where the bridge once existed. Alfredo guided the craft keeping clear of jagged metal edges.

"Why are you peering into the remains of the bridge?"

"I am hoping to discover a name plate." Alfredo hovered the ROV and increased the magnitude of the camera lens. The lighting along with the clear water assisted as he tilted and turned. "There it is as always on the aft bulkhead." He adjusted the camera and read out loud, "Jupiter 1927 Built Harland and Wolf Belfast. At least you might be able to find out who owned her."

The craft backed away and swept across the main deck. "Two hatch-covers missing. One intact. The explosion from the charges that blasted the hull, blew them off. This might be fun," said Alfredo as he pressed the remote arm function. A triple steel claw appeared on the edge of the screen as it grabbed the tarpaulin on the hatch.

"Slowly, slowly," muttered Alfredo.

On the screen, the rotten canvas ripped to reveal broken and distorted planks.

"This is going to take time. Petros, will you make me a coffee?"

"And miss all the fun?"

"I promise I will wait for you to come back before I take Isabella inside."

"Coffee, boss," shouted Marco.

"Looks as if I'm staying," said Petros.

"Be quiet. If I make a mistake I lose my ROV."

Piece by piece Isabella grabbed and ripped the canvas from the hatch. Many of the planks, which formed the cover, tumbled to the seabed. "As she sank and fell on her side, her weight shattered some of the planks," said Alfredo. "If I can shift enough we go in. If not we blow the cover clear, which may cause problems."

Petros shrugged. "Whatever works?"

Limited by its single arm and power the ROV pushed, pulled at the canvas and wood.

"You could drive a bus through a hole that size."

Alfredo turned his head. "A bus does not have an umbilical trailing behind it. My ship maintains its position with a computerised global positioning system. If one of the bow or stern thrusters malfunctions for a few seconds I lose the ROV and cost you a lot of money."

Petros placed his hand on Alfredo's shoulder. "Point taken."

With the dexterity of a surgeon, Alfredo enlarged the opening. Hours elapsed before he declared. "It is time to see what is in this hold."

Tommaso and Simone crowded the entrance, their eyes fixed on the screen. Isabella approached the cavernous hole with caution, her four halogen lights illuminating a dark cargo hold unseen for sixty-nine years.

"It's empty," muttered Simone.

"Think boy," said Alfredo, "The bottom is in front of us."

"Interesting," said Petros. "Those banks of ammunition boxes have metal straps securing them to the deck."

Isabella crept ahead and hovered a short distance away.

Petros laughed as he read the German wording.

"What is so funny?"

"It says, 'This Way Up'."

"They have been secured with cross-straps bolted to the deck so they cannot move. It implies whatever is in them is heavy. The last thing you need in a rough sea is your cargo shifting."

"So we are buggered," said Petros. "Isabella has discovered something we cannot move."

"Never took you to be a defeatist. I am a professional. Simone, have Davide prepare two charges, detonators wired to the surface."

We should check each container," said Petros. "Maybe one is broken."

"German engineering and well constructed. My way may take a couple of hours but saves time." He glanced at his watch. "We will stop, relax, and have lunch but first my Isabella must return."

As the ROV surfaced, Petros hooked the lifting beam. Assisted by Simone they manhandled it onto the deck.

Davide checked for damage before attaching a roll of wire to a fixed arm.

"Fascinating," said Petros.

"Simple, the detonators are placed in the explosive which is held in the remote arm. When the charge is in position the ROV backs away and the wire trails to the surface."

"I imagine placing the explosives is a delicate operation."

"No, it is easy. The difficult bit is not using too much."

Marco brought soup with fresh crusty bread and oranges on the aft deck.

Each man grabbed a mug of soup, a chunk of bread and sat on the deck

When Alfredo finished eating, he stood and strolled around the deck stretching and bending before he returned and spoke to Davide. "Ready?"

Petros and Tommaso lowered the ROV into the sea while Alfredo sat in the control room. With a flurry of foam, the red and black machine disappeared into the depths. Alfredo used the side scan sonar and sat-nav to guide his hand. Sixteen minutes later four sets of eyes watched the screen as Isabella wedged the explosive charge at the base of one bracket. Time elapsed until on the surface they hoisted the ROV onto the deck.

Davide removed the drum of wire and prepared the ends for connecting to a battery. He turned to Alfredo.

He nodded.

"Not exactly dramatic," said Petros.

"Dramatic is a large explosion. An expert uses enough to do the job," said Davide.

"Now we do it again." He rolled the wire onto the cable drum, examined the ends, cut back to fresh ends, and attached a detonator. This he inserted into the explosive. "Ready."

Again, the ROV descended but before the second charge was in place, Alfredo examined the damage caused by the first explosion. "Can you see, one strap neatly severed and the ammunition boxes undamaged, well almost."

With the second charge in place and the ROV on deck, Davide pressed the button.

Twenty minutes later Isabella entered the hold. On inspection, the screen showed many ammunition boxes on the steel deck. Like an inquisitive beast, the ROV hovered over one, drifted to the right and then left.

Petros attempted to quell his excitement. "Can you see the fastenings?"

"Yes and I am deciding on the best way to lift them."

Alfredo drove Isabella until it sat on the steel plates next to a box.

Petros watched the small movements of Alfredo's right hand as he operated the joystick while his left the grab. The first clip broke away as did the others. With a flick of the wrist the cover came off the box. A layer of rust covered the contents until the wash from the thrusters brushed it away.

"Holy Mother of Jesus." Alfredo crossed himself. The box in the centre of the screen contained four cast ingots of what appeared to be gold.

"Can you lift one?" asked Petros.

"Depends on the weight," said Alfredo. "I will try."

The remote arm grasped a handle. Utilising full thrust Isabella rose and glided forward. The four ingots from the top layer tumbled out along with many more. With the empty box discarded, Alfredo settled the ROV next to an ingot, which rested on another. The grab locked its jaws around the middle of the bar.

"Progress out of the hold will be difficult. If I snag the umbilical we lose everything. The extra weight reduces my control." He took his time as the remote arm drew back into the main body of the ROV.

With a steady hand, Alfredo positioned Isabella until the halogen lights illuminated the gaping hole in the hatch cover. The veins on the back of his hand stood out as at full power the ROV raced clear. Free of any obstruction he activated the red button on the consol. The screen went blank and he relaxed in his chair.

"What's happening?" asked Petros.

"Isabella is on her way to the surface. I operated the emergency floatation bags to give extra lift. Unfortunately, it kills the other systems dead. Come, we will have to lift her onboard."

The ROV floated one hundred metres on the port bow. Petros and Alfredo dragged the machine while Simone wound the umbilical onto its drum.

Tommaso hooked the lifting shackle. All eyes were on the grab as it rose out of the water and rested on the deck.

Petros went to remove the ingot but the grab held it fast.

Davide manually operated the release mechanism, which dropped the bar into his palm and smiled. "Hitler's Gold."

Petros read the words. Deutsche Reichsbank – 1Kilo Feingold. "Simone, your knife please." He placed the ingot on the deck and scraped the top. The dull gleam changed. "Looks like and is as heavy as gold so I believe it is."

Alfredo placed his arm around Petros' shoulders. "Our troubles are just beginning."

"I don't understand. I have the salvage rights."

"Your lawyer will have, I am sure, done everything in his power to have the paperwork signed and sealed in triplicate but that was before we discovered the gold. You have commissioned and paid for a search no one was interested in. When we arrive in Palermo you must by law declare what we have found."

"So you're saying, others may claim ownership of the ship and its cargo."

"The ammunition boxes are German. An authority on salvage may claim the ship was under the command of a Kriegsmarine Officer when the British attacked and sunk her. The gold is not marked in any other way so they might state it is German. I suggest you talk to your lawyer but for the moment keep quiet. A day or two might place the odds in your favour."

"We couldn't retrieve a few more ingots to pay for our time?"

"We were lucky to lift one. As I said, talk to your

lawyer."

"Your crew, will they keep their mouths shut?"

"With the promise of a bonus that is not your problem."

"We know where the ship is. That's our bargaining chip. Once the location is known the rats will gather."

Marco arrived with two mugs of coffee. "Dinner is ready. What time do we eat?"

"For once, we can eat at a decent time. Tommaso, make sure everything is secure on deck. Find Davide and tell him to start the engines, we are going home."

Simone shouted and pointed to the sea off the port bow. "Captain, at five miles there's a hulk full of bodies low in the water."

Petros and Alfredo ran to the bridge.

"No one's moving," said Petros.

"The politicians have named this the perfect storm of immigration. These fools place their lives at risk in boats, which are not fit for firewood. I am told the operators charge a small fortune for a single place."

The *Tuna Turner* shivered as the engines started. Alfredo waited until the control indicator lit. "Let us take a look." At minimum speed, he guided his vessel alongside the stricken craft.

Both men stared unbelieving into a mass of men, women and children. An arm lifted and dropped.

"The young man in blue moved," said Petros. He ran from the bridge and jumped the one-metre gap between the two craft. This is insane, he thought, as he placed his feet between bodies. The boy turned his head as Petros felt for a pulse. "This one's alive," he screamed. With care, he lifted the thin frame and handed him to Tommaso. One by one, he checked the others. "There's a young woman with a baby, unconscious but both have a pulse." Again, he lifted and carried them to waiting arms. A wooden ladder led to the flooded deck below. Bodies bloated by death filled the space.

"Alfredo, I can't see an engine."

"There is a rope hanging over the bow. Was it cut or broken?"

Petros clambered over the hulk and pulled the rope from the sea. "Cut with a sharp knife."

"The bastards filled the boat with refugees, towed it into the middle of nowhere and left them."

Petros went to say something but what was the point? He rushed back to the *Tuna Turner*.

"She's sinking. We haven't much time to get the bodies off."

Amadou rubbed sleep from his eyes. "Marco, myself and ZZ will hand them across."

As the number of dead increased Amadou shouted, "How many?"

"At a rough count, seventy from a boat which at best could carry twenty," said Petros.

"ZZ, Marco, time to get off."

The calm sea lapped over the top edge of the aged sides and the craft settled into the deep waters.

Willing hands grabbed Amadou, dragging him inboard. "The dead in the lower deck numbered thirty, give or take."

Davide covered the bodies with reverence securing the tarpaulin with heavy concrete sinkers.

"The little boy, how is he?" asked Petros.

"The three of them might have a chance. Dehydrated and possibly have not eaten for days. Tommaso has been dribbling a rehydration solution down their throats."

"What's the mix?"

Alfredo seemed surprised. "Tommaso served with the army in Afghanistan. One jug of boiled water with a teaspoon of salt and six of sugar. He's using a dripper for the baby and tells me we must continue the treatment until we reach Palermo. Maybe we will berth in Syracuse."

Petros smiled. "I'm impressed but which is nearer Malta or Sicily?"

"About the same but I will check." Alfredo checked his sat-nav and placed a cross on the chart. With a pair of dividers he measured the distance between Valetta and then Syracuse. "Malta is closer by far. Why?"

"Helicopters. Get on the radio, channel sixteen, and tell them we have three survivors from an abandoned boat of refugees. They stand a chance with proper medical treatment. Tommaso is doing his best but a hospital can give fluids intravenously. This will flood their bodies with water and salts much quicker."

Alfredo lifted the handset on the dual frequency radio. "This is *Tuna Turner*. I have an emergency. Out." He waited.

For a few moments the radio remained silent.

"*Tuna Turner* this is the harbour master, Valletta. State your position and nature of emergency. Out."

Alfredo gave the ship's position and the details requested. He glanced at the chronometer on the aft bridge bulkhead and turned to Petros. "Thirty minutes for the helicopter and a doctor."

Petros peered through the bridge windows. "I recommend you advise their man to descend onto the bow. There's plenty of room and nothing will move in the down draught. The pilot will inform you of speed and direction."

The throb of a helicopter's rotors signalled its arrival.

The radio blasted into life on channel sixteen. "This is Gulf Tango Charlie 326 – Channel seven two. Out."

Alfredo switched channel. This is *Tuna Turner*. Course west. Speed three knots. Maintaining steerage way."

"This is G T C 326. Course and speed ok. Don't touch anything."

Everyone except Petros watched as the craft maintained its position over the bow as a dark-haired crewmember in a day glow orange dry bag descended with two stretchers dangling below.

Head down Petros assisted with the equipment.

"Thank you."

"You're a woman."

"Doctor Martese De Martino and yes, I am. Where are my patients?"

"Please follow me."

She examined the casualties in minutes. "I have intravenous drips in the copter. Please carry the woman to a stretcher. Then you can come back for the man. I'll take the baby."

With the utmost care, he lifted the woman, carried, and placed her on a stretcher. As he left, the doctor strapped, clipped the harness and watched it rise and vanish.

Petros returned with the man who opened his eyes. Fear covered his face.

The doctor unzipped the front of her dry bag and positioned the baby between her breasts. She turned. "Thank you."

While they waited for the hook to lower, Petros shouted, "What are their chances?"

She mouthed. "Not good."

Secured, she gave a wave to the wireman.

In minutes the craft gained height and flew in the direction of Malta.

"*Tuna Turner,* my patients are on drips and alive. Out."

The radio crackled as Alfredo changed to channel sixteen. "Let us go home and land the less fortunate." He checked the chart, fixed their position, and drew a line direct to Syracuse, the nearest Sicilian port. "Nine hours means we arrive in the early hours of the morning. When we are in range, I will contact the harbour master. It has been a long day. Eat and rest for tomorrow may be even longer."

***

An orange glow filled the sky above the island.

"The mountain is on fire," said Alfredo. "This year must be a record, thirteen times Etna has grumbled and spewed out its guts."

"Our ancestors, like us, have lived with the danger. The soil in which our grapes prosper came from the mountain. Maybe one day she will be angry...Tommaso tell my crew to prepare for coming alongside."

The *Tuna Turner* negotiated the entrance to Syracuse harbour at three knots. "We will berth opposite Riva Giuseppe. There is a large car park, perfect for ambulances and the authorities."

On approaching an empty berth, a blaze of lights lit the ship. Alfredo swore and covered his eyes with a pair of Ray-Bans. Without a scratch on the paintwork, his ship nestled against the ancient berth.

Marco, Simone, ZZ and Amadou secured the ropes fore and aft. As Davide shut down the engines, the babble of the waiting media took over.

The police formed a line and prevented anyone boarding until the harbour master and another clambered across the gap between the ship and the wall.

Alfredo and his crew waited.

"Alfredo Abruzzi?"

"I am."

The uniformed man held out his hand. "Julio Lucia, Harbour Master. This is Pavlo Silva, the Mayor. Such a tragic mess with the sea becoming a cemetery. A humanitarian problem with no solution. Where are the unfortunates?"

Alfredo pointed. "Seventy two men, women and children are under the tarpaulin. We failed to recover another thirty or so."

Julio, followed by Pavlo and Alfredo, crossed the deck. Julio lifted the corner of the canvas. The stench of the dead filled the night air. "I have trucks and men with body bags on the jetty. Leave this to them. I have good news. The three survivors in Malta are recovering. I understand it will be some time before they will be fit enough to leave the hospital." He shouted to a man wearing a one-piece blue coverall on the jetty. "Seventy plus. Inspector, shift those people so the trucks can come closer."

He turned to Alfredo. "The media are hungry for another disaster. Talk to them and then I'll have the area sealed."

"I will speak to three on the forward deck. You choose."

Julio climbed up to the jetty and walked between the ten trucks adjacent to the ship. "The captain will talk to three of you." He touched two men and one woman. "Let these through with their cameramen. The rest might as well go back to bed."

ZZ, wearing tight cut off jeans, a white T-shirt and flip flops, waited for the media to cross the gap. His eyes never left the blonde reporter who negotiated between the shore and the ship with the efficiency of an athlete. Good looking and has taste, he thought. Her clothes not from a local store. She wore a white blouse, dark blue designer jeans and black Doc Marten boots. In her right hand, she carried a Gucci duffle bag. Their eyes met, she laughed and smiled before lowering her gaze.

The three teams guided by ZZ picked their way forward around wires and items of salvage equipment.

"You have five minutes to set up your equipment," said Alfredo.

Ready, her hair in a French bob, the energetic slim female started to ask questions.

"Wait," said Alfredo. "I do not intend to repeat myself. My crew and I are tired and could use a good night's sleep."

"Where are these people from?" asked the woman.

"I have no idea."

"We have been told three have survived," said a man.

"Three out of over one hundred. If it had not been for the sharp eyes of Petros Kyriades they might have been placed with the others."

For a moment, the cameras focussed on Petros before returning to Alfredo.

"What happened to their boat?" asked the other man.

"It sank. My crew recovered as many as they could but we believe thirty or so went with it."

"Why did you recover dead people?" said the woman.

"I have no idea who they are or where they came from but they deserve a proper burial." Alfredo glanced at his watch. "I have said all I am going to say, except goodnight."

Alfredo, followed by his crew, entered the superstructure and closed the door.

Petros and ZZ guided the news teams ashore.

Before she clambered to the jetty, the blonde held out her hand and whispered to ZZ, "Scarlet."

ZZ stared at her face; it would always photograph well, and grabbed the opportunity to assist. When she let go she flashed her most innocent smile and placed a card in the palm of his hand.

As the last corpse was hoisted and placed on the jetty, the ship's engines started. "Alfredo isn't hanging around," said Amadou."

"No point. Job done," said Petros.

"A coffee and then bed," said ZZ.

"I'll be in the mess in ten minutes. I need to see if Alfredo needs any help with watch-keeping." Petros ascended the ladder to the bridge where Alfredo and Tommaso controlled the vessel as she left harbour. "I'll give you two a break when we're clear."

The night passage through the Straits of Messina remained uneventful.

At noon the following day, *Tuna Turner* entered Palermo harbour and faced another gathering of the media.

Wearing a smart outfit, Alfredo's wife stood on the jetty and waved.

He waved back and laughed. "That is a first. Do you think my wife wants to be on television or is here to see me?"

"I shouldn't worry, she's talking to my girl friend," said Tommaso. "Tomorrow we will be old news. Let them have their five minutes of fame. I'm going for a shower before stepping ashore."

"Help me face the media, Petros," said Alfredo. "Your keen eyes saved three from a watery grave."

Together they stood on the jetty, answered a barrage of questions while Alfredo's wife hugged his arm and Tommaso's girlfriend wound her arm around Petros.

With every question answered at least twice, Petros held up his right arm. "One more and we're finished."

Alfredo pointed to a middle-aged man. "He's a local

reporter, I'll answer his."

The last question answered, Petros took a deep breath and grabbed Alfredo. "Let's get going."

The two women lingered on the jetty before Isabella said, "What time will you be home?"

Alfredo shrugged. "I have things to do. This evening, maybe six or seven."

"We eat at seven."

Petros and Alfredo made their way to the crew's mess.

"Marco, some sandwiches please and two cups of coffee." He turned to Petros. "In a few days a manned submersible with its equipment and driver will be on the stern. I will have it delivered early morning but many may become aware of it before we sail. I have ordered my crew to keep their mouths shut. I have promised them a bonus. You need to contact your man in London."

"Alfredo, take our bar of gold and hide it. If this goes pear-shaped you can give them their bonus."

"If I thought you might cheat on me you would not be here. I know people in Palermo who slit throats for fun."

Petros gave him a strange look. "You mean the Cosa Nostra?"

"Do not say the name. The rules forbid discussing them around outsiders. And some questions are better not asked."

***

Scarlet Orlando returned to her flat in the better part of Syracuse and found the middle-aged, grey-haired, Giovanni Silvio watching the news on television. She noted his pensive expression, strolled into the kitchen and made two cups of coffee. One she placed on the small table in front of him.

He lifted his head and gave a suspicious frown. "Where have they been?"

"They were searching for a wreck but didn't find it. When a boat full of corpses turned up they returned to harbour."

His snappy mood faded. "As a reporter, don't you find that puzzling?"

"No."

"Find a reason to visit that boat."

"I don't need a reason. One of the crew is a dish."

"Most men want to get into your knickers."

She flashed a sparkling smile. "Must be my irresistible charm."

"More than likely your bedside manner."

"Why do you have to lower everything to your level?"

"It's what you do best. You live in this apartment free of charge and have a good job because for the moment, you satisfy my needs."

She bit her lip and remained silent.

Giovanni stood, straightened the jacket of his expensive dark blue suit and pushed her aside. "I'll be back sometime tomorrow. Find out where that boat went and why. Sleep with the guy if you have to."

She heard the door slam. "Bastard, get stuffed. I'm good at my job. I'll show you."

Chapter Sixteen

Irritated, Roland Wallace slammed the handset of the phone into its cradle. "Why do I have to do everything?" His eyes never left the fifty-five inch screen on the far wall as he pressed playback. "I see you, Mr Kyriades, but why are you in Palermo standing on a fishing boat?"

He pressed the memory button on his mobile. "Yes, boss."

"Peter, where the fuck are you? I want you here like yesterday."

"Is there a problem?"

"There will be if you don't get your slack arse over here."

"Ten minutes."

The call ended.

***

Peter Fox's face remained guarded as he entered the private lift to his boss's penthouse.

Roland looked livid. "When I phone I expect you to jump and never ask how high. Have you been watching the news?"

"Why?"

"The man Kyriades is on a fishing vessel in Palermo. I want to know why."

Peter shifted his weight from foot to foot. "Why is that name familiar?"

"He's the guy who found a ship full of gold according to the information Johnston gave us. Your mother's Sicilian; find out why he's in Palermo."

Peter took a deep breath and looked Roland straight in the eyes. "If he's found it, what do you have in mind?"

"Simple. I want it. And if I have to rid this world of a few nobodies, I will. Time you made tracks. Ring me on my pay-as-you-go when you have some information. In fact ring me tomorrow with information or I'll have your bollocks grilled and served on a plate for the dog to eat."

***

Peter Fox arrived in Palermo at six in the evening. Outside the airport arrivals, a chauffeur-driven car waited to drive him to the house of Gabriele Silvio, the Padrino of Palermo.

At the entrance to the grounds, a broad-shouldered guard in a black t-shirt and black trousers assisted by another stern-faced individual, body-searched Peter and emptied his case.

"You know me, why bother?" said Peter in fluent Italian as he shoved everything back.

"The boss demands and we oblige. He's in the main dining room. Don't keep him waiting."

At the main door to the house, a man dressed as a steward ordered him to follow.

Gabriele sat at the end of a long wooden table with the other occupant of the room, his younger brother Giovanni. He stopped in mid-conversation as Peter entered. "Come, wonderful to see you. Your mother, she is well? She's been away a long time."

"Always a pleasure to be with you, Padrino. My mother is well and sends her love to you, your wife, and beautiful children."

"You flew with easy Jet? You must be tired and hungry. Sit at my table and eat, the pasta is homemade."

The steward pulled back a chair for Peter.

"Roland mentioned you have a matter of great

importance to discuss which requires my assistance."

Peter finished one mouthful before speaking. "I'll not waste your time. The vessel *Tuna Turner*, what do you know of her?"

"Ah, Alfredo's boat. An honest man who pays his dues, and works hard. I have no difficulty with him. Why do you ask?"

"Roland believes a man named Petros Kyriades from London guided him to a shipwreck full of gold."

"You have my attention."

"In exchange for a share Roland asks you to supervise the operation."

Gabriele frowned. "I need more information but my first thought is to let Alfredo do the work as regards the recovery. At a predetermined point in time, we highjack the vessel and take the gold. They carry no weapons and another ex-fishing boat lost at sea will not trouble the police. They have enough problems with boats full of refugees."

"So I can tell Roly it's a go."

"No. Tell him I want fifty percent and you, Peter, at my side. If he agrees then it's a go. Remind him I could take it all but a war is not necessary. He has London and I have Palermo. Life is good. You may use one of my phones."

The steward carried a silver tray with six different mobiles. Peter chose an old Motorola.

"When you finish your call, we change the card and the unit is sold. My scavengers, as I call them, deliver twenty a day to one of my shops near the harbour. The passengers from the cruise ships have little time to report their loss before sailing."

Peter smiled and nodded as he spoke. "Good evening, boss. The deal is fifty percent and I go with him." After a few seconds, he replaced the unit on the tray. "It's a go."

"What did he call me?"

"Opportunist."

"Are you sure it wasn't something similar to thieving Sicilian bastard?"

He grinned, "A few of those words sound familiar."

"Let's drink to cooperation and prosperity."

"And why not?"

The two brothers and Peter enjoyed a superb meal and after a few glasses of wine went to their rooms.

Giovanni lay on his bed visualising a ship full of gold.

***

Whenever possible, Petros jogged six to ten miles early in the morning including the weekends. He paused at a busy Palermo crossroads and waited for the lights to change. A few hundred metres along he stopped at a cafe. From the outside, it appeared spotless. He paid for two egg mayonnaise sandwiches and a glass of fresh orange juice from the self-service bar. At an empty table next to a window he sat, ate, and watched the world go by. The noise of conversation throughout the room made it difficult to separate one sound from another. He pressed the memory button on his mobile for James Eden.

"Petros, good morning. Was the cruise beneficial?"

"More than you think. We discovered many large containers in the hold."

"That's excellent."

"We have a name. Jupiter. 1927. Built Harland and Wolf, Belfast. I imagine whoever owned her has long forgotten."

"If she's still on a company's books they may well claim ownership of the cargo. I'll check it out and get back." He paused. "Oh, I've completed my searches in Germany and Greece and found nothing. What are your plans?"

"A few days relaxation and then continue the cruise. I understand from the captain we'll be carrying extra cargo."

"I recommend you contact me before resuming your cruise. I might have something of interest to discuss."

"Give you a bell tomorrow." The line went dead.

For a time, he strolled around the town. In a square, he sat on the worn steps that circled an ornate fountain, and stared at the dark clouds mushrooming from Mount Etna. No one took any notice of him when he contacted and spoke to Maria and Alysa.

***

James Eden lifted the handset on his desk to telephone a long-time-friend at Lloyds Shipping. On the seventh ring, the call connected. "Lloyds, Karen speaking. How may I assist?"

"I'd like to speak to Edward Hammond."

"Your name please?"

"James Eden."

"His line is busy. Please can you call back later?"

"No, I can't. Edward told me to ring him as soon as I gathered certain information for him. You can tell him I'll call when I'm not busy."

Karen replied. "One moment, Mr Eden. I'll interrupt his call."

Edward came on the line in a few seconds. "James, you must want something."

"I require a favour."

"If I charge you the going rate I might be very busy but..."

"Five hundred cash."

"Strange how priorities can change. What do you want?"

"I need all the information you can find on a vessel named Jupiter. Built 1927 at Harland and Wolf, Belfast."

"As a starter for ten, anything that old is either scrapped or a museum piece."

"Tell me something I don't know."

"Give me a couple of hours and I'll get back to you."

"Sooner and with the life history might help."

"Leave it with me." The connection ended.

James stood and stared out of his office window overlooking the Strand. The sun kept disappearing behind the dark rain clouds casting shadows over the buildings. With a grimace he returned to his desk and studied a pile of computer printouts.

***

Edward Hammond pressed the keys on his lap top to gain access to the company records. The screen glowed with the words. 'Records held in the Information Centre'. "Shit." He grabbed his jacket and strolled the one mile to the Centre, housed in a bland red brick building. The security guard made him sign the register before allowing him to enter. In the cavernous ground floor library, he sat at a computer terminal and entered the Jupiter's details.

"Interesting," he muttered as he typed the known information. The screen flashed – 'Records not computerised. Located section C, row 11, shelf 4'.

He strolled into section C and quickly found the heavy leather-bound ledger containing the information. From the records and documentation he read,

SS Jupiter, launched 1926, fitted out 1927 and traded as a general cargo carrier until nineteen thirty. Sold to Jose Maria

Line and renamed Vincente, Nineteen thirty three. Whilst entering the River Tagus in collision with the Argos and sank. Raised and rebuilt in nineteen thirty three becoming the Illueca, trading as a general cargo ship until in nineteen forty, sold for scrap. Prepared for towing to the scrap yard in Thessalonica, Greece.

He photocopied the single sheet and took a London cab to James' office.

Carole, wearing black nail polish and lipstick, a black one-piece body stocking, stopped Edward with a glare of annoyance. "I'll let James know you're here."

He hovered for a few minutes until she returned. "Sorry you had to wait but he was on a call. You know, client confidentiality. Please go in."

"Come in and sit down," said James as he pointed to a chair. "My apologies for making you wait but I was in the middle of an important call."

"No problem." Edward sat and handed across the single sheet of paper. "Can I ask why you're interested in a ship which was scrapped in nineteen forty? She sails no more."

James peered over the sheet of paper and yawned. "You can ask but I'll not tell." He opened the right-hand drawer in his desk, leaned forward and lowered his voice. "Five hundred as agreed and keep your mouth shut."

Edward gave a nod of the head. "I was never here."

"The next time we don't meet, you can buy me dinner."

"I'll do that."

Edward waved to Carole as he left.

She ignored him but mouthed, "Arsehole."

***

James managed a weak smile as he reread the information. He typed, "Thessalonica Ship Breakers,' into the box on the screen. His eyes studied a short list of builders, but no mention of a breaker's yard. For a long time he sat staring at the ceiling, something did not make sense. Again, he checked historical records and noted the Allies bombed every Greek shipyard during the second world war making them virtually useless.

Nothing remained but to sleep on it. Again, he read the single sheet. James thought ahead, the last thing he needed was an owner of the vessel crawling out of the woodwork. On a sheet of paper he made notes.

1. The shipping company no longer exists.

2. Destined for the scrap yard, therefore someone might have paid good money for the vessel.

3. Somehow survived the war. Past its prime, it remained functional, served a purpose and sailed from Thessalonica in July 1944.

4. From the initial salvage, carried a large amount of gold.

5. Sunk by the Royal Navy.

6. Found.

7. Owned by?

He stared at the mess of paper covering his desk and the half-drunk cup of coffee. "Carole." Then he remembered she had left. "There has to be an answer," he muttered. "Time I went home."

***

James woke with a start and glanced at the alarm clock. Becky remained asleep as he slipped silently from the bed and spent ages standing beneath the shower. His hand rubbed the stubble on his face but today he decided not to shave.

In the kitchen, he watched the news on BBC World and drank his first coffee of the day. Without waking his wife, he headed for his office

Chapter Seventeen

Hidden from the hundreds of tourists in Palermo, The Chianti restaurant catered for the privileged few. The rich, the elite, and top class escorts. Gabriele Silvio, along with his brother Giovanni, sat in the simple furnished room at the rear. Six associates smoked and drank coffee around a circular oak table.

Gabriele, their Padrino, refined his notes with suggestions from his team. Each man possessed strengths that he utilised. Experience being their mainstay. Although this appeared to be a straightforward piracy venture, no one deluded themselves. Much could go wrong as they planned alternative strategies. The procurement of an Arab Dhow remained number one on the list. Most of the other equipment was to hand or straightforward to obtain. The much needed part of the operation, the placing of a location device, he left to a paid member of the police department. The man, although weak-spirited, was aware of the price of failure.

"We will assemble here on the day the *Tuna Turner* leaves harbour. Taking possession of the gold will be a major undertaking and will be completed in daylight," said Gabriele. "I will use my own motor cruiser. Anyone damages the paintwork will have the cost of repair taken from his share."

"We are men of honour, Padrino, we know the rules," said Antonino, a handsome young man with pale skin and black hair.

"You will lead the assault on the ship. Three others, well armed, should suffice."

Antonino opened his mouth as if about to speak but thought better of it and simply nodded.

"Our code of silence is the key to this operation. When Alfredo's ship sails we make our move and arrange his burial at sea."

The group shook hands and without another word left.

***

Police Sergeant Calderone walked with a slight limp to the rear of his patrol car and opened the boot. From beneath the spare wheel cover, he removed a small, black plastic-coated electronic device.

For a few minutes he strolled back and forth along the jetty checking Alfredo's limited security. One of the crew would be on the vessel and at this time of night, possibly sleeping. Without making a sound, he traversed the gangplank. As quite as possible, he made his way to the external door, which led into the bridge. The handle turned, but to his disbelief, he found it locked from the inside. He shivered but controlled his fear. His eyes searched for a suitable place. He spotted a steel ladder leading to the top of the bridge. Hesitant, he ascended and saw an opening in the mast. With a definite clunk, the magnet held the device secure. A press of a button and the unit transmitted a signal every thirty minutes.

Sweat ran across his face as he journeyed back across the deck.

"Who's there?" said a man.

He fought off a wave of nausea. "Sergeant Calderone. I thought I saw a movement and came on board to investigate."

Marco shone a torch into the sergeant's eyes. "Good to know our police do some work. I'll see you off the ship. Roaming around a boat's deck at night, especially with your bad leg, can be dangerous. You never know what you might tread on."

"My radio is in the car and I must report in," said the

sergeant.

Marco shone the torch with his free hand as he guided the sergeant off. "Don't forget to report in."

For ten minutes, Calderone sat unmoving before driving away. Later he would nod twice to his contact making it known the unit was in position.

Marco returned to the crew's mess. Strange, he pondered, the sergeant shivered as if he was cold but it is a mild night. He rang Alfredo.

***

James began the task of searching Mediterranean ship breakers' records on his computer. But the thought nagged, why berth a ship ready for the scrap yard in Thessalonica? He read Edward's report and whispered, "Eden, you're a plonker of the highest order. Italy attacked Greece in October 1940 and this vessel remained in a Thessalonica shipyard, serviceable but forgotten. Until in desperation, the German SS needed a ship."

At speed, he checked the internet for the Jose Maria Line. With a broad smile he read, 'Went into liquidation nineteen fifty two.' One more question required an answer. On the demise of the owners, did the company go with them?

Ten minutes later the words, 'No assets,' told him everything. A smile played on his lips. The *Jupiter*, according to available records, no longer existed.

James relaxed into his chair, his mind working overtime. He removed the pay-as-you-go mobile from his desk draw, pressed the memory button and waited. He chose his words carefully, "Hi, Petros, listen. I've researched your missing vessel and it appears she was simply abandoned when the Italians attacked Greece. The shipping company went into liquidation with no worldly-goods. This means whatever you recover belongs to you. Just keep the whole thing under wraps until I give you the nod. Remember people talk and Sicily is the home of the Cosa Nostra."

Petros listened but remained silent.

"When do you intend to sail?"

"Alfredo has ordered some specialised equipment. We're ready to leave the moment it arrives."

"Sail the second it's on board. I guarantee someone will notice and ask awkward questions."

"I'll speak to Alfredo."

"Any problems, contact me on this phone." James terminated the call.

***

Alfredo was in the galley talking to Marco when Petros entered.

Petros searched for the coffee pot. "You look troubled."

"Marco tells me we had a visitor last night. Police Sergeant Calderone."

"Is that a problem?"

"He is a man who sold his soul to the Cosa Nostra. No one trusts him, including his fellow officers."

"Those people don't give refunds," said Petros.

"What he said made sense to me," said Marco.

Alfredo frowned. "He's good at that."

"That's the second time I've heard of the Cosa Nostra in the last five minutes. Where did you find him?"

"On the deck," said Marko. "We seal every door from the inside to prevent opportunist thieves."

"I just spoke to James and he virtually ordered me to tell you to sail as soon as the submersible and its team arrives. He believes the less said about this operation the better. I have a suggestion and before you ask, I'll pay."

"It's my ship but you are the boss," said Alfredo.

"Get the crew, provisions for three weeks and anything else you need on board today. No visits to the cafe for a glass or two of wine. When the crew arrive, we search the upper deck, every nook and cranny. Don't ask what we are searching for, I haven't a clue. You'll know when and if we find something."

"What is this nook and cranny?" asked Alfredo.

"Every possible place something might be hidden."

"I will contact my team. Marco, take Petros and start searching from the bow."

"No time like the present."

***

Petros and Marco checked every imaginable hiding place from the bow to the bridge structure.

"Top of the bridge next," said Marco.

"I'll search the wings."

With the wings proving clear, Petros climbed the steel ladder and rummaged under deck lockers.

"Found it," shouted Marco.

Petros joined him. "Leave it. Now we control the game."

Marco exchanged glances. "I don't understand. This will tell them where we are."

Petros' face remained impassive. "Someone will be monitoring the signal. There'll be a better time and place to throw it overboard."

"I can live with that...There's a fresh pot of coffee in the galley, fancy a cup?"

Petros nodded, followed Marco and savoured the aroma

of ground coffee beans. He sipped the dark brown liquid. "This is good."

"The captain's special. I often make a brew for myself when I'm on my own."

"When you order your provisions, add a few kilos of those beans."

"They are expensive."

"Let me worry about the price."

Amadou stuck his head around the door. "Does the coffee taste as good as it smells?"

"It does, come and join the party," said Petros. "I need you and ZZ to do something."

"Got to be better than doing nothing."

"Both of you pack your bags and stroll along the jetty. Jump in a taxi and find a hotel out of town. Book two rooms for a week."

"I gather we are not wanted."

"Wrong," said Petros. "Stay in the hotel tonight and have breakfast in a nearby cafe. Tomorrow evening, leave and return unseen. I want anyone who's watching this vessel to believe you and ZZ have gone. You're my back up when the Cosa Nostra shit hits the fan."

With a wry smile on his face, Amadou nodded. "I'll collect some insurance while I'm ashore."

"Good idea."

"We'll leave in ten minutes. It might be better if you said farewell and waved as we walk away."

"Grab your gear and leave the theatricals to me. I might even break down and cry on your shoulder," said Petros.

"That, they might not believe."

Petros peered over the ship's side while he waited.

"Thanks for the boat ride," said Amadou.

Petros shook hands with him and ZZ. Together they strolled to the gangway. He waved as they wandered towards the town.

***

Amadou and ZZ strolled into Panini's cafe, found a table, and ordered a coffee. Amadou glanced across to the crowds wandering around the yacht-studded harbour.

A waiter arrived and placed their coffee on the table.

Amadou handed over a ten Euro note, but held it for a few seconds while he asked, "You don't happen to know of any cheap but clean hotels?"

The man was all business. "Ten minutes from here, my mother's sister owns the Ariston, the cleanest hotel in Palermo."

"Can you get us a deal? Two double rooms for a week, bed only."

"Give me five minutes."

He returned in less than two. "I get you special offer, two double rooms, one week but you pay cash."

"How much?" asked Amadou.

"Six hundred Euro."

"Is that each or together?"

"For the two rooms. You will not find cheaper in Palermo and close to many fine restaurants."

"We'll take them. Can you give us directions or better still take us."

"I'll tell my uncle I'm having a break."

They strolled through narrow cobbled streets where with outstretched hands you could touch either side. From a restaurant the aroma of meat roasting on a spit, tantalised senses. Older women dressed in black lowered their eyes as they passed. Feral cats fought for scraps of food until chased by a stray dog.

In less than ten minutes, they entered via a stone arch and flagged courtyard to the cool reception at the Ariston Hotel. Amadou gave the area the once over.

Behind the counter, a pleasant looking woman greeted them. "It is good you brought them, Alexander. Tell your mother I will call tomorrow for my dress. Gentlemen, please follow me to your rooms."

They climbed two flights of stairs and along a corridor to the rear of the hotel.

She stopped at a door. "This is one room, the other is next door."

"I will take the other room," said ZZ.

Her eyes fixed on Amadou. "You have the cash?"

From his jacket, he removed his wallet and handed over six hundred Euro.

She smiled. "Taxes, we pay too much." She held up the money. "My refund from government."

"I couldn't agree more," said Amadou. "ZZ, see you in half an hour. I need to make a few calls."

ZZ held up the card the blonde reporter gave him. "I will contact this one."

Amadou laughed, entered his room and shut the door. The room was spotless, with an oversized double bed and an en-suite shower room. He opened the window, peered out at the streets below where life in many ways had not changed for years. With his clothes hung in the single wardrobe he lay on the bed and let his thoughts wander.

In the adjoining room, ZZ tossed his bag on the bed and made the call.

***

Scarlet Orlando arrived outside the hotel and parked her Red Fiat Abarth close to an historic stonewall near to the entrance.

ZZ walked round to the driver's door and opened it. "Great car."

She gave him a seductive smile. "It reminds me of me, small and wicked."

"Are you?" he asked with a grin.

She jumped out of the car and operated the remote locking. "I can be. It depends."

"On what?"

"If you have a shower in your room."

"My friend told me if I wish to seduce a lady I must wine and dine her before taking her to my bed."

She turned round, unlocked the passenger door. Clothes covered the rear seat. She rummaged through them and hauled out a bottle of red wine.

"I have the wine and there's a bistro round the corner for later."

"I am a man of the desert. I eat to maintain my strength."

She gave him a look, smiled and ran her hand over his chest. "Shower first and then much later, my man of the desert, we eat to restore your strength."

Together they ran to his room.

Showered, Scarlet swept back her wet blonde hair before turning to face ZZ, allowing the towel to fall to the floor.

"You've dropped something," said ZZ.

She was halfway across the room with the cheekiest of smiles. "Have I?"

***

Amadou sat at the bar sipping a beer. "Need to stretch my legs," he said to the barman. He drained the dregs and left the hotel turning right and entering the labyrinth of narrow cobbled streets, which led to the centre of the old town. A family of feral cats ran and hid in a cardboard box as he passed. At the edge of a square he found a payphone. He lifted the receiver, inserted his credit card, and keyed in a number from his notebook.

A child answered.

In poor Italian he said, "Can I speak to your papa?"

"Salvatore Rizzo. Who is this?"

"A friend who requires to purchase a few items for self-defence."

"I have many friends," he rasped. "Where are you calling from?"

"I'm in the city council square close to the Pretoria fountain."

Salvatore's tone softened. "You know I deal in cash."

"I wouldn't have it any other way."

"When do you require these items?"

"Tomorrow morning after the bank's open."

Salvatore paused. "Ten o'clock at the blue boatshed by the old harbour."

"I'll be there." Amadou sighed as he ended the call and strolled to a nearby restaurant to eat. A young dark-haired waitress wearing a skimpy mini skirt directed him to a corner table set for two at the back of the dining room. The surroundings were lively with the majority of the larger tables occupied. Glasses tinkled and voices fortified by the wine rose and fell. Waiters scooted at speed back and forth, their arms balancing plates filled with food.

Amadou ordered bistecca alla Palermo and asked for it to be well done.

On leaving, he hailed a taxi to take him back to his hotel.

***

Alfredo returned towards evening with his crew and a van full of provisions. The next hour passed loading and storing along with Marco shouting.

While eating their evening meal, Alfredo turned to Petros. "Amadou and ZZ, they are not eating?"

"They've gone."

"Why? They were useful."

"They felt out of place and I tended to agree. When is the submersible due to arrive?"

"Sometime tomorrow afternoon."

"We sail the moment it's on deck and secure."

"I agree," said Alfredo. "My crew tell me questions are being asked as to where we went and what was found."

"What were their answers?"

"We went all over the place and found nothing. And by the way," he grinned. "you are a mad Englishman who keeps changing his mind."

He shrugged. "I can think of a few people who might agree with you."

Not being at sea enabled the crew to enjoy a few glasses of wine and play cards. Petros returned to his cabin while Alfredo sat in the bridge and read a book, his eyes constantly scanning the jetty.

***

At ten o'clock Amadou waited. The freshly painted blue gates at the entrance to the Palermo Yachting Association remained shut. A chain and padlock ensured they remained that way.

An air of authority radiated from Salvatore, a large, well-built man in his fifties, as he appeared from a side street. He hugged Amadou. "My friend, long time. How can I be of service?"

"I need some insurance."

"Come and inspect the merchandise, much of which you supplied a year ago."

Salvatore removed the padlock and chain. Together they strolled along a cobbled path to the farthest boat shed. The skeletons of craft from distant days lay rotting on wasteland whereas to their left a well-planned marina contained craft of every shape and size.

Inside the shed, an aged motor cruiser sat in a wheeled cradle.

Salvatore pointed. "My office. Looks like a boat, is a boat but it will never float again."

They clambered up the steel steps alongside, entered a partly refurbished main cabin, and wandered forward to a bedroom.

"Shut the door," said Salvatore.

Amadou obliged.

Salvatore pushed a button on the far wall. A pump started and the bed lifted to reveal a large storage cupboard filled with weapons of every description.

"Not the safest of hideaways," said Amadou.

Salvatore cocked his head to one side. "Not necessary." He grinned. "If the door is left open this boat launches into the air with a big explosion taking the thieves with it."

Amadou selected his weapons, took the bulging white envelope from his pocket, and handed it to Salvatore. "You should check that."

Salvatore shoved the envelope into his trouser pocket. "If it's not enough I pay you less next time I order equipment."

Amadou smiled, lifted two holdalls, one in each hand, strolled out of the boat store and along the street to his hotel.

***

Behind the low-loader, the traffic crawled towards the harbour. Crowds of holidaymakers stopped and watched the driver negotiate the bends in the road as he blocked the oncoming vehicles. Mobile phones photographed the chaos.

An hour elapsed before the vehicle was in position to reverse along the jetty. Unruffled, the driver checked his alignment and reversed the four hundred metres to *Tuna Turner* without stopping. At the ship, he jumped out of his cab and adjusted the stabilisers before hoisting the pillar-box red submersible onto the deck.

Ginger-haired, Adrian Sullivan, exhibited a healthy complexion from years working in salt-laden surroundings. His dishevelled appearance contradicted his expertise as he guided the craft secure in its steel frame to the deck.

Alfredo greeted him as a brother.

"My truck driver will remain in Palermo until my return. We agreed fifty percent of my costs up front, the remainder on completion."

"Your money as agreed," said Alfredo as he handed over a buff envelope.

Adrian jumped to the jetty and gave it to his driver. "Deposit this and find yourself a three star hotel and no gambling."

"The man shoved the banker's draft into his jacket and returned to his cab. With a roar, the air filled with diesel exhaust as the empty low-loader traversed the jetty.

Petros remained on the far side of the vessel. A skilled

observer may have seen the wave of his hand as the red monster swayed above the deck. Amidships and concealed by the superstructure, Amadou and ZZ hauled themselves and two heavy holdalls over the side and entered the ship. ZZ fighting to keep his eyes open blew a kiss to Scarlet who sat behind the wheel of a hired motor boat.

***

Adrian checked the securing wires on the steel frame once more before turning to Alfredo. "When do we sail?"

The deck trembled and exhaust erupted from the funnel as Davide started the engines.

"Silly question. Where's my cabin?"

Petros strolled across and shook his hand. "Petros Kyriades. Follow me. It's the one next to mine. That's a pretty comprehensive bit of kit."

"The Red Devil, self-contained, air-compressor, tools, spare parts, everything I need to do the job. I'm paid for results."

"And as I'm the one paying I couldn't agree more."

"What are we recovering?"

"Gold."

He raised his eyebrows. "How much?"

Petros grinned. "When you bring it to the surface, we'll find out. The mess is at the end of this passage. The captain wants a chat once we're clear of the harbour."

Alfredo arrived twenty minutes later, opened a large manila envelope, and removed a dozen photographs, which he handed to Adrian. "What do you think?"

"Anyone require coffee?" said Marco as he entered the galley.

"Three cups," said Petros.

"Great detail," said Adrian. "The hatch cover has to be removed before I venture inside. I suggest you cut the brackets with explosives. If we're lucky it'll blow the hatch away. If it doesn't, I'll cut and drag. We position a steel basket away from the vessel. I'll remove the ingots and place them in the basket and on my signal, you hoist them to the surface. I reckon maximum ten at a time."

"You describe it as a day at the office," said Petros.

"I'll need an assistant."

"Why?" asked Petros.

"I operate the sub and my assistant the articulated arm. It's not impossible to do both but easier with an extra pair of hands."

"Could I do it?"

"I'll teach you in ten minutes if you want but we work until we can do no more or Alfredo calls us up. No tea breaks and you piss and crap in a bucket."

"Fine by me. I took a gamble there was something on this ship the Germans needed. I guessed gold and hit the jackpot. Alfredo, are you going to tell him the bad news or shall I?"

"You tell him. I am enjoying my cup of coffee."

"We should consider ourselves fortunate the location of the vessel has remained a secret. Somehow, what we have been searching for has the Cosa Nostra placing a transmitter onboard. If it were me, I'd wait a few days until the recovery is almost complete and move in. Pure speculation on my part and I'm open to suggestions. But, I don't intend to give whatever we recover away, so I've taken out insurance. Wait a moment."

Petros left and returned a few minutes later with Amadou and ZZ carrying two holdalls.

Alfredo inhaled sharply. "I admit you baffled me by leaving. Do I need to ask what's in the bags?"

ZZ unzipped the nearest and removed eight new pump action Remington shotguns. A box of stun grenades and two boxes of regular grenades. "One shotgun each and four boxes of shells."

"For defence," said Petros.

Alfredo picked one of the weapons up. "These are the best. Where did you get them without a permit?"

"You don't need to know," said Amadou. "I have contacts who, when asked, help."

"Amadou and ZZ will keep their eyes skinned for anything out of the ordinary while the rest of us work our balls off. The Cosa Nostra aren't stupid and more than likely kept us under observation during our time in harbour. They will count on Alfredo and his crew to give little or no resistance as they and their families are part of Palermo. Me, as an individual, they can deal with. One bullet in the head and no questions asked. Between you and me, I know how these people operate."

"You talk as if they will come," said Alfredo.

"My gut instinct kept me alive in some of the most dangerous places in the world. With what's at stake, I'm sure."

Adrian selected one of the shotguns and worked the pump action. "If it comes to the gunfight at the OK Corral, I'm in. No bastard's going to take my life for a bar of gold."

Alfredo chewed his lower lip. "Petros, I really do not want a stand-up fight with these people. Trust me, they follow their own rules. My crew will support me but once a shot is fired, we declare war. The Cosa Nostra will fight and one side will die."

"I have a saying, for evil to exist it takes good men to do nothing. Our deaths are inevitable if we do nothing. And I've no intention of underestimating the Cosa Nostra," said Petros with a smile. "In the meantime, we have three, maybe four days, before anything might happen. I suggest we carry on as normal. Adrian can teach me to operate the arm and if your crew require a bit of target practice so be it."

The idea of a fight stimulated the crew beyond imagination. How they might attack and defend their ship and livelihoods became the main topic of conversation as they ate dinner.

As the *Tuna Turner* sailed through the Messina Straits Petros removed the transmitter and tossed it over the side. "Should give us another day," he muttered.

The night was dark and the passage uneventful.

***

Scarlet grabbed her few possessions from the hotel bed she had shared with ZZ and shoved them into a plastic bag. With the bag over her arm, she descended the stairs and made her way to her car. For a second she hesitated before contacting Giovanni.

He answered his mobile on the third ring. "What did you find out?"

She cursed under her breath. "They have a submersible on board and I believe will be sailing this evening."

"Did you find out what they are looking for? My brother believes it is gold."

"I did the business with my contact but it's difficult to speak when you're with a real man. I did ask him about his job and he replied, bodyguard. Does that tell you anything?"

"Nothing which can't be dealt with. Keep your contact interested."

The line went dead.

Scarlet tossed her mobile onto the passenger seat livid at Giovanni. She liked ZZ and his young agile body. She smiled, anyone would be better than the slobbering, overweight creep.

She returned to ZZ's room, closed and locked the door. He'd told her it was booked for a week. Lifting the telephone she ordered a bottle of Merlot and lay back on the bed. Softly she hummed to herself while she thought, I'll wait."

***

In a telephone box outside Victoria station, Roland Wallace gripped the handset, his expression serious as he spoke to Gabriele Silvio.

Gabriele explained. "The transmitter my man planted on board is working. As we speak, my state-of-the-art computer plots the position of their vessel. I love technology that saves so much hard work. I'll give them a couple of days before I relieve them of the gold. Don't worry, the ship will be lost at sea with all hands. On completion, my motor yacht will berth in Rome and the gold transferred. Your share will be in your Bermuda account, soon after."

"Just let me know when you have the gold. I intend to implement an insurance policy of my own. I've been informed Kyriades is an ex-soldier and I detest heroes who get in my way. They tend to fuck things up."

"You worry too much. The crew of a fishing boat are unarmed and will be easy to overpower."

"Make sure he's shot first." The line went dead.

Gabriele turned to his brother Giovanni. "The English always worry." He glanced at his watch. "Time we went and found ourselves some refugees."

"If we don't there's plan B which I prefer."

When you are Padrino, you may decide. For the next thirty years, I decide."

Giovanni stood and shoved his hands in his pockets to regain his self-discipline. He strolled round the room then perched on the arm of a chair. "Why can't I come on this mission? I can deal with fishermen as good as any of the men."

"Do I not take care of you, brother? You want for nothing so leave the business side of our family to me."

Giovanni smiled. "You are right, brother." He hugged the man before saying, "I must go. Have a safe and profitable trip."

Chapter Eighteen

The *Tuna Turner* arrived over the wreck of the *Jupiter* late in the afternoon. Alfredo set his ship to hover and the six electric motors started and stopped automatically as they maintained the vessel's position. He turned to Petros. "When do you want to start?"

Adrian interrupted. "May I suggest something?"

"Be my guest," said Petros.

"Use your ROV to set charges and blow the brackets. I need to see the hulk before I descend. A good night's sleep before a long day works for me."

"I agree," said Alfredo, "but then I am not paying."

"You two are the professionals. So long as we recover the gold and no one gets hurt another few hours doesn't matter. What's the saying, early to bed and early to rise? Let's get the ROV ready for a dip."

No sooner had the ROV secured the charge, surfaced and Tommaso pressed the button, it dived again. Isabella repeated this process eleven times before the multiple steel straps securing the cargo were all fractured.

"The hatch cover has taken some damage," said Adrian, "but it can wait."

"Silly question," said Petros. "but are there any large sharks in the Med?"

Adrian smiled. "You'd better believe it, although not often seen. If my memory serves, there's at least forty different types. The big three are around and have sunk their teeth into a few tasty morsels."

"And they are?"

"White, Bull and Tiger. They only bite to see if you're good to eat."

"Great whites can't have much to eat in the Med."

They continued stowing the ROV and other gear.

"Great whites can't have much to eat in the Med."

"Dolphin and Tuna are in abundance and the occasional holiday-maker. Last one I heard of was off the coast of Malta. Honeymoon couple, he swam way out to impress his new bride and a Great White took him. She thought he was waving until he disappeared."

Petros grimaced. "On that wonderful thought, it's time for dinner."

"Adrian walked around his red submersible checking. Satisfied everything was in order, he joined the crew in the mess.

The meal over, everyone, apart from Amadou and ZZ, retired to their cabins, showered and rested.

On the bridge, Amadou checked their position from the sat-nav and glanced at the sweeping line on the radar display. The nearest vessel remained over thirty miles distant. He stared out of the starboard window relieved that the sea remained empty. For six hours, on the hour, he repeated the procedure. At the rear of the bridge, ZZ dozed in a chair.

Amadou was checking the radar when ZZ said, "See any ships?"

"Nothing except the sea and stars."

"When do you think the Cosa Nostra will arrive?"

"Soon."

"You talk as if you know."

"I don't know exactly, but they will."

"Funny, isn't it? We always tell ourselves not to get involved."

"You're not wrong."

"So why do we?"

***

At first light ZZ woke everyone except Amadou who had fallen asleep in a chair. Marco produced coffee and toasted ham and cheese sandwiches for breakfast.

Adrian supervised the launching of the Red Devil.

Within the hour, Adrian and Petros dropped into the submersible. Being last Petros pulled the hatch closed and sealed it before sliding into his rigid seat. His eyes gazed at the electronic control panels in front and to the sides.

Adrian completed the pre-dive check-list, ticking each item on his sheet.

Simone, wearing a wet suit, floated at one of the viewing ports, waiting. When he received thumbs up from inside he released the securing shackle and pulled himself onto the *Tuna Turner*.

In the control room, Alfredo completed a radio check with Adrian.

Those on deck watched as the submersible slipped under the surface.

***

Adrian angled the craft as it descended. The gentle hiss as air bled from the ballast tanks was unmistakable.

Petros stared through the viewing ports while Adrian controlled the descent. The daylight diminished into dark as the depth increased until Adrian switched on the searchlights.

He tapped Petros on the shoulder and pointed to a gauge. "Alfredo's depth was spot on. We're at two-fifty metres and your ship is right in front of us."

The craft banked, rose over the hull and descended with

the main viewport facing the cargo hatches.

"Time you put into practice what I taught you. I'll hover while you remove the remains of the cover."

Petros grabbed the single control. "Don't shout at me if I get this wrong." The robotic arm extended, jerked and prodded until with concentration he began to think of it as an extension of his own.

The numerous detonations the previous day had loosened the planks still in place. When Petros secured the three fingered clamp, Adrian reversed the craft, turned one eighty degrees allowing it to be dropped clear of the operating zone. Three hours later the Red Devil with every light operating entered the hold.

"Bloody hell," said Petros as he saw the scattered boxes.

"Time to surface."

"We could shift a lot of this ready for lifting."

"We could," said Adrian. "It's a monotonous process but easier if we place the ingots into steel baskets and to do that Alfredo may have to reposition his ship."

Fifteen minutes later the craft floated on the surface. Simone secured the shackle and the hydraulic crane hoisted it inboard.

Petros shielded his eyes from the sun as it reflected off the sea.

Adrian laughed. "Take your sun glasses next time."

"Good timing," said Alfredo. "Marco's made soup for lunch."

***

"Bastards," screamed Gabriele Silvio as he struck the computer keyboard with his fist. "They found the transmitter."

"We can still find them, can't we?"

"Rocco, you idiot. It might take days."

"But we know where they found the boat people."

"Go, get me the paper."

"The cleaner threw it away."

"Don't stand there. Search through the rubbish until you find it."

"Yes, Boss."

Full of rage, Gabriele placed a chart on the table and marked the position where the transmitter stopped. From the Straights of Messina he marked the maximum distance the *Tuna Turner* could have travelled in twenty-four hours.

"The paper, Boss."

He grabbed it tearing it in two." Go and wash. You smell like an overworked whore."

Rocco shrugged and wandered to the bathroom.

"Not there, idiot. Use the kitchen." Gabriele's eyes devoured the front page. "Sixty-five miles from Valletta." With a pair of compasses, he scribed an arc, which bisected the maximum distance line. "I'll have you on my radar, Alfredo, you cannot escape. Rocco."

"Yes, Boss."

Gabriele shook his head. "As my nephew I employ you but I often wonder why. Give the order and I'll meet you and the rest of the crew in an hour on my motor yacht."

***

With two steel baskets gripped in its claw, the submersible descended, trailing a lifting wire to the wreck. These Adrian placed on the seabed fifty metres from the open hold. The wire Petros secured by a slip hook to one basket.

Adrian peered through the viewport, his voice relaxed. "See how the wire bends? We have to position the ship above so that the baskets don't snag. Thankfully, the current in these parts is slight."

He switched the radio to transmit. "Alfredo, move to port twenty metres. Stop. Move to starboard a tad. Stop. Ahead ten metres. Stop. That should do. Petros, let's start collecting."

The first basket hoisted contained sixteen bars. The second was ready as they waited for an empty basket to return.

"Where is it?" muttered Adrian.

"I see it."

"Alfredo, another ten metres to starboard."

The afternoon vanished as baskets containing ingots ascended and when empty, descended.

Adrian glanced at the digital clock on the consul. "I can't speak for you but I'm knackered. Time to call it a day and believe me, your right arm will be sore tomorrow."

"Agreed."

On pulling themselves out of the craft, both men stretched cramped muscles.

"Don't you want to see it?" asked Tommaso.

"I've seen every damned bar," said Petros as he flexed his right arm. "What's for dinner?"

***

In a foul mood, his smile as warm as a January day at the North Pole, Gabriele Silvio manoeuvred *Belladonna,* his luxury motor yacht, away from its berth in Palermo harbour. Behind him stood Rocco ready to take over. Like each of Gabriele's men, he obeyed the rules of the Cosa Nostra without question.

The bow of the luxury yacht lifted in the slight swell as

she cleared the harbour.

"Rocco, take the wheel."

"Yes, Boss."

Gabriele drew a line on the chart, set the autopilot, anti-collision radar, and inserted a disc into the computer. He turned a switch to fully automatic and the *Belladonna* followed a programmed track at eighteen knots. "Keep your eyes open and call me if any vessel comes inside the two mile range on the radar. I'll have the others relieve you when they've eaten."

Rocco nodded, sat in the captain's chair, and stared out of the windows.

Gabriele summoned his team of eight into his stateroom. From a jug, he poured a cup of coffee and sat at the head of the ornate table. He tapped the fingers of his right hand on the polished wood before speaking. "Tonight we rest, tomorrow we work. First, we find a boat full of migrants, not difficult these days. Four of you suitably armed will kill them if they're not already dead. The *Belladonna* will tow whatever to a suitable position and allow the wind and tide to do the rest. You will hide onboard until spotted by the *Tuna Turner*. They will, as good seafarers, come to your assistance. I suggest as soon as the craft touches the side, you kill the crew and take over. I repeat, no one is to remain alive. On the bridge you will find a radio, check it is on channel sixteen and transmit, 'We are into fish,' I will reply, 'On my way'."

A burly, hard-faced man wearing blue jeans and white T-shirt, leant on the table. "Who is included in this party of four?" asked Antonino.

"You can take the three men on my left. The others will assist when we come alongside and transfer the gold. Rocco will need to be relieved after you've eaten. The fridge in the galley is full of micro-wave meals. There's no alcohol, so don't bother to look for it."

"You can go and eat. Don't forget Rocco." Gabriele poured himself another coffee. The eight men stood, nodded and left.

Satisfied with his plan, Gabriele strolled into his private galley, opened the fridge. From a selection of meals provided and prepared by a local restaurant, he chose a lobster salad.

On the hour, he went to the bridge, checked course, speed, and position. Once clear of the Straits of Messina he relaxed on his double bed. Sleep was a long time coming.

The light from the morning sun shone through the porthole and woke him. In less than a minute, he stood on the bridge staring at an empty sea. He glanced at the sat-nav and marked a cross on the chart; they had made good speed. "Keep your eyes open, Antonino. It's time for my breakfast and I look forward to a financially rewarding day."

"I'm sure it will be, Padrino."

Breakfast consisted of fresh orange juice, toast and three cups of strong black coffee. As a man who left nothing to chance, his mind considered every option.

***

On a mirror calm sea and a sunny morning, the *Tuna Turner* hovered over the wreck. Alfredo and his crew sat on the aft deck eating breakfast.

Petros turned to Adrian. "How much longer?"

"If it goes as well as yesterday, we'll be finished tonight."

"I'll feel a whole lot better when we unload the gold in Malta," said Petros.

"Why not Palermo?"

"If today brings what we've planned for, I prefer Malta to Palermo and the police will not ask awkward questions."

"The man has a point, Alfredo," said Adrian."

"I know. Let us get moving. Marco, clear the deck. Ready Adrian?"

"I need a pee. Give me a couple of minutes."

The Red Devil bobbed on the surface as Adrian completed pre-dive checks. Simone trod water while he waited. With the shackle released and the diver clear, Adrian angled the planes and descended. "Time to start work."

"You were right about my arm. It aches."

"Once you grip the controls you'll soon forget."

"A bar of gold is as good a cure-all as anything I know."

The work and time progressed until the final bar dropped from the grab into the basket.

"Take a last look at the old girl," said Adrian. "At this depth, I doubt if anyone will see her again."

Both men peered through the view ports as they circled *Jupiter's* hull.

"Well look at that, a Great White having a nose," said Petros

They watched as it glided across the hull, flicked its tail and vanished into the dark.

"Told you they were around... Going up, next floor, lunch. I'm famished."

"Any idea how many bars?" asked Petros

"Lost count after one hundred."

As the craft surfaced, sunlight from the late afternoon flooded the tiny cabin. Simone tapped the hull as he secured the lifting shackle.

Once on the aft deck and nestled in its cradle, Petros opened the hatch and clambered out followed by Adrian.

"We have stowed the gold in the engine room bilges. It will not move and cause any problems with ship handling," said Alfredo.

"It's your ship and as temporary ballast it's in the perfect place," said Petros. "Did you count them?"

"One thousand, one hundred and twenty bars as far as I can tell. You're a rich man."

"If I can keep it."

"Alfredo, Petros, some gate-crashers are about to join the party," said Amadou quietly. "Fifteen miles due south, a boat low in the water."

"If it is the Cosa Nostra under cover of refugees," said Alfredo, "they know we must offer assistance."

"Who's going to shout if we sail in the opposite direction?" asked Davide.

"It might not be them. We could be leaving a boat load of women and children to die," shouted Tommaso. "The baby we rescued is alive because we care. A ship is not a democracy. Alfredo is the captain and whatever he orders I'll agree."

"We take a look."

"Never underestimate your enemy. Amadou, break out the shotguns," ordered Petros. "Where's ZZ?"

"Sleeping."

"You'd better wake him or we won't hear the last of it."

On the bridge, Alfredo switched the computer and autopilot to manual. A roar and a plume of exhaust from the funnel indicated engines running. He waited until the red lights on the consul changed to green before setting the throttles to slow ahead. At a range of one mile, the *Tuna Turner* circled the drifting craft.

Tommaso and Simone gazed across the calm water with binoculars as they checked for signs of life.

"I will go closer," said Alfredo. He turned his head and noted Petros, Amadou, Adrian and ZZ concealed behind the steel bulkheads.

"Nothing," said Tommaso.

"You two go below or join the others. I am going alongside."

From the bridge wing came the clunk click of shells entering the firing chamber.

Continuing to circle, Alfredo sailed closer until the boat filled with the dead nestled alongside in the shade of *Tuna Turner*. A corpse shifted. A man stood, shoved the body to one side, dropped on one knee, raised his automatic weapon and fired into the air. Three others appeared from amongst the dead brandishing AK47s.

Alfredo dropped to the deck and pushed the throttles hard over. The four men on the boat fired. A wall of bullets streamed towards the *Tuna Turner*. Shells ricocheted off steel bulkheads and shattered the windows. Flat on the deck he steered using his feet.

Petros and his team stood, shouldered their weapons and produced a barrage of accurate fire straight into the boat. At minimum range, the multiple shotgun charges carved into the living, dead and through the worm-infested planking.

One man scrambled to find cover, slipped and fell blood-covered into the sea. Another brought his AK to his shoulder and fired.

With bullets whining past their heads, three shotgun blasts ripped the opposition's chest to ribbons.

From aft, Amadou and ZZ fired a nonstop barrage until their magazines emptied.

At a safe distance, the men on the *Tuna Turner* stared as the aged wooden craft filled, sank by the stern and disappeared.

Gulls dived, screeching for the scraps of dead flesh floating on the surface.

Amadou fired several shots but the scavengers circled the remains, swooped and snapped at each other.

Alfredo shouted from the bridge. "I see someone in the water."

"Leave him. Maybe a shark will smell his blood," said Adrian.

"Let him flounder for a while. In fact for ten minutes sail in the opposite direction," Petros shouted. "When we've dragged him out, he'll be tired and less of a problem. There's a few questions I want to ask."

Alfredo laughed and headed away from the swimmer. Those on the deck waved.

Thirty minutes later Tommaso and Marco tossed a rope at the floundering middle-aged man with a red face and chuckled as he attempted to climb.

"Tie the rope under your armpits and we'll haul you inboard," shouted Tommaso.

A few minutes elapsed before he hung as a drowned rat from a davit.

"Tommaso, does he speak English?" asked Petros.

"I'll interpret for you."

"I have a few questions," said Petros as he stared into the man's eyes. Deliberately he pushed his shotgun into the captive's crotch. "Tell the truth and you live. Lie and I promise you, your head will leave your shoulders."

Tommaso repeated the words.

In Italian the man screamed, "If I tell you anything I'm a dead man. Shoot me."

"We don't have much time and I understand the code of silence that forbids you from betraying your comrades. So you die, but not by my hand. My friend who once worked for Gadaffi," he pointed to Amadou, "is a master of interrogation. When he has finished you will want to die."

From behind, a knife flashed through the air and into the suspended man's thigh. Blood flowed from his lower lip as he stifled a scream.

"I forgot to mention he has an assistant who loves to practice his knife-throwing. The other leg, ZZ." The second blade found its mark.

"Kill me," screamed the man.

Are you ready to answer my questions?" asked Petros in a quiet voice.

"You know I cannot."

"Then we will leave you suspended and give you time to reconsider." He wrenched both blades out of the bloodied flesh. "Feel better? Mind you, you're losing a lot of blood. I'll give you an hour at best before you die. I'm told it's not painful. Time for coffee. I'd bring you one but you won't be in a fit state to drink it."

With his face contorted by pain he spluttered, "My Padrino will have his revenge."

Petros glanced left and right. "I don't see him."

"You will."

***

Roland Wallace and Donald Mercer stepped out of the dark green Jaguar and strolled towards the front door of Petros' home.

Donald pressed the bell push and stepped back.

The moment Maria opened the door, Donald grabbed her throat and slammed her against the wall.

"Shut your mouth," said Roland. "Who else is in the

house?"

At that moment Maria understood fear. "I'm on my own."

"Where's your little girl?"

Maria stared through the window as Charlie loped towards the house. "She's at my mother-in-laws'. I'm picking her up later when I join them and the rest of the family for dinner."

"You will call them and say you have a headache and will they look after the child."

Her hands shook as she gave a defiant stare, "And if I don't?"

"Then you will be responsible for others being hurt. He pointed. "My man Don loves a fight."

A growl, deep and intense came from the kitchen.

"What the fuck..."

The weight of a full-grown Alsatian smashed into Donald and sank his teeth into the flesh of his right arm.

The animal's sharp fangs found bone as he pulled.

Donald shrieked and kicked out.

Terror gripped Maria. "Bastard," she screamed as she powered her right knee between his legs and raked his face with her fingernails.

With an ear-splitting yell, he staggered backwards and collapsed to the floor dragging the animal with him.

She went to kick him while he was down but Roland shoved her away and armed with a nine-millimetre pistol, lashed at the dog's head.

"You bastard. Run, Charlie," screamed Maria.

With a yelp, the animal ran through the open kitchen door, into the garden, disappearing into the foliage.

Blood dripped on the polished wood floor. "I'll kill that

fucking animal. When I've done with the dog, you're next."

With a mocking smile, Roland's tone akin a teacher addressing a naughty pupil, "Don, keep your mouth shut and your hands to yourself. Go outside and he'll rip your throat out. She'll bandage your arm and you will not touch her unless I say so."

Scorn filled her voice. "He needs a hospital, preferably mental."

"Be reasonable. Soak it in antiseptic and bandage it."

Donald dragged Maria by the arm to the kitchen as blood poured from his wounds.

Roland, gun in hand, followed. "Nice place. Your husband must be worth a bit."

She washed and poured TCP into the torn flesh and grinned. "Not such a big man now, are you?" The bandage she wrapped as tight as she could. "Keep it raised."

Roland pointed. "You will sit in the chair by the window and make your call." He wandered to the lounge window and sat on the built-in seat overlooking the Thames.

Numb, she made the call, cutting her mother-in-law off.

"What do you want?"

"Your husband to do as he's told."

"That'll be the day."

"For you he'll do anything."

"You don't know him. When he returns, he'll fry your balls and eat them for breakfast."

He struck out with a clenched fist, hit the side of her face, grabbed her hair, and pulled her head back. "One word from me and Don will fuck you, and when he's done you'll wish you were dead. Is that what you want?"

Her mind raced. Could she deal with these morons? She stared at him and her eyes blazed. Her right hand grabbed his balls, squeezed and twisted.

"Roland screamed and smashed her between the eyes.

Out cold, she crumpled to the floor.

"Let me do her," said Donald.

"Later. Remove her clothes and tie the bitch up."

Semi-conscious she lay on her side and curled into a ball.

***

Alfredo shouted from the bridge. "Petros, someone is asking for you on the radio."

Petros charged up the steel ladder to the bridge.

"Channel 7."

"Petros Kyriades."

"Mr Kyriades, you do not know me but you have something I want very badly. When my transmitter stopped sending a signal and my men failed to return I assumed the worst."

"We rescued one but he's bleeding to death as we speak."

"Toss him overboard, he is of little importance."

"What do you want?"

"What you found on the wreck."

"Get lost."

"May I suggest you contact your wife. My partner holds her as insurance. If you cross him, I guarantee her health will deteriorate. The choice of your wife living or you attending her funeral is yours."

"I don't believe you."

"I give you until the sun shines over the horizon to see sense. After that your little girl will have lost her mother. Your decision, Mr Kyriades." The transmission ended.

"Give him the gold," said Alfredo.

"Not yet. I have one possibility, but first I'll phone home as they expect." He returned to his cabin, found his sat-phone, went on deck, and pressed memory key one.

"Maria Kyriades."

"Are you all right?" He listened to a scuffle and muted scream.

"Pleased you contacted your wife, My Kyriades. She is quite beautiful."

"You touch her. I'll string you up on a butcher's hook and hang you from a tree as bird food."

"Don't threaten me. I have the advantage and don't give a shit. The legal system in this country is so fucked up I won't even be charged. What you need to worry about is my associate. She kneed him in the bollocks and your dog took half his arm off. Unlike me, he's a bit of an animal and will fuck her in many ways before he kills her. I don't believe you'll let that happen. If the transfer of the gold goes ahead tomorrow, I'll let her live."

"Touch her and I'll swing but as sure as eggs is eggs you'll die the most gruesome of deaths," shouted Petros.

"I've lost count of the number of times someone has said that to me. Everyone of them ended up in the mortuary or pig food."

"There's a difference. I'll send you, your mother, father, sisters, and brothers to hell. If you don't believe me, touch my wife."

The line went dead.

With little hesitation, Petros pressed memory button two.

"Yes."

"Bear, I have a problem."

"What's new?"

"For once I'm deadly serious. Some arsehole has Maria hostage and if I don't hand over the gold she'll be murdered. I must make my decision by sunrise tomorrow."

"You know he'll kill her."

"Of course. The best witness is a dead one."

"I've no idea what I can do but don't worry. I'll ring you when Maria's cooking my breakfast."

"Thanks. I really don't know..."

"Get off the line, you're wasting my time." Bear terminated the call.

Petros turned, everyone stood there.

"We are agreed. Give him the gold," said Alfredo.

"We die if we do. There's no way the Cosa Nostra will let us live. No witnesses make life simple. No, tomorrow morning we take that bastard down."

"And your wife?"

"Plan B is in motion. In as much as I want to I can do no more. Is our friend still alive?"

"Just about," said Tommaso.

"Good. I'm going to throw him overboard."

"What will that do?" asked Marco.

"With luck attract a shark or two. We need to know how many men are on the Cosa Nostras' vessel."

Amadou and ZZ let the man drop to the deck.

He opened his eyes and gasped, "Kill me."

Petros placed his feet either side of the man's torso. "You are finished. My idea is to drag you astern and watch the sharks have dinner. With luck you'll live a few more hours but in agony unless you tell me how many men are on the other vessel."

"Mother of Mary, take me now."

"Alfredo, two knots please. Amadou, ZZ, take this creature to the stern and toss him over."

The man screamed as they dragged him and suspended him from the rail.

"Tell him what he wants to know and I will treat your wounds," said Alfredo.

The man attempted to lift his head as he whispered, "I cannot."

Alfredo cut the line and let him fall into the water.

"Good move," said Petros. "How much plastic have we on board?"

"Sufficient to blow us to heaven and back to hell," said Davide.

"Time to make a few fireworks."

"Your wife?" said Alfredo. "You must be worried."

"Whatever happens to my wife, tomorrow I'll have my revenge in part. Later I'll claim payment in full. If my friend can do it, my wife will be safe."

"How can you be so sure?"

"I'm not but what can I do?

Davide and Petros placed the plastic explosive, plus a selection of nuts and bolts of various sizes into old paint tins.

"Petros, this is crazy."

"It could even work."

Davide nodded his approval as he taped a timed fuse to each tin.

Chapter Nineteen

Bear parked his car in the station car park and strolled to the entrance of Petros' Pangbourne home. Shielded by a giant holly bush, he waited in the shadows and out of sight of the road.

Ten minutes later a black van stopped at the river's edge. Its driver turned off the engine and lights.

Although a big man, Bear moved like a ghost and tapped on the van window before the driver sensed him being there.

The driver wound it down. "What's the score, Night-Fighter?"

"Don't know. I waited for you to arrive before I moved in. Are you sure you want to help? It could cost you your jobs."

"We're here, aren't we?" said James.

Three men dressed from head to toe in black jumped out.

"God, I miss the old days," said Zack.

"Everything's PC and bound by the rules," said Brian.

"Night scopes?"

"Two," said Brian, "and we have a phazzer each."

"Won't you get into trouble borrowing those?"

"No chance, bought them off a friend in Portobello market. Most of the street girls have them these days."

"That would make the earth move," said Bear. "Right, two teams. James, you're with me. A recon first then meet back here."

"What's in the bag?" asked Zack.

"Crossbows, silent and effective."

"Are we going to take these bastards out?" said Brian.

"You're not but I might," said Bear. "Can't have Special Branch hurting the bad guys, can we? Whatever next?"

Alert, the two groups split, Bear and James to the front and nearside, Brian and Zack, rear and far side.

Both teams listened to their own footfalls and watched the house for any sign of movement.

"What's that noise," whispered James.

As they circled the garage to gain the best view of the house, Bear raised his hand. "I hear something." He edged forward searching with his night-sight. In a soft voice, "Charlie." The animal nuzzled Bear's hand.

"Stay," said Bear, his senses sharpened by experience. "What's this?" He smelt his hand. "The dog's hurt, which tells me one of them has a nasty bite. "Good boy."

The view from the tree line and across the lawn gave them a perfect view of the house.

"Shit, they've drawn the curtains," said James.

"Which means they're in the lounge or kitchen," said Bear. "Back to the gate. Charlie."

Two men and a dog returned to the entrance and waited for the others to return. They emerged out of the gloom.

"Nothing," said Zack. "Where did the dog come from?"

"He belongs to the daughter. Right, we go in through an upstairs window. There's a ladder in the garage." Bear jangled a set of keys.

"There was a time when we abseiled, swung on ropes and smashed through windows," said Brian.

"Iranian Embassy, fifth of May 1980, and we were a lot younger," said Zack.

"The ladder," said Bear.

Zack and James carried the wooden ladder to the rear of the house. Bear, with the two crossbows slung across his back, climbed quickly and silently and waited on the balcony for the others. He pointed and whispered, "This is the guest bedroom, it opens out onto a long uncarpeted landing and stairs to the right." With his stiletto, he slipped a window catch and slid over the sill.

"Have you been practising?" whispered Zack.

"Not lately."

From the shadows, the others followed.

He crossed the carpeted floor and cracked open the door. The hallway was in darkness. He slipped the crossbows from his shoulder, loaded, and handed one to Zack. The other he kept. "You have one shot, make it count."

James and Brian readied their phazzers.

The four men sidled along the passage to the top of the stairs, stopped and listened.

Someone walked across the ground floor, their footsteps distinct.

"Don, take a look in the fridge and make me something to eat."

"Yes, Boss."

"How pathetic. You serve him as if he's your lord and master."

"Bitch." An open-handed slap across bare skin came next.

"Leave her."

"I'll look forward to having you every way possible before I break your neck"

"I bet you can't even get it up," shouted Maria.

Bear turned to Zack and nodded.

They descended the stairs two on each side and paused at the bottom. With Bear leading, they strolled into the lounge.

"And what do we have here? Breathe heavy and I'll fire," said Bear.

Donald lunged at Maria.

Bear fired, the bolt entered Donald's thigh.

Roland raised his hands. "Don't shoot." Diverting attention.

Donald shifted his right arm to his back and received another bolt in his shoulder.

Roland seized the moment to grab his pistol. Confusion filled his face as two phazzer darts struck him in the chest. He convulsed and collapsed unconscious to the floor.

Maria lifted her clothes, forced a cheerful smile and ran to Bear, hugged and kissed him.

"You okay?"

"Bit shaky but now you're here I'm fine. I must look a sight."

"You look good to me but before you go up west, I'd cover those bruises with makeup."

"Thankfully, Alysa is at Zena's. I'd better get some clothes on."

"What do we do with these two?" asked James.

"I have an idea. Leave me a dozen of those black cable ties."

Maria stood in her shower, leant against the white tiled wall, cried and shook. She turned up the pressure and the jets pummelled and stung her skin. The force of the water drove out her fear. Fifteen minutes later, she descended the stairs, dressed in blue jeans and a T-shirt. "Coffee. Who wants one?"

"Best thing I've heard since we arrived," said Zack.

"Maria, are you sure you're alright?" asked Bear.

She ran her hands through her damp hair and gave a half-hearted smile. "Five cups it is."

Bear secured both men and retrieved the two blood-covered bolts. From his pack, he removed two wound dressings and tied them in place. Brutally he dragged the unconscious man off the floor and onto the settee as Charlie bounded into the house.

He barked at Bear and growled at Donald.

"You can bite him later," said Bear. "Let me look at your head." He examined Charlie's head. "Superficial, a lot of mess but no permanent damage."

The clatter of mugs on the kitchen table signalled the coffee was ready. Three men still wearing their black balaclavas grabbed a cup each.

"The oaf will need a hospital," said James.

"Later," said Bear. "Do you know who the other man is?"

"Roland Wallace. The Met have been trying to pin something on him for years but he keeps his hands clean."

"Did," said Bear. He wandered over and removed one set of car keys from Donald's pocket. "Can someone give me a hand?" He bent and lifted the nine millimetre pistol and pushed it in his pocket.

Zack strolled over and between them they dragged a screaming Donald and dumped him into the boot of the Jaguar.

"Time you and the others left."

James glanced at his watch. "Thanks for a great night out. Must do it again sometime."

Bear shook their hands. "Cheers."

"Anytime, my friend," said Brian. "We owe you our lives from Iraq."

"In fairness I'm getting too old for this. Consider the debt paid."

Bear checked the road, nodded to the three men, who at speed ran to the van, started the engine, and drove away. He waited a few minutes before returning to the boot of the Jaguar.

The horror of what was happening swept across Donald's face. "And you can go fuck yourself."

"Interesting turn of phrase but it's you who's fucked. Scum like you deserve nothing and I know what Maria would have suffered before you killed her." He pressed the pistol into

Donald's forehead. "The boot's on the other foot now and I hate men who hit women."

Grimacing, Donald stared into Bear's eyes. "What are you going to do, big man? Shoot me? This is Britain and I deserve a fair trial."

"Don't get lippy with me, arsehole. My rules are simple, I throw the ball, and you catch." A wicked smile crossed his face before he taped Donald's mouth shut. Next he positioned the pistol on Donald's right knee and pulled the trigger. "Left next." He repeated the process. "Try walking without knees." He ripped the dressings away from the bolt wounds, allowing blood to flow. "If you could crawl to a hospital you might live." The boot slammed shut.

As Bear entered the house, Maria asked, "Did I hear two shots?"

Bear laughed. "Sorry about that but I needed to scare the shit out of your boyfriend."

"The other one's coming round." With gusto, she booted Roland in the stomach three times.

"The rough stuff's my job but with a boot like that West Ham need you for their next game." Bear sat on the settee and prodded. "Time to go, arsehole."

He stared at Bear in pain and shock. "Do you know who I am?"

"No and I don't give a shit. The best part is you don't know who I am. You fucked up. You should have stayed on your own manor. This one's private, invited guests only."

Ashen-faced, Roland groaned as he tried to sit. "Who are you? How much do you want?"

Bear smiled. "A couple of million would boost my pension fund."

"I pay my dues to the police. I'll give you fifty thou if

you let me walk."

Bear raised the pistol. "Give me one good reason why I shouldn't blow your brains out?"

"One-hundred thou."

Bear lied with a smile. "No thanks, my boss pays better."

Terror filled Roland's face as he stammered, "You can't be the police, so who the hell are you? I can use men like you. Why not work for me?"

"I'd rather shovel shit than work for an arsehole." He dragged him by the collar, out of the house and tossed him into the back seat of his Jaguar. "Time for sleep." He removed a plastic container from his pocket, flipped the lid allowing a full hypodermic to drop into his hand. With no hesitation, he shoved it into Roland's arm and injected the colourless liquid.

Roland held up his tied hands defensively, his eyes wide with fear. "You can't do this."

"Nonsense. Just did."

He entered the house. "Maria, will you be okay?"

"I've a bit of mess to clean up and then I'll drive over to Zena's and stay the night."

"I'll give you a hand. Your face will have a few nice bruises. How you going to explain them away?" He removed the pistol from his pocket and wiped it clean with kitchen tissue.

"I fell down the stairs."

"I'd believe you. I'm going to tell PK you're at his mum's. Unless you want a word."

She smiled. "Tell him I'm on my way. I'd rather not talk until I'm ready. He'll only ask awkward questions."

Bear punched the buttons on his mobile and as soon as Petros answered, "Don't talk and for once in your life, PK, listen. Maria is going to stay at your mum's for the night. You can call her there."

"Any problems?"

"Piece of cake."

"Is Maria okay?"

"Right as rain."

"Thanks. I owe you one."

"I'll send you my bill." He terminated the call.

"Charlie," said Maria. "Jump into my car, we're going for a ride."

The animal ran outside and waited for her to open the door.

With the alarm set, Bear closed and locked the door as Maria drove away from the house. He put on a pair of black leather gloves and from his jacket pocket, he removed the pistol.

He dragged the unconscious Roland from the rear seat and dumped him along with the pistol into the boot on top of the moaning Donald.

After one final glance back at the house, he sat behind the wheel, drove towards London and the M25. For the time being he kept within the designated speed limit and concentrated on the road ahead. The journey ended in a rundown housing estate on the outskirts of Basildon. His eyes checked out the CCTV cameras, everyone smashed. "Perfect," he muttered. He parked the Jaguar with the doors unlocked behind a mass of overflowing refuse bins and left the keys in the ignition. A quick glance around and he strolled towards a bin store with the door hanging askew. Concealed in the shadows, he leant on the wall, folded his arms, and waited.

Three young men drinking from cans ambled by the car. One dragged something along the paintwork.

"The keys are in the ignition," said one.

"What are we waiting for?" said another.

The three piled inside slamming the doors. With the

engine racing, the tyres screeching, they hurtled across the car park and exited along the main road.

Bear smiled as from a nearby payphone he dialled 999 and reported the Jaguar stolen and hung up. In the centre of town, he hailed a passing cab. With the roads almost empty, the drive to Upminster tube station took less time than he anticipated. A train arrived minutes later and within the hour, he entered his own home.

Jocelyn rushed into the hall. "How did it go?"

"No problems. As I thought, people can be cooperative if treated correctly. It's been a long evening, Fancy a Ruby?"

She laughed. "Let me get my coat."

***

The owner of the Bengal Lancer knew Bear and Jocelyn as regular customers and guided them to their favourite table in an alcove.

Bear raised his head as the aroma of different spices tantalised his senses.

Jocelyn appeared concerned. "How did it really go tonight?"

"As I said, no problems. East end amateurs attempting to emulate the Krays."

"Your order, sir, madam?" asked the manager.

"You first, Jos."

"To start, Garlic King Prawns. Main course Chicken Shashlik Masala."

"For me, Miah, A large portion of Garlic King Prawns. Main Course, a double Lamb Shashlik Bhuna and a bottle of your best dry white wine."

Jocelyn waited for Miah to depart. "If my memory is

correct the Krays killed or had people killed."

"Ronnie and Reggie were proper villains, the hard men of their day and the east end of London their empire. Both paid the price. Reggie died in prison and Ronnie a month after his release. Albeit they topped some of the competition, they did love their mum."

Miah returned with their starters, a large platter filled with fresh garlic prawns. Two finger bowls and napkins.

With the prawns decimated, Miah sent a member of staff to clear the table. Minutes later the main course arrived sizzling on cast-iron platters. "I know Mr Bear will enjoy. It is his favourite."

"It's food," said Jocelyn. "He enjoys all food."

His platter clean, Bear pushed his plate away and cleaned his mouth with a napkin. He glanced at Jocelyn's half empty plate. Finished or just taking a breather?"

"Yes, I'm stuffed. I enjoyed what I've eaten."

"Miah makes a great Ruby."

They stood and a waiter assisted Jocelyn with her coat while Bear wandered across to Miah. "I think you'll find this satisfactory." He shoved a couple of notes into Miah's top pocket.

Miah removed and handed them back. "On the house. You are my best customer."

Bear laughed and thanked him.

"Come on," said Jocelyn. "Tomorrow we need to discuss the plans for our wedding."

"Goodnight, Miah." He raised his eyes. "No peace for the wicked."

***

The three boys drove the Jaguar at high speed, laughing as the traffic cameras flashed.

"That's twelve points on his licence, Harry," said Martin.

"Can't this wreck go any faster?" said Joe.

"Fancy doing some handbrake turns up by the reservoir?" asked Harry.

"Yeah, and later we wipe it clean and dump it in the water," said Martin.

***

A semi-conscious Donald attempted to shove the weight on top of him away. With little strength, his hand slipped onto the discarded pistol. Pain jangled his nerves as he managed to cock the weapon.

The car veered to the left, braked, shot forward and stopped.

Donald listened to the laughter from those in the car. Kill, kill, kill, his only thought. He grasped the weapon with both hands and aimed at the partition securing the rear seat.

The car accelerated as he applied pressure to the trigger. He kept firing until the magazine emptied. Exhausted, he tossed the pistol aside.

The car hit the water with an almighty splash. For a few minutes it clung to the surface. Through damaged windows dark brown water flowed. It sank in less than five minutes, still upright, with its four wheels nestled in the mud. A cloud of silt rose, settling on the polished paintwork.

***

The following morning Bear watched breakfast television as the local news station broadcast,

Murder inquiry launched after three men were found inside and two more in the boot of a dark green Jaguar recovered early this morning from Hanningfield Reservoir. Police have sealed off a section of the reservoir.

It is understood the victims could be linked to gang warfare and drugs. An Essex police spokesperson said the investigation continues but refused to comment further.

The car was eventually removed with the bodies inside.

Detective Superintendent Leslie Holmes of the Essex police did not mention how the men died.

A local resident stated drug trading was commonplace in the reservoir car park and cars were often stopping late at night and then driving away.

Bear looked on in astonishment and switched the television off. "There endeth the lesson." He whistled as he strolled to the kitchen and prepared his breakfast.

Chapter Twenty

Petros awoke at four, dressed and wandered onto the deck. The moon cast its reflection on a mirror-flat sea. "Time," he muttered before clambering up the ladder to the bridge. "Good morning, Tommaso."

"Hi. Great day for a fight."

"I need to use the radio."

"Go ahead, you know the procedure."

Petros switched to channel seven on the radio. "Good morning. This is Petros Kyriades. Out." He repeated the message three times before someone answered.

"I gather you have reconsidered my proposal. You must love your wife. I suggest you come to me one hour after sunrise. My vessel is thirty miles north of your present position. Remember, my associate is taking care of your wife. Out."

"You are up early," said Alfredo as he entered the bridge.

"Need time to get my brain in gear. Our friend is thirty miles north."

"One moment. Tommaso, set the auto-pilot to north, speed ten knots. I will stay here while you have breakfast. Do not take too long."

He turned. "Petros, have you a plan?"

"Yes, and with luck no-one on our side will get hurt." He explained to Alfredo what he wanted him to do. Checking the time he said, "Two hours until our appointment. Breakfast calls."

To his surprise the mess was full. "What's up with everyone? Couldn't sleep?"

Tommaso turned his head towards Petros. "Like you, we'll be glad when this day is over."

During breakfast, tension played games with the crew's minds. Tempers flared but subsided just as fast.

Petros stood and scanned the faces around him. "Anyone who would rather avoid the action can stay below deck."

Apart from the throb of the engines, silence filled the space.

"We might have a problem with that," said Marco. "This is our boat and no man is going to take it from us. Well not without a fight."

"Amadou and ZZ have their instructions."

"Can't wait to see those bastards' faces," said ZZ.

Adrian sipped his coffee and nodded.

"I'll go and relieve Alfredo," said Tommaso as he refilled his coffee cup.

"Just keep your head down and don't get shot," said Petros. "The rest of us will cause confusion and mayhem."

Alfredo entered the mess as Petros said, "I'll take control of the ship."

Alfredo shook his head. "I know my ship, my bridge, how she reacts and I am a better ship-handler than Gabriele Silvio."

Petros nodded. "I have a feeling he's in for a bad day."

Davide entered. "Tommaso has them at ten miles and closing."

Each member of the crew grabbed a shotgun, a box of ammunition from ZZ and made their way to the upper deck. Davide and Petros pushed the timed detonators into the plastic explosive. ZZ and Amadou took up their positions out of sight on the stern. Alfredo stood erect on the bridge.

The deck trembled as two vessels at slow speed came together, their hulls separated by fenders of rubber tyres.

Davide, Petros and Adrian tossed the half dozen paint tins along with grenades onto the bow, waist, and upper bridge of *Belladonna* while multiple shotguns peppered the superstructure.

Almost in slow motion the two vessels drifted apart.

ZZ and Amadou waited for the moment when the stern of one crossed the stern of the other and vaulted over.

On *Belladonna*, four men stepped into the open and blasted away at *Tuna Turner* with semi-automatics. Empty cartridges filled the air before they fell to the deck.

From behind the steel bulkhead, Davide, Petros and Adrian hurled more grenades across the gap.

ZZ and Amadou raced for cover. Another burst of gunfire filled the air.

Gabriele screamed abuse as Alfredo's vessel at full power manoeuvred away. Furious, he pushed the throttles hard down.

Alfredo reasoned his opponent's reaction and altered course.

ZZ and Amadou entered the superstructure, located the engine room entrance, tossed in two stun-grenades and closed the door. Thirty seconds later, they descended the steel ladder.

ZZ utilised the ladder as cover, while Amadou removed a block of plastic explosive from his backpack, broke it in two and inserted a detonator in each piece timed for ten minutes.

He nodded to ZZ as he stuck them on the ready-use-fuel tanks but below the water line. With a quick glance around, they raced up the metal stairs and through the entrance. Amadou stopped long enough to fasten the door clips.

"Time for a swim," said ZZ.

Once on the deck they charged for the stern. Shots ricocheted off steel posts as they criss-crossed the deck. Both men gripped their weapons tight as they slid behind the aft winch.

At deck level, ZZ peered round the winch drum. Two men approached, their semi-automatic rifles firing.

Amadou removed two grenades and handed one to ZZ.

With hand signals, he indicated he would go left and for ZZ to go right. They waited.

The firing ceased as the men changed magazines.

Two grenades hurtled towards the gunmen.

With their shotguns ready, ZZ and Amadou rolled, fired, cocked and fired in the general direction of the men.

Flat on the deck, they raised, aimed their weapons; one man's mangled corpse lay on the deck. They turned their heads and watched the bow of *Tuna Turner* ride high over the amidships section of the *Belladonna*.

Their eyes scanned the deck as they searched for the second man. Wounded, he tumbled from behind a life-raft container. ZZ and Amadou fired together.

The constant noise of shotguns pounding the *Belladonna* thumped the air.

"Let's get wet," said Amadou. In a few long strides both men dropped their weapons and jumped into the water. On surfacing, they watched the *Tuna Turner* go astern and the *Belladonna* limp away.

"You just killed your wife, Kyriades," screamed Gabriele over the radio. "Alfredo, you will never see your family again."

Gabriele grabbed the semi-automatic from his one surviving crewmember. "Steer out of shotgun range so I can achieve one good shot."

Petros checked the time and shouted, "Get the hell away from them, max revs." He felt the engines power and the ship turn.

Gabriele calmly raised the weapon to his shoulder and prepared to take the shot. "What are they doing? Full power, they can't escape."

"The throttles are at full," shouted the man on the wheel. "The controls are smashed."

Petros stood alongside Alfredo. "Any moment."

"What about your two friends?"

The explosion blasted *Belladonna's* engine room. Pieces of steel flew into the air trailing black smoke and flames. Jets of blazing diesel sprayed the superstructure.

Those on the deck of the *Tuna Turner* shivered as the vibration from the blast washed over them.

The ship split, flooded and in seconds vanished. A slick of black smoking oil marked her sinking.

"Petros, I will pick up your men first and then we search for survivors."

"I've a feeling he and his crew went down with the ship."

"I will still look," said Alfredo. "It is right."

The *Tuna Turner* stopped twenty metres from the swimming ZZ and Amadou. The slight breeze drifted the ship towards them.

Marco and Davide tossed lines and hauled them inboard.

"The water's great for swimming, not too cold once you get used to it," said ZZ.

"If you have to get used to it, it's too bloody cold," said Petros. "Well done. Any problems?"

"A couple," said Amadou, "but we shot them."

For a time Alfredo cruised the area until he was satisfied no one from the *Belladonna* survived. He wandered to the radio and for a few moments gathered his thoughts. "This is the *Tuna Turner*; my position is Latitude 35 degrees. 40 north. Longitude 15 degrees. I am reporting an explosion on a white motor yacht some ten miles north of my position."

"*Tuna Turner*. This is Valletta Harbour Master. Please repeat."

Alfredo repeated his message.

"*Tuna Turner*, how many survivors?"

"I have searched the immediate area and have found no survivors."

"Thank you, *Tuna Turner*. Out."

Alfredo turned to Petros. "It is right to report an accident at sea."

"I agree. I like the flare of your new bow... Don't worry, I'll meet the cost of repairs."

There was a shout from below. Petros glanced towards the deck where ZZ and Amadou collected and tossed the shotguns, the spare ammunition and grenades over the side.

"A precaution," said Petros to Alfredo.

"A waste of fine weapons but I understand. In the meantime, I will have the minor damage painted over. Looks better that way. I will set a course for Malta and with luck we should arrive this evening."

"Tomorrow we might have to unload the gold but first I contact my legal beagle. I want him here to deal with this," said Petros.

Chapter Twenty-One

James woke from a deep sleep and groped for his vibrating mobile. His thumb found the mute button. The scent of perfume gave rise to other thoughts. Not to wake his sleeping wife, he slid out of bed, let his feet find his slippers and made his way downstairs to the kitchen. He pressed recall.

"Hi, James, sorry to wake you."

"Petros, you pay me good money for the privilege. What's the news?"

"One thousand plus ingots of Hitler's gold."

"I'm your lawyer, so listen to what I tell you. Under no circumstances, unload the gold. Nazi gold usually belongs to others, which Hitler's storm troopers stole as they plundered Europe. When will you return to Palermo?"

"At the moment we're on passage to Malta. I reckon it's better for our health and wealth."

"Tell me when I arrive but don't forget you're paying for Alfredo's boat by the day and it doesn't come cheap."

"I can pay him a bonus with the gold."

"Don't count your chickens. I've completed the paperwork for the next stage and now have to convince the authorities on the law of finds as opposed to the application of maritime salvage law. The process is more like the series Law and Order than Jonny Depp and the Pirates of the Caribbean."

"Don't understand a word but then as you said, I pay you to figure out the detail. When will you arrive?"

"I'll call you once I've landed." The call ended and he wandered to his study and searched the web for a flight to Malta. A BA flight departed from Gatwick at midday. He made a first-class booking and emailed two associates in Malta. The time on his computer sidled past eight. He crept up the stairs and returned to bedroom.

"It must have been important."

"It will buy you a new Porsche."

"How long will you be away?"

"Depends, with luck less than a week."

While he showered and dressed, Susan readied his case.

Clad in a purple tracksuit she drove him to Gatwick Airport.

***

The following morning, James, dressed in a dark pinstripe suit, his face expressionless, took his seat at the head of the table. He positioned his Admiralty and Maritime Law Guide along with his Journal of Maritime Law and Commerce in front of him and smiled. He acknowledged the two lawyers both with Honours from the Universities of Glasgow and London in Maritime Law who sat on either side and shook hands across the table. "Good morning, Kevin, Allan. Thank you for agreeing to see me and to arbitrate on this matter."

He handed across copies of the initial claim forwarded to the UK and European Receiver of Wrecks and a confirmation of receipt plus previous published papers on the law of finds.

"James, always a pleasure to welcome you to Malta," said Kevin Attard in a clipped BBC accent. As usual, he wore a double-breasted blazer, crisp white shirt and public school tie, his uniform of choice. He brushed back his dark hair. "I know you are fully cognisant with the letter of the law but does the law of finds apply in this instance?"

"It is our duty to decide whether there is enough evidence to prove abandonment," said Allan Vella, a man in his early fifties with a tanned face from sailing, surrounded by an unruly mop of light-grey hair.

In contrast to Kevin, he dressed casual, open-neck white sports shirt and grey trousers.

James leant forward dispensing with any formalities. "The sooner we come to an agreement the better. I have every fact I can find but accept there may be something out there which may prove my claim in error. The vessel Jupiter. Built 1927 at Harland and Wolf, Belfast, was sunk by the Royal Navy in October 1944 outside this island's territorial waters."

The door opened and a short, plump, dark-haired woman entered with a large envelope in her hands. With a smile on her face, she strode towards Kevin and placed it in front of him.

"Thank you, Mikaela." He waited until the door closed. "Like you, James, after a long night we came to the same conclusion. The Jose Maria Line, the final owners of the Jupiter, abandoned her in Thessalonica sometime in 1940. We are of the opinion she was either sold or was about to be sold for scrap when Germany invaded Greece"

"The Jose Maria Line has long gone," said James as he churched his fingers, "and I can find no will disposing of the company of which I understand included large debts."

Allan checked the time. "We should take a break. I've arranged for lunch upstairs in the boardroom but I made a few notes which are for our agreement and approval.

"One, as far as can be reasonably ascertained, the Jupiter was not insured.

"Two, there are no records of any party attempting to recover the vessel.

"Three, the location of the sinking, although clear in the Royal Navy records, has never until now been investigated.

"Four, there are no heirs as far as we know to the Jose Maria Line and from available records, we believe they abandoned her.

"Five, the German Navy reconfigured her upper decks to bear a resemblance to a hospital ship named Gradisca. That's everything for now."

He pushed himself back from the table. "Let's eat."

They climbed the stairs to the boardroom where other partners of the practice relaxed during their lunch hour. In the far corner set for three, stood a polished oak table.

A pleasant-looking young, dark-haired, slim woman entered pushing a silver trolley laden with food. In less than a minute smoked salmon, various cooked hams and a selection of salads covered the table.

"I gather this will be on the bill," said James.

"What do you think?" said Allen.

James shook his head. "In that case pass the salmon."

Allan carved a chunk of a smoke-darkened ham and added salad to his plate. "Out of interest, how did your client discover this wreck?"

"He was searching for a train."

Allan's brow wrinkled. "And he found a wreck. I'm sure you realise the seriousness of our findings. It could make your client a rich man."

"He is already," said James.

"Will you be here for the weekend?" asked Allan

"Hope not but any particular reason?"

"I'll be playing with my new toy."

"Must be expensive," said James.

"Second-hand, but good as new. I've treated myself to a Sunseeker Predator."

"Good boat. Rather fast if my memory is correct."

"Forty knots, well almost. For a bit of fun, I've installed an automatic clay pigeon trap on the stern."

"If I'm here, I'll join you. Long time since I've fired a shotgun."

"I've four. Two single shot and two pump action. Why don't you stay over?"

James grimaced. "I have little enough time with my wife as it is. She's far more fun than a fast boat with shotguns."

"Must be love. I'm not going to argue."

They finished their second cup of coffee and returned to the silence of their secure room.

As the sun began to set, James finished discussing the laws of salvage and of finds.

"So we are agreed," said Kevin. "The abandonment of the *Jupiter*, although not confirmed by letter or with the agreement of the previous owners, happened. Furthermore, for the purpose of this claim abandonment is inferred by the vessel remaining untended in Thessalonica and the law of finds applies."

James and Allan nodded.

With the signed originals of the documentation in his briefcase, Kevin handed signed copies to James and Allan. "I'll have these processed in three to four days. Tell your client to do nothing until you give him the word. Relax and enjoy our island. It has much to offer. Where are you staying, James?"

"The Phoenicia."

"Showing its age these days but still up there with the best," said Allan, "Need a lift?"

"Thanks but no thanks. I'll walk and clear the head."

James strolled to his hotel enjoying the hustle and bustle of daily life as it went on around him.

Once in his room he ran a hot bath and for the next hour relaxed and gathered his thoughts.

***

Petros waited for a phone call from James, his mind deliberating the possibility other claimants might exist.

Late in the evening his mobile rang, it was James. "How did your day go?"

"As well as could be expected. We agreed the law of finds is appropriate but it requires the signature of a judge familiar with the laws of salvage. Your claim will be confirmed in three to four days. In the meantime, relax, enjoy the thought of the gold belonging to you. Go stay in an expensive hotel."

"And what about the gold itself?"

"Leave it where it is and don't tell a soul. Special arrangements will be required to deliver it to the central bank vaults."

"And you?"

"I'll make myself and my associates available at a moment's notice if the judge wishes to discuss any issue we may have overlooked. I can assure you between the three of us every detail is correct."

"Okay, great idea to stay in a hotel. Might just do that."

"Better than on a cramped salvage boat. When I have the final decision, you'll be the first to know."

"Thanks, James. Must have dinner one evening."

"Look forward to it. Bye." The line went dead.

Petros strolled to the upper deck where Amadou stood staring across the harbour. "Where's ZZ?"

"He's collecting Scarlet from the airport. He can't get enough of that one."

"Were you any different at twenty-two?"

"Much the same but never as lucky. He appeals to women, like flies to camel dung. Heard anything from James?"

"Three to four days before a decision is made."

"Could be worse. At least Alfredo can have the bow fixed while we do nothing."

"True. I'm off to find a hotel and a comfortable bed."

Amadou shifted his position and scratched his head. "Good idea. Do you mind if I come with you? Alfredo's bunks are passable but a large double bed, which doesn't move, is better."

***

The evening flight from Rome touched down ten minutes late. Scarlet, with her overnight bag, avoided the luggage carousel and headed straight through customs to arrivals. She scanned the crowd of people waiting to meet someone and in seconds spotted ZZ.

He ran towards her and they held each other as if parted for months instead of days.

With more haste than was necessary, he grabbed her bag and dragged her into the chaos of slamming doors and taxis racing away.

To the sound of a shrill whistle a taxi stopped, waited for them to jump in and with a grinding of gears drove away before ZZ had a chance to tell him where.

ZZ tapped the driver on his shoulder. "Sliema Chalet."

The driver grunted, pressed his horn and cut up a slow moving car.

ZZ gripped Scarlet's hand as the car veered in and out of the traffic. In what seemed minutes the vehicle stopped.

The driver grunted again as he shifted his carcass around. "Twenty Euro."

ZZ paid and jumped out of the car. "His breath smelt of

garlic and the stench of sweat made me gag."

Scarlet studied the front of the hotel. "Not the best in the world."

He laughed. "We have a bedroom for as long as we are here. What more do we want?"

She laughed as they strolled into reception.

ZZ waved to the bored receptionist as they wandered across the foyer "The view from the balcony is awesome and on the top floor we can't hear the noise from the road."

He inserted the electronic key card into the lock. The curtains were drawn and the room lit by one table lamp. An open bottle of red wine rested on the table and a bottle of white in an ice bucket.

She grabbed the white, poured two glasses and handed one to ZZ. "To us."

With a grin on her face, she pushed him back, rolled on top of him, placed her hands on his chest and kissed him hard on the lips. It was the kiss of life. Spent and breathing heavily they parted and lay side by side.

The next morning he woke early. In the dimness he saw her gaze follow his every move. "I'm tired."

She sat up, her olive skin dark in the half light. "Whose fault is that?"

"I didn't hear any complaints. I'll have a quick shower and then we find breakfast."

"Wait. I'll join you."

"It's a small shower."

"I know."

Chapter Twenty-Two

Petros rose early, showered, shaved and dressed. With a full English breakfast eaten and washed down with two cups of coffee, he contacted Alfredo on his mobile, simply to ask how the repairs were going.

"One more day, a couple of coats of paint and good as new. When do we unload?"

"I hope in two to three days."

"Not a problem. My crew is enjoying being paid for doing nothing."

Petros laughed. "I'll try and speed things up." He disconnected the call and decided to stretch his legs.

Halfway along Strait Street he saw ZZ holding Scarlet's hand wandering towards him.

He stopped and waited. "You two look happy."

"I met you on the boat in Syracuse," said Scarlet.

"Meet Petros, my boss," said ZZ.

"Temporary boss," said Petros. "With luck we'll be finished here in two to three days and you and Amadou can go home."

"What have you been doing?" asked Scarlet.

Petros' eyes met ZZ's. "Searching for a ship which the Royal Navy sunk before any of us were born."

"Did you find it?"

"We wasted a lot of time and money," said Petros. "With luck I'll be flying home in a couple of days."

"So why stay in Malta?"

Petros hesitated. "Two reasons, our ship struck something during the night and it's being repaired and I have some friends here I haven't seen for a long time."

"When you've finished whatever you're were doing, how

much longer will ZZ stay?"

"That's up to him and I imagine you being here might influence his decision. We must have dinner." He paused. "What's wrong with tonight? I'll ask Amadou, Alfredo, and James, my lawyer?"

Scarlet frowned at the sudden change of subject. "I'd like that. I can learn more about ZZ."

"Tonight, my hotel, The Silver Sand, seven thirty. We'll meet in the dining room."

"See you," said Scarlet as she dragged ZZ away.

"Shit," said Petros as he pressed the memory key for Amadou on his mobile but the line was busy.

***

ZZ and Scarlet strolled to the gardens overlooking Grand Harbour. At the cliff edge, he pointed to the marina. "The *Tuna Turner* is berthed over there."

Scarlet gave him a huge smile. "Wait here for a few minutes, I have to do something."

He paused before answering. "I'll come with you."

She pointed and smiled. "If you follow me you might get arrested."

He watched as she wandered off, his mind a mixture of excitement and fixation for her.

Out of sight, Scarlet contacted Giovanni on her mobile and relayed the gist of the conversation she had with Petros.

"Did he definitely say two to three days before they leave?"

"That's what he said. Oh, and for some reason his lawyer's in Malta."

"Are you certain?"

"If I wasn't, I wouldn't have told you."

"Don't get lippy. My brother and his motor yacht have vanished, which, until they arrive in Palermo, makes me Padrino. So anymore back chat and I'll dump you as the expensive trash you are."

"I'll pretend I didn't hear that. What are you going to do next?"

"Not for you to know. You keep lover boy out of the way and he'll not get hurt. Understand?"

"Hurt him and you'll end up in prison for the rest of your life."

Giovanni's voice became menacing. "You made your bed. One word to the authorities and I'll have you fitted for concrete boots."

"I'm not an idiot. Remember women can be useful. Where are you?"

He ended the call.

She was in a foul mood but with several deep breaths and a little cold water splashed on her face, her unruffled character returned. She swore, dried her face and returned to where ZZ stared at the deep blue sea covered in white horses.

"Penny for them?" she asked.

"Fancy a holiday in Libya?"

"If I take more time off work, I'll get the sack."

ZZ gripped her hand. You know you really are something else."

Her eyes sparkled. "You're not so bad yourself. I'm hungry."

***

Petros had the table place settings suitably arranged so he sat directly opposite Scarlet.

Amadou and Alfredo arrived first, followed by James.

Petros pointed to the table and motioned for them to sit. "I'm not surprised ZZ and Scarlet are last." As he finished the sentence, they entered the room. He signalled to the waitress. "Fill the glasses, red or white and keep them full." Out of sight, he handed a sizeable tip.

She smiled. "Thank you, sir. May I inform the chef you're ready for the main course to be served?"

"Please do. I could eat a horse."

The waitress arrived pushing a trolley loaded with steaks, fillets of various fish and roasted vegetables.

Petros glanced at the food. "My choice, Hope you enjoy."

"Sea and turf, an excellent combination," said James.

They scooped the food from the platters and ate with passion.

"First-class," commented Alfredo. "I must ring Tommaso. My new bow was being painted as I left."

"I'm sure that can wait until you return," said Petros.

"My boat is my life. As my wife tells me, I think more of *Tuna Turner* than her. Sometimes she is right." He turned away and pressed the memory key on his mobile "My phone is not connecting. Can I borrow one?"

James handed over his iphone.

"Yours too is not connecting. I have tried every member of my crew. Something is wrong. I must return to my ship."

***

In Vittoriosa yacht marina, vessels rocked gently as craft of varying sizes transited their berths. For ten minutes the entrance to the area remained unattended as the security staff busied themselves elsewhere.

Giovanni Silvio, having bribed the Maltese gate-keepers, sauntered along the jetty followed by three men. He stopped at the *Tuna Turner* cupped his hands around his mouth and shouted, "*Tuna Turner* anyone on board?"

Five minutes elapsed before he made his move.

Their rubber-soled shoes made little noise on the steel deck as the three men drew their pistols and entered the superstructure. In minutes, they found the crew playing cards and drinking wine in the mess room.

Tommaso jumped when he saw the three men but on catching sight of the dull metallic gleam of the pistols pointed at him, froze.

The man leading the trio said, "Good move. Go get our boss."

Giovanni Silvio, an overweight man in his forties, glanced around the room as he entered. He stopped in the centre of the deck. "I see four of you. Where's Alfredo? I need to inform him I'm the new Padrino of Palermo. For years I suffered being number two to a weak man. I will make the Cosa Nostra strong, an organisation to be feared."

He pointed. "You're Marco the cook. Tell me what was found on the wreck and I'll not touch your mama. She's a buxom woman and will satisfy many of my men."

"We found nothing. The Englishman is mad spending so much money."

Giovanni turned, removed the pistol from the nearest man's hand, cocked and with a steady hand, fired. Marco, with a bullet in his right shoulder, collapsed, screaming abuse.

Giovanni scowled "The next bullet will be in his left shoulder and I'll work my way from limb to limb until he's dead.

I told you I'm the new broom that sweeps clean. I'll ask my question once again. Anyone of you may answer but I'll shoot Marco if it's not what I want to hear. What did you recover from the wreck?"

Davide forced himself to resist the impulse to go and help Marco. He would have loved to ram his fist down Giovanni's throat but thought better of it. "We found Hitler's Gold. It's in the engine room bilges."

"You could have saved Marco so much pain. Tommaso, you will sail this vessel to Palermo where my gold will be unloaded. If you do this I'll let you live."

"And if we don't you'll shoot us," said Simone.

"Refuse and then three of you will die in the next minute. Tommaso might live if he does as he's told."

Davide, carrying the first aid box, bent over Marco and eased his T-shirt clear from his shoulders. "You're lucky, the bullet has gone straight through." He stood and from the kit removed a bottle of medicinal alcohol and two large surgical pads.

"This might sting a bit but it'll slow down any infection." Using a swab, he washed away the excess blood. He placed the pads front and back before bandaging the shoulder. "Sit back and rest. I've done the best I can but I'm not a doctor."

"Thanks," said Marco. "There're cold meats and bread in the galley if you need to eat."

"I'd better start the engines before his highness starts shooting."

Tommaso checked the bridge controls. "I must have men on the bow and stern to release the ropes. As you shot one of the crew, your men aided by Simone will have to work the ropes."

Giovanni pointed a pistol at Tommaso. "One wrong move and I shoot you in the leg."

"Do that and you drive this ship."

"Shut up."

"You're the Padrino of Palermo. Who am I to argue but I still need men on the bow and stern to release the ropes."

From the funnel came two streams of exhaust. Tommaso watched as the gauges settled and Davide switched to bridge control. "Are your men going to help or do we stay tied to the wall?"

Giovanni relented and gave the order. "You two on the bow and you help on the stern."

"We know nothing about ropes and ships," said one man.

"Then you will learn or lose your fingers."

Tommaso gave the orders in a straightforward manner. With the ropes clear, he used the engines to manoeuvre the hull away from the wall.

Shots sounded from the stern.

Giovanni turned and glanced aft and saw one of his men. From the man's head blood gushed as he blasted the water behind the ship. "What's the fool doing?" The firing stopped.

"If the police or the Maltese Navy tell me to slow down or stop, I'll do as I'm told," said Tommaso. "These guys have their own set of rules."

He laughed. "If you stop you die."

A smug smile covered his face. "If I don't stop I die but the best part is, you die."

"Then pray to the Virgin Mary you don't have to. Increase speed."

Tommaso reported their departure to the harbour master who, although irritated by the short notice, wished them a safe voyage.

The moment they crossed the line between the calm waters of the harbour and the open sea the bows lifted before they plunged into deep troughs.

Tommaso grinned as he watched the three thugs throw up into the wind. "Your men are not sailors. They just covered themselves in their own vomit."

Giovanni leant against the rear bulkhead. "Do you think I care?" He laughed as a touch of madness filled his eyes.

One of the men, his face covered in dried blood and with the complexion of an elephant's skin, staggered onto the bridge. "The bastard hit me with something and jumped overboard."

"For your sake, I hope you didn't miss," said Giovanni.

"I never miss. Hit him at least three times."

***

Simone dived deep into the clear water of the marina. With strong strokes, he pulled away from the departing vessel, finding refuge under the twin hulls of a large catamaran.

"Are you staying there or do you want a hand?" shouted a tall, thin man dressed in denim shorts and a ragged but once white T-Shirt.

Simone grabbed the offered hand and heaved himself onto the deck. "Thanks. Have you a telephone I can borrow?"

"Sure have. I came on deck when some idiot blasted away with a cannon."

"That idiot was shooting at me. Don't worry I'm not the problem. Four men just hijacked my ship."

"Jeez," said the man. "Here's my cell."

Simone pressed the keys. Alfredo answered on the first bleep."

"The ship's gone, Captain. Giovanni Silvio and three men came on board and shot Marco. He threatened to kill him if we didn't divulge what we recovered from the wreck. I managed to escape."

"Are you okay?"

"I had a great swim and I'm fine. There's an American fussing around like my mama. When I've dried out I'll get a cab to Petros' hotel."

"If you can, stay where you are and I'll contact you later."

Simone turned to the man. "Can I stay with you until my captain returns?"

The man chuckled. "Only if you drink bourbon and play poker."

"The name's Simone and I deal a mean hand. Thanks." He lifted the mobile, "I'll be here for as long as it takes, Captain." The line went dead.

"Bill Martin, my pleasure. I'll get the cards, one bottle and two glasses."

***

Alfredo turned to face Petros. "Giovanni has my ship and your gold. There's nothing we can do."

James tapped Alfredo on the shoulder. "What's the maximum speed of your boat?"

"Twelve knots in a calm sea. Why?"

"A stupid idea but why don't we take your boat back?"

"How?" asked Petros.

"My friend has a power boat. We could catch them in less than an hour."

"They must be heading straight to Sicily," said Alfredo. "But they have guns, we have nothing."

"Wrong again," said James with a huge grin on his face. "I know my friend has four shotguns on board."

"Get on that phone and talk to him," said Petros as his brain went into overdrive. "Where's his boat berthed? I'm up for a crack at this insanity. Anyone else?"

"I'm with you," said Amadou and ZZ in unison.

"My idea, so I'm coming," said James as he waited for Allan to answer. "You'll need an independent witness when this shit hits the fan."

"It's my ship and I'm coming but I'm too old for heroics," muttered Alfredo.

"I need to borrow the Predator, Allan. Where are you?"

"Manoel island marina, prepping her for the weekend."

"Tell him I'll buy him a new one if we bend it," shouted Petros. "The fuel tanks, are they full?"

"Filled half an hour ago. Why?"

"Allan, don't ask questions. Move your boat to the Sliema ferry terminal and we'll meet you there."

"But..."

"Allan, for fuck's sake just do it. I'll explain later." He ended the call.

"Will he play?" asked Petros.

"He'll be at the terminal. Let's go."

Scarlet turned and faced ZZ, her lips trembled but her look remained determined. "Please don't go. Giovanni's an animal and will kill anyone who gets in his way, Stay here with me."

"Petros is my friend. I'll not let him down." He kissed her on the lips. "It's time to go."

"Giovanni is a maniac," said Scarlet.

Everyone froze.

"You know this man?" asked Petros.

"He is the Padrino of Palermo. Everyone knows the Cosa Nostra in Sicily."

"Leave her. We're wasting time," said Petros.

"Goodbye, Scarlet." ZZ raced after the other four men and crammed his frame into the taxi.

"I can only take four," shouted the driver.

Petros handed him a fifty-euro note. "Five. Sliema ferry terminal fast and you can have another."

At the sight of another crisp note, the engine roared into life and the rear tyres left long black streaks on the ground. With horn blaring, the aged vehicle rattled and shook its way along the Great Siege Road at over eighty kilometres an hour.

At the terminal Petros handed over another fifty-Euro note. "Thank you."

"I see Predator," said James.

Allan, unused to the power of his craft, eased her gently alongside the pontoon. Five men jumped onto the aft deck.

"Allan," said Petros. "You have five seconds to make a choice. Stay or go?"

From the authority in his voice, Allan could tell this man made decisions on the run and possessed a level of confidence, which must have come from military training. "My boat. I'm staying."

"Okay, but don't get in the way. Alfredo, go below and check the radar for a vessel running at ten knots heading for Sicily," said Petros as his eyes scanned the controls.

"Can you drive one of these? They are rather powerful," said Allan.

"Watch and learn." Petros centred the rudders and thrust the two engine controls hard astern.

Allan staggered and struck the console.

With the wheel turned hard to port, he slammed the controls full ahead. With ease, he steadied their course towards the open sea.

"There's a speed limit in the harbour you know," shouted Allan above the noise of the engines.

"So what? Alfredo, have you found our craft?"

"Yes. Steer 010 and we should intercept in twenty to twenty-five minutes. I'll track its course."

Petros nodded.

"Are you sure this will work?" asked Amadou.

"No. But it's worth a try. Allan, where are your guns?"

"I'll get them."

"No, show this man." He pointed to ZZ.

ZZ nodded, smiled, and followed Allan.

Alfredo wrote on a white board, 'Fifteen minutes distance to target,' and showed Petros as Allan returned to the deck.

"You drive," said Petros, "I need to think."

Allan grinned as he positioned himself behind the wheel. "You trust me?"

"Keep on course 010 and make no sudden turns." He motioned to James and Amadou as he entered the main cabin and slumped into the soft leather sofa. "I need a plan and quick. Anyone, any ideas?"

***

Tommaso switched on the navigation lights as the Mediterranean dusk turned into night.

"What are you doing?" shouted Giovanni.

"With age comes wisdom and you've failed the test. Go on, shoot me. Remember Marco's the cook and your men are spewing their guts up." He pointed at numerous red, white, and green lights. "See them? They belong to other vessels. I can see them and with our lights on, they can see us. Or would you prefer a giant tanker to plough over us?"

Giovanni realised that he would have to content himself with watching and waiting until they reached Sicily. "Shut up or I'll shoot you in the foot, just because I want to."

Tommaso checked the radar again. The vessel on the same course as the *Tuna Turner* would soon go past them. "Interesting," he thought.

***

Alfredo lifted his head from the chart table. "Petros, you have one chance. Jump on board from the stern. It is dark and I doubt they have thought of being attacked. No one in their right mind would dare."

"Says a lot for me. Great idea but we need someone to drive this boat and a grappling hook. One cock-up and we're fish food."

"I'll drive," said Alfredo. "I have more experience than the rest of you put together."

"He's right," said Amadou.

"How close can you get?" asked Petros.

Alfredo turned and laughed. "Close enough."

"ZZ, we have four shotguns. How much ammunition?"

"Plenty, but two are single shot."

"I'll take those," said Petros. "I'll head for the bridge. You two the accommodation section." He nodded to Amadou and ZZ. "I don't need to tell you what to do."

"I think he wants us to earn our money," said Amadou.

"Shoot first. We'll worry about the questions later. James, start making notes. Alfredo, time to get your hand in and I have to find a grappling hook." Petros clambered back to the driving position and stared ahead, He could just make out the stern light of *Tuna Turner*. "Allan, you're gripping the wheel too tight. Think of this machine as a beautiful woman you want to take to bed. Caress and she'll give you everything. Hold too tight and she'll fight you every inch of the way."

Without any hesitation, Alfredo edged Allan out of the way and grasped the wheel with his left hand, easing the craft to port and then to starboard to stay directly astern. With his right, he decreased the power. "Tell me when you're ready."

In ten minutes, Predator cruised half a mile astern.

"Allan, where's the lifejackets and grappling hook?"

He pointed. "Grappling hook is in the aft under-seat stowage. Life jackets are in the main cabin, I think." He ducked his head and began lifting the seats until he found them. He shouted. "Four enough?"

"Three will do." Petros and the others donned the jackets and crawled to the Predator's bow, sat and waited. "Link arms just in case Alfredo catches a wave the wrong way."

Alfredo relaxed as he stared at the stern-light of *Tuna Turner*. With a slight movement, he turned the wheel to starboard and pushed the throttles to maximum. The Predator jumped across the sea and at one hundred metres distant, passed the *Tuna Turner*. After a few minutes, he glanced astern and extinguished the navigation lights.

"What's he playing at?" asked Amadou who noticed the red and green lights turn off.

"I hope he has a plan," said Petros.

"I hope so too," said ZZ. "I'm soaked."

"Sea air is refreshing and good for you, stimulates the heart and clears the mind," shouted Petros.

"At the moment I don't care what it does," said ZZ.

"Something's wrong, the lights keep going on and off," said Amadou.

Petros watched. "He's sending a message. Tommaso will

be on the bridge reading every letter. There you are, Tommaso has acknowledged."

"Didn't see a thing," said Amadou.

"He flicked the main masthead light off and on. Hold tight, something's happening."

Alfredo extinguished the Predator's navigation lights again and in a long sweeping curve turned to port at maximum speed until he disappeared into the gloom. Ten minutes elapsed before he was again astern of *Tuna Turner*. Remaining at high speed, the Predator charged through the sea. He throttled back at the last moment. With well-judged throttle control and boat handling, he maintained a distance of less than one metre from the steel stern. The bow lifted and fell as predicted.

With illumination from *Tuna Turner's* stern-light, Petros, his face taut with concentration, stood and heaved the grappling hook at the submersible's steel frame. He pulled in the slack and prepared to jump. *Tuna Turner's* hull dropped and the moment it began to rise, he jumped across the gap.

Safe on the deck and hidden by the submersible, he turned, tossed the rope's end back, grabbed the shotguns and cartridges from Amadou. "On the rise is safest."

In less than a minute the three men, weapons ready, progressed along the deck. Petros lead his men towards the main transverse bulkhead. Tense, they took a breather on reaching the access door to the accommodation.

Petros signalled his intentions and began to ascend the ladder to the bridge.

Amadou grinned at ZZ as they opened the bulkhead door and checked for movement. The well-lit passageway was empty. Both men ignored the fact that if someone appeared they were exposed. Amadou covered ZZ while he shuffled along on his knees and stole a look into the crew's mess hall.

He spotted Marco on a bench seat, his eyes closed, with a blood-soaked bandage wrapped round his shoulder. Ahead, someone vomited.

Amadou changed position and edged along the bulkhead. ZZ slithered towards the opening, stood and stepped into the galley. Two men lay on the deck. Both never realised what happened until it was too late. The stock of ZZ's shotgun slammed into one's face destroying bone and teeth. The barrel of Amadou's weapon entered the other's mouth.

ZZ placed one finger over his lips.

"That was a stupid move," whispered Amadou.

"When I saw these dogs were incapable, it seemed the easiest thing to do."

Amadou flashed his eyes as he caught a flicker of movement in the passage. He slid behind the large freezer cabinet.

A man holding a pistol in his right hand entered. On the balls of his feet, he edged forward while pointing the weapon at ZZ's back.

He went to speak as the butt of Amadou's shotgun struck the side of his face. The man staggered, fired his weapon, and the bullet entered one of his prostrate associates.

Petros, his position tight against the bridge superstructure, heard the shot and took a gamble. With his left hand he slammed open the bridge door.

"What the..." said Giovanni.

Petros' shotgun blast struck the man's chest.

Giovanni staggered backwards across the deck to the far bulkhead. His face twisted as he slithered to the deck. A bloody red streak marked his passage from life to death.

No one moved.

"There's three more," said Tommaso.

Footsteps pounded the stairs leading to the bridge. Petros shifted position and took aim.

"Hold your fire, it's Amadou ."

"Where's ZZ?" asked Petros.

"Securing the prisoners."

"Tommaso says there are three."

"Agreed. Two out cold and one bleeding to death."

Petros pointed. "My man's going nowhere except the morgue."

Amadou chuckled, retrieved Giovanni's pistol from the deck and fired a shot through the window nearest the door.

Petros felt the bullet roar past his head. "What the fuck."

"Self-defence. He fired first and missed, you didn't." Amadou wiped the weapon clean and inserted it in Giovanni's dead hand.

"I can live with that." Petros set the radio to channel sixteen. "Predator this is *Tuna Turner*. Job done. Time to go home." At the rear of the bridge, he watched as Predator's navigation lights came on and the curving wake trailing astern as she dashed for the Marsamxett harbour.

He put down the microphone. "Unfortunately, the police must be involved."

Tommaso looked at the two men as if unsure what to say. "Piracy is a crime and you three acted in self-defence. I saw this one," he pointed to the bloody corpse, "raise his weapon and fire. One moment's hesitation and you'd be dead and he did shoot Marco."

Petros held up his right hand. "I get the message but thankfully we do have two legal beagles on the Predator."

"Coffee," said ZZ, balancing a tray. "We have a corpse in the galley and two men tied to the heavy steel oven."

Petros grabbed two cups and handed one to Tommaso.

"How long before we're alongside?"

"An hour at most."

The radio operated. "*Tuna Turner* – Channel One."

Petros set channel one on the radio. "Unknown caller – This is *Tuna Turner* – out."

"James here. When you arrive, there will be a police superintendant Hawksworth and his team waiting on the jetty. I've briefed him on the situation but he has to inspect the crime scene and take statements."

"Hawksworth is rather English," said Petros.

"I understand his father was a sailor and married a local girl."

"No problem, James. Thanks. Speak later. Out."

Chapter Twenty-Three

Late in the evening, the *Tuna Turner* came alongside the same berth in the marina she had left hours before. On the jetty, Alfredo and Simone stood in front of a police car. An ambulance, its siren wailing arrived seconds later.

Petros, with Tommaso, watched from the bridge as an overweight man in his late thirties, black hair brushed back from his forehead, and with the face of experience, stepped out of the police car. He gave orders to two police officers to block the gangway.

Petros raised both eyebrows. "Must be the superintendant. He's certainly efficient. I'll go and meet him."

Once the gangway was secured, the superintendant strolled across.

"Superintendant Hawksworth." Petros held out his hand.

Hawksworth ignored the gesture. "I need a room where I can interview and take statements from everyone on board. You have a casualty who may leave after being questioned." He pointed to the ambulance team and said, "Go and give emergency treatment."

The two men carrying a stretcher nodded and scurried across the gangway. "Where is the casualty?" one asked.

Petros' gaze shifted to the men. "I'll take you. Mind your feet on the ropes and wires." In a line, they walked to the crew's mess where Marco rested.

One of the medics removed the dressing, inspected the wound and applied a fresh dressing.

"Three heads turned when Hawksworth entered.

He pointed. "Your name?"

"Marco Russo."

"Who shot you?"

"Don't know his name."

Petros butted in. "His body is on the bridge, where I shot him."

Hawksworth, with a troubled look in his eyes, nodded as he glanced around the room. "I'll question you in a minute. You may remove the casualty."

With a bit of help, Marco stood and assisted by one medic walked out. The other followed with the stretcher.

Hawksworth allowed himself a faint smile as he sat at the mess table and waited.

One of his officers entered. "Two dead and two suffering from head injuries. The crew are lined up outside." The sergeant, with a serious but intelligent face, removed a folder and a miniature recorder from his case and sat in the chair next to his boss.

"Recording a conversation concentrates the mind, Mr Kyriades," said Hawksworth. "You may sit if you wish. In your own words, explain the part you played in the repossession of this craft. I will stop you to ask questions as appropriate."

Petros began from the time he and the others met for dinner and finished with his shooting Giovanni.

"Did you aim to kill this man?"

He shook his head slowly. "He did, I didn't. If I hadn't fired, I'd be dead. Ask Tommaso, he was there."

"Thank you, Mr Kyriades. And I will ask. Please send the next man in and remain on board as I may wish to question you again."

Tommaso strolled into the mess as if he had all the time in the world and sat facing the two men. Hawksworth lifted a sheet of paper as if to read it but signed the bottom. He repeated the same opening statement to Tommaso, leant back in his chair and listened. "Why do you think Mr Kyriades shot the intruder?"

"Because the bastard fired at him. What would you have done, asked him to hand over his gun? The pig shot Marco and would have killed him. He threatened to shoot me just for fun."

Hawksworth smiled. "You didn't answer my question."

"If he hadn't you'd be carrying another body off on a stretcher. Self-defence is the way I see it."

Hawksworth nodded thoughtfully as his eyes scanned the statement taken by his assistant. "Your comments are noted. Please send the next man in and wait outside."

Alfredo stormed into the mess and screamed. "Why haven't you arrested those men who stole my ship?"

Hawksworth folded his arms. "And you are?"

Alfredo fixed him with a stare. "Captain Alfredo Abruzzi and owner of this vessel"

Hawksworth unfolded his arms. "Please sit. Captain. I need a statement from you and your part in the recovery of your vessel. Two men are dead and I'm sure you understand it's my job to investigate the circumstances in which they died. Would you not agree?"

After three hours had passed, Hawksworth's the sergeant came out of the mess "The Superintendant asks that you attend his summing up of this affair before he leaves."

Hawksworth shut his file and pushed it to one side, stood, stretched his legs and back. He turned to the waiting men. There was a moment's silence as his hand rested on the file. "I have statements from everyone involved except the cook, Marco, two lawyers, James Eden, Allan Vella, and an Adrian Sullivan, plus the two surviving hijackers." He paused for a moment. "When I have those statements I'll have completed the evidential stage of my enquiries. My team will scrutinise and produce an event schematic for our National Crown Prosecutor to analyse. A decision as to a realistic prospect of conviction will result. The hijackers will relax in our prison. You, Mr Kyriades, are to remain in Malta until a conclusion is reached as to the killing of Giovanni Silvio."

Petros angled his head. "No problem. I wasn't going anywhere."

Hawksworth fixed him with a stare. "And I'll take your passport."

"Bit difficult - it's in my hotel room."

"Mr Kyriades, I'll have an officer waiting at reception when you return to your hotel." Their eye contact was enough to say everything.

With his sergeant trailing two steps behind, Hawksworth left the mess and the ship.

***

James Eden and Allan Vella sipped their drinks while they waited in the bar of the Silver Sand Hotel.

James peered over his glass. "Our mutual friend has arrived along with a uniformed police sergeant."

"Hawksworth will have demanded his passport. Wait here." Allan, still in his boating kit, sauntered across. "Sergeant, why are you with my client?"

"Orders from Superintendant Hawksworth. I have to take this man's passport."

"Really and you have the necessary paperwork?"

"I'm obeying orders."

"I suggest you return to your station and come back with the appropriate paperwork. In the meantime, I'll vouch for and hold my client's passport. You can collect it from my office tomorrow morning. Goodnight."

Petros was sure the man flinched.

The sergeant, his face-hardened, thought for a few moments. "I will inform the Superintendant." He turned and strolled out of the hotel.

"Can you do that?" asked Petros.

"No," he grinned. "You have accomplished tonight what most men would have walked away from. The superintendant might agree self-defence but knows it's not his decision. In the morning, I'll talk to the Crown Prosecutor's office. They decide whether prosecution is needed in the public interest. I will suggest another course of action to follow."

"Petros shrugged. "I couldn't have done anything without the use of your boat."

"One thing bothered me. Would you have bought me a new boat if you had trashed Predator?"

"Yes and no. If I was alive to tell the tale, yes, but if the operation had gone pear shaped, no."

Allan laughed. "All well that ends well. You must be knackered." He checked the time. "Any problems with the law give me a ring."

"No doubt I'll see you tomorrow. Thanks again. Drive carefully."

Allan shook his head. "This is Malta, he who sounds his horn first is in the right."

"Great legal judgement." He waited until Allan exited the building before strolling across to James. "I'm off to bed. Appreciate your help. See you in the morning."

Chapter Twenty-Four

Petros sat in the breakfast room with Amadou and ZZ. "You're here early. What's so urgent?"

"The job's finished and ZZ's girlfriend high-tailed it last night. I could be home with my wife."

"I agree. I'll have your money wired to your usual bank account." He glanced around and whispered, "plus when I know what the gold's worth, one percent of the total. Happy with that?"

Amadou nodded and helped himself to a glass of water.

"Thanks for your help, ZZ. Pity about Scarlet."

"I liked her a lot but apart from the sex, we both lived a lie. You have a saying in England, ships that pass in the night."

Petros stood and held out his hand. "Very true. If there's another job could you be interested?"

Amadou cleared his throat. "The next year might be a busy and profitable one for me in the arms trade to Syria. Unlike many, I trust you PK. Life with you has its exciting moments." He checked the time. "Must go, we have a flight to Benghazi at midday." They shook hands.

ZZ fidgeted with his right ear. "Time to go." He hugged Petros, looked him squarely in the eyes, smiled then walked away.

"Don't think about it, PK. He has the greatest admiration for you."

"He's growing up. Look after him." Petros strolled with Amadou to the hotel entrance and waited while he and ZZ jumped into a taxi and it drove away.

"Morning, Petros," said James.

"And I thought I'd have a quiet breakfast and read the paper," said Petros as he returned to his table.

James sat opposite. "I've a suggestion. Land the gold and send Alfredo and his crew home. At the moment you're spending a load of money for no return."

"That thought did cross my mind."

"I can arrange for an armoured car to collect it, with luck today or tomorrow."

Petros accepted James' point. "You make the arrangements and I'll talk to Alfredo."

James nodded thoughtfully and pointed to the coffee pot on the table. "Is that still hot?"

Petros shook his head. "I'll order another." He lifted the pot and made eye contact with a passing waiter.

"Certainly, sir." The man grabbed the pot and scurried away, returning moments later with another. "He filled two cups and took a half step back. " Anything else, sir?"

"Brown toast and lime marmalade, please"

James sipped his coffee and when the toast arrived helped himself to a slice. He glanced around making sure no one was within earshot. "How many bars did you recover?"

Petros shrugged. "Not sure but I'll count each one prior to depositing them in the bank."

"Well if you'll excuse me, he doesn't know yet but I've an appointment with the director of the Bank of Valletta."

Petros folded his arms. "Have a good look in the vault before you leave."

With a nod, James smiled. "Do you know there was a time in Malta when the locals would only deposit their money with the bank on the clear understanding they would be allowed into the vaults to see where it was kept."

Petros grinned. "Better than under the mattress."

"You may be right. Give you a call later."

Petros poured his fourth cup of coffee and sipped the

luke-warm dregs. Outside the sunlight filtered by the one way glass gave a comforting glow to the room.

***

Later that morning Petros, wearing blue jeans, trainers and a white polo shirt, left the hotel. At a steady pace he threaded his way towards Quarry Wharf and the water taxi station.

Once on the wharf he discovered to his surprise, not one water-taxi. He thought of jumping in a cab but glanced at his watch and decided he would wait. Five minutes elapsed before a water taxi arrived.

"How much to Vittoriosa Yacht Marina?"

The driver's eyes sparkled. With a wrinkled face from too much sun, wearing a peaked cap and light blue cotton overalls he replied, "Today special offer, thirty Euro."

"I'll give you forty if you can do the distance in less than ten minutes."

He laughed, sensed a kindred spirit. "Jump in and hold on."

The yellow fibreglass hull rocketed across the calm waters of Grand Harbour and passed Fort St Angelo.

Petros pointed to the *Tuna Turner*.

The sensation of clinging onto the side of a craft hurtling over the water concentrated his mind. The driver slammed the throttle shut and allowed the hull to glide alongside the jetty.

Petros handed over forty Euro and stepped onto the wooden plank-covered pontoon.

He straightened his back on seeing Hawksworth alight from his black Mercedes.

Hawksworth stood with his feet apart and waited for Petros to arrive on the quay. "Mr Kyriades, you were next on my list but first I must talk with Captain Alfredo. You may wait in my car."

"Can you tell me what this is about?"

"I have a few more questions."

"Questions about what in particular?"

"Who, Mr Kyriades, who?" He stomped across the *Tuna Turner's* gangway and entered the accommodation section.

Petros sat in the front passenger seat and waited.

Ten minutes later Hawksworth returned, sat behind the wheel, started the engine and drove sedately away from the marina.

"Adrian Sullivan, Mr Kyriades, what do you know about him?"

"Apart from the fact he operates a submersible for a living, nothing."

"Well he robbed my men and me of what little sleep we might have had last night. Shortly after leaving the marina, I watched him being pulled out of St Julian's Bay at four this morning."

"Bloody hell. I assume as he was pulled out he was dead."

"Unfortunately he is and I want you to see him."

"Could it have been an accident?"

"I keep an open mind until the facts tell me different."

They stopped in the small car park outside a building, which stood on its own to the west of the Mater Der Hospital.

"Mr Sullivan wasn't in the water long."

In a room at the far end of a long corridor and on the other side of a glass petition, two men wearing green surgical gowns and matching wellingtons waved at Hawksworth. On a stainless steel slab the body of Adrian Sullivan lay naked.

"Mr Kyriades, can you confirm the man on the slab is

Adrian Sullivan?"

"From what I can see and the colour of his hair, it is."

"When did you last see him?"

Petros paused in thought. "I'll be honest, I can't remember. Maybe two days ago. I booked a room in a hotel and never saw him again."

"Thank you. That's all I need to know. You have confirmed the name on the driving licence in his wallet. We can now leave."

"Do you know who did this?"

"I have my suspicions."

"Who?"

"I believe it's the same men who stole the *Tuna Turner*. We have a video from a shop's security camera, which shows them and the victim walking from a car park. Only four returned." He looked Petros straight in the eyes. "You mix with the wrong people, Mr Kyriades."

"I don't know any of them."

"Somehow they knew you and what you discovered. I understand you have employed the services of Allan Vella. He's a good man to have if you're arrested."

Petros felt sick and did not reply.

Hawksworth laughed. "I think you need a drink." He drove from the hospital to Msida yacht marina and pointed. "My bar and restaurant. It will supplement my pension when I retire."

They entered an open door on the left. The area was spacious, each table set for dinner on pristine white table clothes.

"Looks up-market," said Petros.

"My customers are from those obscene motor cruisers in the marina. But then their money is as good as anyone's. What would you like to drink?"

"A fresh orange juice and tonic, please."

Hawksworth signalled to a waitress standing nearby. "Christina, two fresh orange juice and tonics, please." His mobile rang. He checked the display and switched it off.

Their drinks arrived.

"Mr Kyriades, who knew you were searching for gold?"

Petros shook his head. "You've interviewed most of the crew, and my associates I'd trust with my life."

Hawksworth shrugged. "From information I've received, the man you shot came from Palermo and his older brother, who appears to have gone missing, was the leader in the Cosa Nostra. Someone talked but I doubt if we'll ever discover who. They beat Mr Sullivan before throwing him in the sea. If he talked and I believe he might have, that would explain their attempt at piracy. Once back in Palermo the gold would have vanished. You, Mr Kyriades, are a brave, if somewhat foolish, man but then it's the business you're in. The Collectors is the name of your London-based company."

Petros folded his arms. "You've been busy."

Hawksworth smiled. "The internet is a wonderful tool and these days gathering information from other police forces is so much simpler. I know you acted in self-defence and my report will indicate that. The Crown Prosecutor's office will rubber stamp my recommendations and another file will gather dust in the archives. You're free to go but I'll be a lot happier when you leave my island."

Petros downed the dregs of juice in his glass. "I'm off the hook?"

Hawksworth chuckled and nodded. "You are. I'd give you a lift back to your hotel but I'm going to grab some sleep. Not as young as I used to be. Goodbye, Mr Kyriades."

Petros stood and they shook hands.

Outside the marina's gated entrance three white taxis

waited. He jumped into the first one and returned to his hotel.

Chapter Twenty-Five.

Scarlet's flight arrived back in Palermo where she hired a taxi to the flat she shared with Giovanni in Syracuse. Once inside she threw her coat and bag onto a chair. Outraged by the way Giovanni treated her she sat on her bed. Then a thought struck her. She cursed, and began to pack as much as she could into two suitcases.

Her packing complete, she entered Giovanni's office and with the aid of a steel letter opener forced the drawer to his desk. What she hunted were his keys that lay on the top of some correspondence. She picked them up and walked over to a large wardrobe. In seconds, she unlocked the doors. "I'll show you how good I am," she shouted as on her third attempt the old-fashioned safe inside opened. The top two drawers contained account books, which she placed to one side. The third and largest held what she wanted, thousands of Euro in cash. This she removed without counting, filling large white envelopes. When the drawer was empty she placed one envelope in her handbag and divided the remainder into her suitcases. She then gave the books a cursory once over; dates and names with figures alongside. Interesting, she thought, reading more.

Although second in command, Giovanni controlled a major part of Sicily's drug trade. Many a cheating dealer's body turned up tortured, disfigured or in two or more pieces. Giovanni was protected by his brother on one side and with the assistance of the police on the other. She laughed aloud; these volumes contained enough information to put him in jail forever.

With the books wrapped and addressed to the senior police officer of Palermo, she left the flat and strolled to the local post office. When her turn came she paid the clerk behind the counter and left. Her next stop, her bank where she closed the account.

Back in the flat she forced herself to have a shower and relax. Wearing a light grey suit and the darkest of sunglasses, she left. She placed the two cases on the rear seat of her car before returning to the flat for a final look around. "Almost forgot," she muttered as she emptied the contents of her jewellery box into her bag. A quick rummage in Giovanni's bedside cabinet revealed a gold Rolex and several pairs of gold cufflinks, one pair encrusted with diamonds. As she hurried to her car she looked pleased. She dumped her shoulder bag on the front passenger seat and jumped in. Very gently she rubbed her stomach. "Looks like I might have something to remember you by, ZZ." With the turn of the key, the engine started and she drove away.

***

Petros glanced at his watch. Lunch time had come and gone. He strolled across the *Tuna Turner's* gangway and went straight to the crew's mess room.

"The wanderer returns," said Alfredo. "I was wondering how the investigation was going. Had a call from James. He tells me an armoured car will be arriving sometime this afternoon to take the gold. I told him you gave the orders not him."

"Alfredo, it's been an exciting twenty-four hours with little sleep. I'd love a cup of your fabulous coffee and a sandwich or two."

"I'll do it," said Simone. "Ham and cheese?"

"Perfect." He sat on the bench seat. "The bad news. Adrian was murdered by the men who stole your boat. The good news is those in custody have been charged with his murder and the theft of your boat. I understand from Hawksworth they have confessed and will be pleading guilty."

"Your coffee and sandwiches, Petros."

"Thanks, Simone. Alfredo, I have in fact agreed with James to have the gold taken off your ship and stored in The Bank of Malta's vault. When completed I intend to fly home. But first, as a bonus, I'm giving you one bar of gold each. Does anyone know if Adrian was married or had dependants?"

"I believe he lived with his mother in Rome. I can check it out," said Davide.

"Take an extra bar and see his mother receives the money."

"What will happen to his body?" asked Tommaso.

Petros rubbed his chin. "Don't really know but his mother will have to arrange for it to be transported to a destination of her choice. Without attempting to sound insensitive, Alfredo, make sure he's given a good send off and I'll meet whatever it costs. As one of the good guys, he deserves a descent funeral."

Alfredo paced the room and stopped. "With the number of bars in the bilges it is time to start bringing them up."

Petros scratched his nose. "If we form a chain it'll be quicker."

"I suppose I'm the bilge rat."

"Davide, it's your engine room."

Tommaso laughed. "Petros, as it's your gold I suggest you watch over the pile on the upper deck."

In less than an hour one thousand, one hundred and twenty ingots were stacked in piles of ten on the deck.

Petros removed six bars. "One each."

"I already have the first bar we found," said Alfredo.

"Keep it as payment for Adrian's funeral. Donate what's left over to his mother."

The roar of a heavy vehicle made them turn towards the

jetty. James alighted from his taxi and waved.

Petros and the others stared at what appeared to be a Mercedes plain white van reverse towards the gangway.

It stopped and two armed men wearing full body armour jumped out and took their positions. The two rear doors opened."

From the jetty, James shouted, "What are you waiting for?"

Petros strolled to the side of the ship. "It's a bog-standard white van."

James laughed. "Fully armoured glass and steel. Just looks like a white van."

"Right team, one more time," said Petros as he began shifting the ingots.

"I never thought I'd say this," said Tommaso, "but I'm fed up shifting this gold."

"You'll appreciate it when it changes into paper money," said Davide.

"True."

Forty-five minutes elapsed before the rear doors to the armoured van shut remotely. The two men ran to the front and clambered inside.

"I need you, Petros. The bank will weigh and log every bar. You, I and the manager will sign the receipt notes."

"Petros turned. "Alfredo, when are you sailing?"

"At ten twenty tomorrow on the tide."

I'll be back later. If you work out what I owe you I'll arrange for an electronic transfer to your bank in Palermo."

"I will have your invoice ready."

***

Petros glanced anxiously at the van as it pulled away. With long strides, he ran to the taxi and jumped into the rear seat alongside James. "Somehow I'll feel safer when that lot is deposited inside a bank vault."

James stared wide-eyed. "Stop worrying, those trucks are bulldozer proof."

Petros clearly did not understand the comment. "Bullshit always baffles brains. Can you explain?"

James shook his head. "Several months ago four men with guns, a white van, and a bulldozer attempted to steal an armoured truck identical to the one we're following. It started well when their van blocked the road and the bulldozer began pushing from the rear. It appears the two security guards released the brakes and several tons of armour hit the van and squashed it against a wall. These men didn't have a clue, as now their escape van was useless. Needless to say, they didn't give up and continued to ram the rear doors with the dozer while others fired shots at the windows."

Petros interrupted. "The glass in those vehicles wouldn't crack if an RPG hit it. Bullets bounce."

"Exactly but these morons hadn't done their homework. Which way do the doors usually open?"

"You generally pull them open."

James raised his eyebrows and smiled. "Correct. The more they pushed with the dozer the longer nothing happened. The force required to burst them open must come from the inside or alternatively if someone forced a guard to open them with a key. These men had no idea as to the construction and function of these vehicles."

"How far are we from the bank?"

"Five minutes at most."

"I assume the bad guys were arrested."

James laughed. "Not only arrested but they pleaded guilty

when the police showed them pictures of the failed robbery. They didn't even wear hoods. Tourists took pictures with their Iphone by the dozen and contacted the police, who blocked the two escape routes."

"I think we've arrived," said Petros as armed guards surrounded the van.

"Follow me," said James. "As I said, we and the manager have to witness the ingots being counted, weighed, and stored in the vault."

One hour later Petros and James signed the last document.

"One moment, gentlemen," said the immaculately dressed manager. "Please follow me."

They strolled to the rear of the building and into a windowless room where a young woman sat hunched over a machine. She lifted her head.

"Martese, what are your findings?"

She smiled. "This bar is twenty-two karat. But three of the bars I have tested have given the strangest of readings."

"Use the electronic test machine to check the conductivity just to be sure," said the manager with a serious face.

She wrinkled her nose. "The readings I obtained were from the tester."

The manager thought for a moment. "How long will you require us to store your gold, Mr Kyriades?"

"As long as needs be."

"Can the bank conduct further tests? I'm certain the results so far are from an error with the machine."

Petros paused. "It's marked with the stamp of the Deutsche Reichsbank. I see no reason it's not what it seems."

James jumped in. "When we have confirmed legal

ownership, arrangements will be made to sell. With luck in less than a week."

"My point exactly," said the manager. "You cannot sell if it's not verified. At the moment, I and my staff have a minor cause for concern. I'm sure it is as we believe a fault with the machine but we must be sure."

Petros turned up the palms of his hands. "I agree. How long do you require?"

"A day at most."

"I'm intrigued as to why your machine validates some but not others. You can contact me at the Silver Sand."

"I will make sure you are kept informed, Mr Kyriades."

"Thank you." Petros shook his hand, turned and with James left the room.

"Hope he doesn't take too long. Once your claim is confirmed I have someone interested in purchasing every bar at a good price."

"And who might that be?"

"He has a large place in Saudi and his staff bow and call him 'Your Highness'."

"I'll bow when he transfers the money. Must return to the *Tuna Turner* and pay my dues."

On the bridge, Alfredo leant with his back on the chart table while Petros studied the sums on a single sheet of foolscap.

"Seventeen days, you haven't included your return journey, that's at least another two. The submersible didn't come cheap but worth every penny. I've spoken to the engineers who repaired your bow and replaced the windows on the bridge. All in all, I believe I owe you sixty thousand dollars, American."

"Agreed."

Petros removed his mobile from his pocket.

"Yes," came the reply.

"Bear, I need you to transfer sixty thousand dollars from the company account to Captain Alfredo. I'll hand my phone over and he can tell you his account details."

Alfredo took the phone as Petros strolled out onto the port bridge wing and waited. Two minutes later he handed it back.

"When did you say you were leaving?"

"Tomorrow morning." He chuckled. "Life will be dull without you."

"But a great deal safer. Will the Cosa Nostra be a problem?"

Alfredo laughed. "I would be surprised. Why would they? Neither my crew nor I will tell them what has happened. They will fight amongst themselves to gain power. Babies are born and people die, life goes on."

"Very philosophical."

"Take care, Petros. You never know our paths may cross again."

"If I ever holiday in Palermo with my wife and daughter, I'll let you know."

"That would be good." Alfredo grabbed Petros and hugged him. "Stay out of trouble."

Petros stepped back. "I'll try. Must say goodbye to your team. Without their help none of this would have been possible."

Twenty minutes later Petros strolled along the jetty. Clear of the marina he hailed a taxi and returned to his hotel.

***

At breakfast the following day, Petros watched as James strode towards him. His look was serious as he pulled out a chair and sat with his elbows on the table.

"There's a problem with the gold," whispered James. "The bank manager wishes to see you."

"Can you be more precise?"

James studied Petros. "All I know is twenty bars failed the test."

Petros narrowed his eyes as he picked up his glass of fresh orange juice. "Twenty out of one thousand plus. I can live with that."

James leaned forward. "He still needs to talk to you."

"Have a coffee and when I've eaten my breakfast we'll visit the bank."

"James signalled a passing waiter for a cup and ordered more coffee."

One hour later the two men strolled across the marble floor and out of reception. At a fast pace they walked along the road, which led to the bank. James telephoned the manager as they walked. On their arrival he and his assistant waited by the main entrance.

"Thank you for coming, Mr Kyriades." The man gave a bleak smile. "What we have discovered is most unusual. Please, follow me."

Once again, they strolled to the rear of the building and into the windowless room. On a bench lay twenty gleaming ingots.

Petros smiled. "I assume that," he pointed, "is my gold. What's wrong with it?"

"Let me explain and please understand the tests we have undertaken are fully justified," the manager said offhandedly.

"Are they worth anything?" asked Petros. "If not, toss them in the bin."

"They are worth more than you think.

Petros' gaze remained fixed on the manager. "So what's

wrong with them?"

The manager paused. "Rather than resort to drilling or cutting the bars to verify their integrity we use a simple ultrasonic test. The results give us a confidence in the purity of the gold. The readings obtained from these bars showed strange reflection from the inside. On your behalf, I instructed our inspector to cut through one bar. This proved more difficult than we initially thought."

"I always believed gold to be soft when compared to steel," said Petros.

"A normal metal saw will not cut diamonds, Mr Kyriades. These bars contain diamonds."

"Well, I'll be damned, Hitler's spoils from the Nazi work camps," said Petros, "it fits."

"As I see it," said James, "this was the final shipment. To save time, those in charge placed everything remaining into the melting pot. The route they chose was deliberately diverse but the destination more than likely South America. The *Gradisca* would have made contact with a German submarine in the Atlantic, transferred the gold and then scuttled the vessel with no one any the wiser. Unfortunately, for them the Royal Navy intervened."

The black telephone on the table rang. The manager picked up the handset. The call lasted a few minutes.

"Mr Kyriades, for us to remove the diamonds will be expensive. There are those who are experienced in the process."

Petros levelled his eyes at the manager. "What James described has more than an element of truth but we don't know. Box those twenty bars and send them to the Simon Wiesenthal Centre in Los Angeles. From what I understand, their members promote human rights and teach the lessons of the Holocaust for future generations."

"I'm not sure I understand."

"From what we assume, twenty bars rightly belong to them. The rest are mine."

"We estimate fifty-two million plus, Mr Kyriades,, less our commission."

"James, when can I sell?"

"When I know, you'll know."

"What do you reckon, days, weeks or months?"

With thinly concealed impatience. "Days. Go home. I have your power of attorney and can deal with everything. Don't worry; I'll get you a good price. I want my one percent after tax to be as large as possible. "

"I agree. Don't forget to put a note in the box for LA. Tell them it's a gift." He turned to the manager. "Thank you. Any more problems, James will deal with them. That's why I pay him."

He grinned. "I should have charged you two percent."

"It was almost one percent of nothing. See you in London."

Chapter Twenty-Six

Maria and Alysa waited in arrivals and watched passengers from other flights meet their loved ones. Petros strolled into the open but the minute he spied her, concern flitted over his face. Whatever happened, she had undergone a horrific experience yet thankfully remained whole.

She lifted Alysa, put her free arm around his shoulder, and kissed him.

"Me kiss papa."

Petros grabbed Alysa and kissed her. "Happy?"

"Mama fell down the stairs when you were working."

"Papa knows," said Maria.

He pulled Maria close. "My questions can wait."

A smile spread across her face as she interlaced her fingers with his and led him to the car park. "Do you want to drive?"

"Papa drive," shouted Alysa. "Mama always drives."

Petros shrugged and took the ignition key. "I have a choice?"

On exiting the car park, torrential rain struck the windscreen. "When did this start?"

"Early this morning," said Maria.

"Yarlie got wet."

"I bet he did," said Petros. "From wall to wall sunshine to an English summer, can't be bad."

They drove in silence, each with unanswered questions. At the end of two hours' difficult driving, Petros entered the driveway, parked as close to the house as he could and jumped out. Maria opened the main door and Alysa scooted inside. Seconds later Petros followed and Charlie charged, sliding straight into his legs.

He rubbed the animal's coat. "You're still as daft as ever."

Alysa grabbed Charlie and disappeared into the lounge.

"Coffee?"

"Love one." He touched her face dreading to ask. "How bad was it?"

Her eyes brimmed with tears. "Could have been worse." She spooned coffee into the cups. "Charlie tried his best but they smashed him around the head and I ordered him to run. Bear arrived and with his team did the business. It taught me next time to check who's knocking on the door before opening." The kettle clicked off and she filled the cups. "And before you ask, apart from ripping my clothes off, they didn't."

He wrapped his arms around her soft body and pulled her close, her tears wet on his face. "Thankfully, Bear solved the problem. I felt so useless. I owe him my life and now yours." He smiled. "With friends like him God help my enemies."

She broke the embrace, squeezed her eyes shut and then opened them. "Drink your coffee before it gets cold and Alysa sees me crying."

"She's happy watching cartoons on television with Charlie."

Both of them remained quiet as they listened to Alysa laugh and Charlie bark.

"Anyway, apart from a few bruises and my pride dented, it's over. How was it your end?"

He gave a modest smile, aware her wounds mentally and physically would heal given time. "With Amadou, ZZ, and the team backing me, not a problem. The Cosa Nostra is short of a few men. We suffered one casualty, another with a bullet in the shoulder and when I left the ship, he was cooking dinner." He glanced at the kitchen clock. "Anyway, I'd better give Bear a ring."

The doorbell chimed. "That should be Bear, Jocelyn and one of her bridesmaids. I invited them for dinner."

"Isn't Alysa her bridesmaid?"

"She is but you'll love number two."

Bemused, he stared at her. "Who is it?"

"Open the door, it's raining."

Petros sprinted to the door. Bear grabbed and hugged him. "Even without me you found trouble."

"You were where you needed to be, rescuing my wife."

"I forgot to play by the rules. They won't be bothering Maria again."

"You didn't?"

"Not in a million years."

"Hi, Jocelyn. My God, Lucy. You've grown so much since I last saw you."

Lucy grinned. "Mother Superior tells me I'm twelve now."

She was the last person he expected to see. He lifted and drew her close.

Jocelyn frowned. "Can we come in?"

"Sorry. I'm so thrilled to see Lucy." Petros carried her into the kitchen. "Alysa, come and meet your adopted sister."

Alysa, with Charlie, at her side ran into the kitchen. She stopped when she saw Lucy in the arms of her father. "Daddy has a picture of you in his office. You're African and my daddy found you."

Petros lowered Lucy to the floor.

Charlie wagged his tail and nuzzled Lucy's hand.

Alysa saw the strange look on Lucy's face. "Yarlie my friend and he likes you. I like you. Want to see my bedroom?"

Lucy glanced at Bear and Petros and smiled. "Yes

please."

Alysa grabbed her hand as they raced up the stairs. Charlie chased after them but slid to a stop at the bottom.

"She's still a little girl but I doubt for much longer. Great choice for a bridesmaid. Why didn't I think of it?"

"We didn't either," said Jocelyn, "until the mother superior from her convent school in Luanda telephoned."

"Is there a problem?" asked Petros.

"It would seem our Lucy has outgrown her schooling in Luanda. She dreams of becoming a doctor and used to assist in the convent infirmary. The difficulty is she requires academic qualifications to enter medical school.

"While you were away playing with boats, we decided to help. The mother superior discussed the situation with Lucy and explained she would have to leave the school and her friends. She jumped at the chance to come to England, knowing you and Bear could be trusted. Let's face, it you risked your lives saving her from those people traffickers. She'll never forget. Anyway, she arrived a week ago and lives with us for the time being."

"We'll need to arrange a school."

They smiled at each other.

"Dusted and done," said Maria.

Petros laughed. "Good job I know what you mean. May I suggest the company continues its donation to Lucy's old school and we share the fees for whatever school you've chosen?"

Charlie pushed Petros and barked. "He wants to go outside."

"In this rain?" said Jocelyn.

He shrugged, let the dog out and watched as the animal headed for the trees. He vanished for a few minutes before charging back, his paws pounding the saturated ground. Once in the house he stood on his carpet and waited. Petros rubbed him with a towel.

He looked at his wife and friends. "I suppose we'd better discuss your wedding."

"You're my best man."

"I know. Two weeks Saturday, Marylebone Registry Office, two o'clock."

"Right in one but while you've been away cruising in the Med, arrangements for the wedding and reception have been organised. You need to be brought up to speed."

A thin smile creased his mouth as Petros shook his head. "It's getting late. Tell you what, rather than Maria cooking, let's discuss your plans in the local restaurant. Bear, they make a brilliant beef and ale pie. You can have it with chips or baked potato and we can take Alysa and Lucy."

"Give that man a coconut. How far is it?"

"Top of the hill. I'll give them a ring."

***

Maria ran up the stairs to Alysa's room to find the two girls side by side on the carpet. Alysa's eyes never left Lucy as she showed her how to use her Ipad.

"Wash your hands, girls. We're going out for a meal."

"Mama, is Lucy my real sister?"

Maria sat on the edge of Alysa's bed. "You understand the story of how daddy and uncle Bear found Lucy?"

Alysa nodded.

"Well daddy and uncle Bear decided to help and sent money to the village where she lived and later to her school. It appears Lucy is a clever girl and so she's come to live with uncle Bear and go to another school. So in answer to your question, she's not a real sister but an adopted one. She's adopted us and we her."

Alysa frowned, thinking. "But if I want she can be my real sister?"

Lucy grabbed her hand. "We are sisters. Come, we must wash our hands."

Maria returned to the kitchen. "The girls are getting ready. Charlie watch the house."

When the two girls descended the stairs Bear ran outside and drove his Mercedes as close to the door as he could. They all jumped in as Petros locked the door and set the alarm.

Bear engaged gear and drove out of the drive.

***

Maria came out of the en-suite naked and grinned at her husband. "I missed you."

"Are you tired?"

She crawled onto the bed and sat astride him. "I'm demanding payment in full."

"Be gentle with me."

She turned out the light.

Chapter Twenty-Seven

Two days prior to Bear's wedding, Petros stood in the doorway of his house and watched the rear lights of Maria's car disappear through the entrance.

Petros glanced at his watch and turned to Bear. "Time for a shit, shave, shower, and change of clothes, then we're off to the Black Swan. The owner has given us the backroom and promised a beef curry to end all curries. Once eaten we'll drink and tell stories until..."

"Until what?"

"Until you're rat-arsed and I bring you home."

"Couldn't we simply have a night in front of the tele and a takeaway?"

Petros chuckled. "You're getting old. You're here with me until Saturday, when I deliver you, booted and suited for Jocelyn. Back out now and you're a dead man."

Bear gave him the sort of smile meant for idiots. "I'm staying sober. I know you and the others and what you're likely to get up too.

***

The Black Swan was an old pub with numerous rooms on the ground floor. The landlord, an ex-soldier from the guards, met Petros and Bear as they arrived in the public bar. He guided them to a large room at the back. "You can make as much noise as you like and not disturb my regulars. He pointed to a tall, thin girl with long black hair. "Susie will serve drinks and keep a tab running and with regards to bad language, she knows more than you do. She was a red cap and can kick arse with the best of them. Oh, and by the way, her husband's my chef and he'll serve the curry in half an hour."

As the door opened, a cheer rang out from those present.

"About time. We're on our third pint," said Zack.

Bear shook hands with everyone and sat in the largest chair.

"Bear, do you remember that brothel in Bagdad?"

"It was a sweat box. Fifty men getting pissed and five women working overtime for the fat slob who owned the place. How could anyone forget? If nothing else it kept the medics busy."

"Didn't those two Bulgarian women with legs all the way to their bums fancy you?" shouted Brian.

"In the thick smoke and with the lights out they were still ugly. And no I didn't."

"They closed the place down after six nutters with AKs walked in and shot the place to ribbons."

"Wouldn't be surprised if it opened a couple of days later under different ownership but with the same girls."

The stories continued and the beer flowed until the steaming curry and a ton of rice arrived.

Each man ladled the sweet smelling brew onto a soup plate, grabbed a nan and returned to a table.

In a short time spoons rattled in empty plates.

Bear wandered over to the bar and spoke to Susie. "Your old man does a mean curry."

She smiled. "Staff Sergeant in the catering corps for twenty two years. If you've all eaten your fill I'll clear the table."

"Leave the pot, there's plenty left. I might need a top up after a few more beers."

She laughed. "I'll leave some clean plates."

"As I'm paying, if you fancy a tot or two, help yourself."

"Maybe later. I need a clear head to keep score for the

boss."

Bear strolled over to where Petros' three brothers and Andreas sat. "Did I ever tell you the first night out your brother and I had in town?"

George, Pavlo and Stavros glanced at each other.

"If we said you have," said George, "would that stop you?"

Bear sat and took a gulp of beer. "We'd arranged to meet in The Crown of Thorns, my local. Not the most salubrious of establishments. You know the type, drab interior, smoke-stained walls and ceiling but it served a good pint. For my sins, I arrived late to find PK ready to take on the whole bar.

"The blonde barmaid, Fiona, hated the world and if she didn't like you filled a pint glass with slops. Anyway, she thought he was a copper and told him to fuck off. PK eventually convinced her he was waiting for me and she served him.

"While he leant against the bar three of the local yobs came in and told him to take a hike.

"Your brother decided to finish his pint which wound them up. As half-wits they decided to have some fun. Petros floored the three of them with a bar stool. That's when I arrived and told him to wind his neck in, replace the bar stool and drink up."

George lifted his head as the music to the stripper blasted out of twin speakers on the far wall.

A leather-clad motorcyclist with curves in the right places entered the room. With long strides, she stomped across the floor and stood legs apart in front of Bear. In time with the music, the crash helmet fell to the floor.

A red-haired woman shook her hair free, the smile on her face tantalising. "Hello, big boy."

In controlled movements, she undid the heavy metal zip

on her jacket revealing her bare breasts.

Bear attempted to stand but James and Zack held him on the chair while the others formed a circle.

He shrugged as she straddled his knees and pushed her pert breasts into his chest.

She stood, turned, and sat on his lap, gyrating her hips to the music.

Bear sat there with his hands behind his head, smiling.

Her hands grabbed his and attempted to pull him onto the floor.

With a grin, the dance continued until she circled the others, discarding her clothes until naked.

The music stopped, she bowed to Bear and gave him a big kiss on the lips, collected her clothes and vanished into the toilet.

"Passable," said Bear, "Bit thin, small tits but a nice arse."

"Any more than a mouthful is a waste and when you're stoking the fire, size doesn't matter," said Zack.

"When did you last get your leg over?" asked James.

"You know when. You had the ugly sister."

"Don't remind me. She was a proper double bagger. Get the beers in."

Throughout the evening, they consumed beer after beer.

"I know how to avoid a hangover," slurred Andreas.

"Really," said Bear.

"Stay drunk."

"And you are," said Bear. "Park your arse in the corner and go to sleep."

After midnight the landlord entered. "Gentlemen, your three taxis have arrived."

Brian, James and Zack tumbled into one. As they

shouted goodnight it raced away.

George, Pavlo and Stavros, supporting each other, fell into another.

Bear holding Andreas by the scruff of his shirt sat in the third car and waited for Petros.

Two minutes later he arrived and jumped into the front passenger seat. "You know the address, driver. Time for bed."

***

At ten o'clock, the smell of bacon, eggs, beans and tomatoes filled the kitchen. Petros stood by the cooker and banged a cast iron pan onto the range.

Bear, followed by a pale-faced Andreas, descended the stairs. "No need for the racket. The aroma of breakfast woke me. I've showered and ready to eat."

Petros grinned. "You're always ready to eat. Plates are on the counter, toast in the toaster. I'm not a waiter, help yourselves."

Andreas grabbed a cup and poured a coffee.

"Not eating?" asked Petros.

"That curry was a bit strong for me."

"Nothing to do with the ten pints and numerous brandies you threw down your neck."

"What he doesn't want I'll eat. Must build my strength up for tomorrow," mumbled Bear as he covered his eggs with brown sauce.

Charlie lay in his basket, his eyes alert to any crumb, which fell to the floor.

Petros drank fresh orange juice from a tumbler and made himself an egg and bacon sandwich. "Today we relax and make sure everything's ready for tomorrow"."

I wouldn't worry, Jocelyn, Maria and your mum will have sorted everything. PK, Any more eggs and bacon? And while you're at it, pass over a couple of slices of toast."

"You want it, you cook it."

Andreas drank his second cup of black coffee and nibbled a slice of dry toast. "I'll take it easy."

Bear placed the remaining rashers into the frying pan until they were crisp. Three he placed between two slices of buttered toast. The others he allowed to fall to the floor.

Charlie barked but did not move.

"It's all yours, Dog," said Petros.

In two strides, his long tongue pulled the bacon into his mouth.

"Don't tell Alysa," said Petros.

Charlie barked and settled back into his basket.

"We'd better give this kitchen a good clean after breakfast or Maria will ban you from this house forever. Tonight, I've booked a local restaurant for dinner, then it's back home and an early night."

Chapter Twenty-Eight.

The morning of the wedding day arrived. "I'll get my car," said Petros.

Bear turned to Andreas as the aged BMW stopped in front of the door.. "With all his millions you'd think he'd buy a new car instead of that old banger."

Petros slapped him on the back. "That old banger is a classic. BMW don't make them like that anymore."

"Thank God," said Bear.

"You can always walk."

"I have a choice?"

"I'll drop you and Andreas at the registry office and drive on to Mayfair. Should be back in less than fifteen minutes.

"Have you got the rings? Where are they?"

"For the tenth time, I have and they're in my jacket pocket. Get your arse into gear and go sit in the car. Andreas, you're with me inside the registry office directing the guests. I'm the groom's side and you're Jocelyn's."

"How do I know who they are?"

Petros gave a half smile. "You could ask them."

Andreas shrugged, opened the door, and walked to the car.

Wearing a hired morning suit, Bear glanced in the mirror. "I've scrubbed up okay." He touched his shaven head as he turned and examined the tailoring, which covered his large frame. "She's a lucky woman."

"Dog," said Petros.

Charlie lifted his head from his pillow.

"Look after the house."

As if to say I always do he closed his eyes and gave a little yelp.

Petros lifted the mail from the mat, shoved it into his jacket pocket, and slammed the door.

With forty minutes to spare, Andreas and Bear climbed the steps of Marylebone registry office, located the room, and entered.

"Take a seat, Bear, the man who does the business will want a few words."

Andreas checked the time and glanced around.

Petros returned and ran up the steps.

Andreas commented, "If more guests arrive, it's standing room only."

Petros swept his gaze along the rows of unknown faces. Jack, Zena and his brothers arrived and Phoebe, Andreas' wife.

Jack nudged his stepson. "I see Jocelyn's boss has arrived."

Petros acknowledged Derek Fisher, Captain of HMS President and his team all dressed in their best uniforms with medals glistening, at the rear of the room.

Andreas directed Bear's army pals and their wives to seats near the front.

When Amadou, along with his wife Durrah, ZZ and Scarlet strolled through the door, Petros almost fell over. "No one told me you were coming."

"Maria contacted me when we were in Sicily but asked me not to tell."

Petros turned to ZZ. "Nice to see you two back together."

"She couldn't live without her man from the desert."

Scarlet, wearing a low cut dark green dress slit up to her thigh, nudged him in the ribs. "I thought I'd have a holiday in Libya and bumped into Amadou." She lifted her left hand where a large diamond sparkled. "I intend to make an honest man out of ZZ."

"Talk later. Find some seats if you can." Petros checked the time, motioned to the registrar and left the room.

On the top of the stone steps at the entrance, he waited underneath the carved architrave with Derek Fisher.

The approaching white Rolls Royce flashed its headlights and stopped.

Petros descended the steps as Maria, matron of honour, wearing a sleeveless burgundy, full-length silk dress with straight skirt, exited the car. Jocelyn followed wearing the same style but in ivory with a long train over one arm. Her two bridesmaids, in yellow and white dresses jumped out and waited.

The driver removed from the boot, one large bouquet of lily of the valley, three posies of yellow and burgundy carnations. When ready he gave Jocelyn a kiss on the cheek, wished her good luck and handed the flowers over.

"Papa, I'm a big girl. I'm five and a quarter."

He chuckled. "Can you two promise me something?"

Alysa and Lucy looked at each other and nodded.

"When we are in the room full of people can you stop talking for ten minutes?"

"Yes papa, mama has already told us."

Maria adjusted Jocelyn's dress as they climbed the steps.

At the top, Derek took Jocelyn's right arm and they walked inside and waited until Petros gave them the nod and vanished.

The doors opened and Jocelyn with Derek walked towards the table where the registrar waited. She nodded to those she knew and smiled at the others.

The ceremony was short but delightful.

When it came to the vows, Bear said in a clear and loud voice, "I, William Montgomery Morris, take Jocelyn Linda Scott to be my lawfully wedded wife."

Everyone giggled when Jocelyn stuttered with William Montgomery Morris.

Petros contacted the cab company to be ready to pick up. "Maria, you and the girls are in the first cab. I'll be in the last."

With the register, signed the bride and groom hurried out to the waiting Rolls Royce.

As the bride's car drew away from the kerb, six black cabs formed a line. Petros directed the guests, five or six to a cab. When one pulled away, another joined the queue until he jumped into the last one.

The Savile club in Mayfair opened its doors as Bear and Jocelyn arrived.

The event manager directed them to the old staircase where the photographer and twelve Royal Naval Reserve Officers, six either side, waited as the guard of honour.

Bear and Jocelyn fixed the smiles on their faces as the photographer snapped away.

"I'm starving," said Bear. "If we don't eat soon your new husband will fade away."

"Be quiet and smile," whispered Jocelyn. "Remember you asked me, so this is your fault."

"You could have said no."

"Thank you," said Rodney the photographer. "I'll glide around during the meal and speeches, taking random shots for your album. As requested, I have positioned three cameras in the building filming the complete event."

"Do whatever you do," said Bear. "I'm sure they'll be okay."

"I don't do okay. Every one of my pictures is a masterpiece of creation."

Jocelyn grabbed his arm. "Go and do what you do best. My husband is not favoured with an artistic disposition."

"I understand," said Rodney. "At least I know who the better half is."

"Ready?" asked Petros.

"For what?"

Jocelyn nodded and grabbed Bear's hand. "For you the best part of being married. Dinner is served."

Petros stood by the dining room door and announced Bear and Jocelyn.

"Smells good," said Bear as they paraded in.

At the head of the table Bear waited for grace to finish before he seated Jocelyn. "Now that's what I call a steak," On the platter placed in front of him was the largest T bone steak he'd seen outside of a ranch in the USA.

In between each of the four courses, the required speeches came and went, a decision made by Jocelyn.

"Time you and your wife changed into your travelling clothes," said Petros. "Here's the key to my bedroom. Your cases are by the bed. You have thirty-five minutes."

Bear nodded, beaming.

"You still haven't told me where we're going," said Jocelyn.

"We're going to lie on a beach on the island of Montserrat. Drink the local plonk and watch the sunset over the Caribbean."

"And when the sun sets?"

"Do you need to ask?"

"Come on, we'd better change or we'll miss our flight."

The envelopes in Petros' jacket pocket dug through his silk shirt and into his chest. He glanced into the bar where the guests either drank or danced. One by one, he scanned the envelopes, the last, postmarked Malta. He sat in the nearest chair, ripped it open, and read James Eden's account.

"The bastards."

"Papa said a naughty word."

In front of him stood Alysa, Lucy and Maria. "Now I suppose she'll be telling all her school friends your naughty word. I'm taking these two up to their room."

"Fair enough but read this first. My gold has been taxed? After expenses they've charged forty percent."

"But there's millions of people out there who would love to earn what you pay in taxes."

He shook his head. "That's not the point. They stole twenty million."

"Say goodnight to the girls. Oh, by the way, Lucy will be living with us until Bear and Jocelyn return from honeymoon and she attends her new school."

"Whatever."

"Kiss the girls goodnight."

"Which school is Lucy attending?"

"She'll be a boarder at Woldingham."

Petros shrugged. He kissed Lucy on the cheek. "I don't envy you, you're sharing with Alysa." He kissed Alysa. "No talking when the lights are out."

Alysa grabbed Lucy's hand.

Maria led them away passing Bear and Jocelyn descending the main stairs. She stopped. "Have a great time. See you when you get back. PK's complaining because the tax man just stole twenty million."

Bear beamed. "Amazing. Where is he?"

"In the dining room."

At the bottom of the stairs, Bear said to Jocelyn. "The laugh is, ten million belongs to me. Ah, here's PK. Great party. Pity we have to miss it."

"I'm glad you're married and on your way."

"I hear we lost twenty mill to the revenue."

"Still have thirty-two. Sixteen apiece."

"I bowed out remember."

"Not entirely. You did save my wife from being murdered and you're a fifty percent partner in the company."

"True." He glanced at his watch. "Our carriage awaits. See you when we get back."

Petros watched them disappear via a side door.

Maria returned, stood next to him and said, "Time we had a dance."

"Your wish is my command."

As they danced, his eyes scanned the room. With full glasses the babbling groups of two, three and four, meandered around. "You did a great job."

She lifted her head. "Combined effort. You didn't do so bad yourself but you need to have a word with your mama and papa before they leave."

"We can chat at breakfast."

"True."

The dance music increased in tempo. Couples danced and congregated around Petros and Maria.

"Great party," said one.

"Splendid venue," said another.

Andreas danced with Phoebe and winked when they circled by.

"He was rather the worse for wear the other night. Bear virtually carried him and put him to bed."

Maria went to say something as an almighty crash reverberated across the room. Two figures could be seen attempting to lift each other up.

"Zack and Brian appear to be rat-arsed. Better go and sort them out." Petros strolled across the floor, grabbed their collars and hauled them to their feet. "What happened?"

Brian leant on Petros' shoulder. "Time to go home, PK. Sorry about the mess."

James appeared. "There ends the free booze lesson. Brian, Zack, we're out of here before you do more damage."

The three men nodded to the guests surrounding them and headed for the exit. Petros caught up with them. "Thanks for coming. Bear appreciated it."

"Send us the bill for the damage, PK," slurred Zack.

He watched them negotiate the steps as James flagged a taxi.

The music started with a Status Quo number. The floor filled with dancers many with air guitars.

Midnight approached, the bar closed and the last dance of the evening played.

Petros and Maria stood at the entrance until the last couple departed. Jack, Zena and his brothers along with their families had gone to their rooms earlier. Amadou and Durrah sat with ZZ and Scarlet, chatted and sipped their drinks in a far corner.

Phoebe waved as she helped Andreas up the stairs.

Petros gazed at the bar and dance floor. It appeared a shambles at the end of a wonderful day but he was aware the dining room was clean and ready for breakfast.

***

Showered, Maria and Petros entered the dining room together.

"From what I can see we're the last to arrive. Even Lucy and Alysa are eating," said Maria.

As they joined the two girls Alysa raised her head. "Lucy dressed me."

Petros kissed both girls and sat next to Lucy.

"I'll get fruit juice and toast for two," said Maria.

"More toast," said Alysa.

"Coming right up, madam."

Amadou wandered across and stopped by Petros. "Great night. Thanks for the bonus. Can we have a chat?"

"No problem. I'll meet you in the bar in, let's say thirty minutes."

"He placed his hand on Petros' shoulder and gave a gentle squeeze. "Thirty minutes."

Maria gave him a strange look.

"He's one of the good guys, brave and down-to-earth. Without his help Libya might have been rather difficult."

"He has a beautiful wife. American from her accent."

"Worships the ground she walks on."

Petros refilled his glass with fresh orange juice and wandered around the dining room saying good morning to his family and the others who stayed the night.

Returning to his table he said, "I need to chat with Amadou and after we can go home."

"I'll take the girls and get packed but you collect our cases."

He chuckled. "Take note, girls, mama's the boss." He wandered towards the bar that looked soulless without people.

Amadou and ZZ waited in the sumptuous red leather armchairs. "Right on time," said Amadou.

"One of my plus points," said Petros. "Okay, what do you want to discuss?"

Amadou churched his fingers. "I've been approached by a Syrian refugee who informs me a fortune in gold coins and diamonds are hidden in a vault under his shop in Aleppo."

"No way. In Syria you're up shit creek, with no paddles

and your canoe's sinking. It's gun law, back to the wild west with no sheriff to shoot the bad guy. Out of interest, who is the bad guy? There are so many different factions fighting each other. The vault is more than likely under a ton of rubble. Being sarcastic, operating a JCB in those conditions might interest others. If either side catches you, you'll be shot. The last news item I heard stated the government troops were demolishing the city with barrel bombs. My best guesstimate is wait until it calms down."

"I understand," said Amadou, "But I know the risks."

Petros laughed. "Don't tell me you're going ahead with this?"

"It's a challenge," said Amadou. It's dangerous and there're no easy options."

"You need someone who knows the city."

Amadou raised his bushy eyebrows. "The truth is I, we, don't know enough to start planning a collection. You're right, PK, but I might go in and have a scout around when I have business in the area. To be fair if we can't get out in one piece, I'll give it a miss."

"Let me know how you get on?" said Petros.

Maria entered the bar with Durrah and Scarlet. "Told you, and they say women talk. If we stay much longer we'll be charged another day for our room."

The men laughed, stood and gave Petros a hug

"I'll get the cases," said Petros.

"They're at the entrance," said Maria. "A member of staff brought collected them."

"I'll get the car, five minutes." He returned, loaded the cases in the boot and made sure Alysa and Lucy were correctly strapped in.

As soon as Maria fastened her seat belt, the rain started.

"Papa, play songs," said Alysa.

He pressed the play button. Maria and Alysa started to sing. Lucy remained hesitant until the second time of playing.

"Damn, I've taken the wrong turn," muttered Petros.

"Slow down, if you take the next left it takes you home."

"How do you know that?"

"When we first moved, I took the wrong turn off a few times," said Maria above the noise of the rain and two girls singing.

The road appeared empty. In these conditions, no one was out driving.

"The rain's heavier than when we left London," said Petros as Maria wiped the windscreen with a chamois.

"You should have used my car."

He glanced at her, concentrated on the road, and drove on. At the base of a hill, fast flowing water streamed across the road. Petros drove through; muddy water plastered the windscreen and ran down the windows. Then he saw an animal in the centre of the road. "Shit," he shouted as his foot hit the brake pedal.

The car slid as if on ice. Petros pumped the brake pedal as he attempted to correct its erratic course. The huge bull eyed the car, raised its head and bellowed. Out of control, the vehicle bounced off its haunches, slithered sideways across the road, and destroyed a hedge. Screams filled the car as it rolled onto its roof. For what seemed an age the vehicle slid like a toboggan, descending the steep field, stopping when it struck the trunk of a pine tree.

On its roof, steam spiralled from the engine compartment. The drumming of rain on the underside drowned any other sound.

Petros opened his eyes and instinct warned him time was

his enemy. His voice shook as he stared up the slope. He turned his head. Maria, held by her seat belt, had her eyes closed. "Speak to me, girls."

"Papa hit a cow," said Alysa.

"I'm upside down," said Lucy.

"My head hurts," said Maria.

Petros pressed against his door, it remained solid. He released his seat belt and twisted his body until he could place his feet on the crazed windscreen. Drawing his knees up to his chest, he kicked out. The screen shattered into a thousand pieces. "Maria, you crawl out and I'll help the girls. Ready?" He released her belt and lowered her to the roof.

She crawled through the gap and stood, wary of broken bones. Her legs ached but supported her. Back on her knees, she peered into the car. "Ready when you are."

He supported Alysa and released her belt. "Crawl towards the window and mama will help you." He waited until she was clear.

Lucy followed.

He grabbed Maria's handbag and crawled out.

As they stood on the sloping ground, the wind and driving rain stung their faces.

With care, Petros checked the girls for broken bones and cuts. "The seat belts saved us but there'll be a few nasty bruises tomorrow. He glanced at Maria and then up the slope. "We walk up there and into the village. I'll come back for our cases later."

"Thank God we survived," said Maria.

Petros lifted Alysa and grabbed Lucy's hand. "How about singing a song, girls?"

They looked at him, dazed and bewildered.

In a line, they climbed, slipped, and slid across the muddy slope until they reached the road.

He pulled his mobile from his trouser pocket. The crack along its centre told him it was useless.

The rain continued as they shivered and walked towards the village. On rounding a curve in the road, Maria spotted a large house, which might offer shelter and warmth. Almost running they headed up the drive and knocked on the door.

It opened on a security chain and a man peered through the gap.

Maria spoke softly. "Sorry to bother you but our car's been in an accident. Can we use your telephone?"

Before the man could answer, the door slammed shut and opened wide. A short, overweight, dark-haired woman wearing a floral print dress, roared, "Come in. Girls upstairs and get those clothes off, or you'll die of pneumonia. Albert, sort this young man out. Your new dressing gown will fit him." She gazed at the girls. "My grand-daughters' clothes might fit you young ladies."

Albert smiled at Petros and motioned for him to follow. "Don't worry about Gertrude, she used to be a headmistress at a girls school in Zimbabwe." They entered a large warm country kitchen filled with every modern accessory.

"If I can use your phone for a taxi, we'll be on our way."

Albert smiled. "You're in my house and my wife's the boss. She wants you warm and dry." He filled the kettle and turned the power on. "A nice hot drink will work wonders." From behind a door, he removed a maroon bathrobe. He pointed. "Cloakroom's over there. Have a shower to warm up and your coffee will be ready when you come out."

Petros showered and entered the kitchen wearing the robe.

Albert poured boiling water onto instant coffee and handed him the mug and milk carton.

Maria and the two girls arrived followed by Gertrude.

"Sit at the table. Albert, tea for the ladies and I'll have a cup of mint tea."

For a while they talked of the weather and other mundane matters, until Gertrude stood and said. "You've stopped shaking, your colour has returned. Albert can take you home. You mentioned you live in Pangbourne by the river." She peered through the window. "Use the Range Rover, Albert. No problem if you drive carefully."

Petros held back a smile as Albert simply said, "Yes dear," put on his coat and went outside. "We'll take our own clothes and have yours cleaned and returned in a couple of days."

"It would be an insult to offer you money," said Maria, "but next weekend I'd be happy if you came to our house for dinner."

"Love to," said Gertrude," and you are correct. Offering money for human kindness is insulting. Albert's outside with the car. I'll get your clothes."

Maria and the girls stood and stretched bruised arms.

Gertrude returned with a bulging laundry bag. "Your wet shoes are by the front door. Make sure Albert drives slowly; he can be a bit of a tearaway at times."

Petros gave Gertrude a hug. "Thank you. You saved our lives."

She shoved him away. "You men can be so silly."

Alysa and Lucy waved. Maria gave her a kiss on the cheek. "Don't forget dinner next Saturday."

With the door open the four of them dressed in their strange attire ran and jumped into the waiting Range Rover and slammed the doors.

"Bet you a pound to a penny my wife told you to make sure I drove slowly."

Petros, in the passenger seat nodded.

After a few miles of crawling along flooded roads, they entered Pangbourne and in minutes drove into the drive of Petros' house.

Rain pounded on the vehicle's roof.

"Wait in the car until I open the door," said Petros. "Albert, fancy a hot drink or something stronger."

"Better get back or she'll worry. What time next Saturday?"

"Sevenish," said Maria.

The moment Petros opened the house door Alysa and Lucy leapt out and ran. Maria grabbed the wash bag. "Thank you, Albert."

Petros and Maria stood by the front door and waved as he drove away. Inside Charlie welcomed Alysa and Lucy.

Charlie sniffed, barked, and lay in front of Lucy with his head between his front paws.

"See Yarlie love you," said Alysa.

"I'd better contact the police and tell them we're okay. You never know some bright eyed bobby may have spotted my car."

"You loved that car, didn't you?"

"I did, we've been together a long time. If it's fixable, I'll have it repaired but it didn't look too good on its roof. I'm going to change."

"Alysa, get into your pyjamas. Lucy, you can wear one of my night dresses and it's an early night for both of you." She watched as the two girls ran up the stairs passing Petros coming down.

"I feel a whole lot better wearing my own clothes."

Tears flooded from Maria's eyes as she wrapped her arms around him.

"Mama why are you crying?" asked Alysa standing in her

pyjamas at the bottom of the stairs.

Through watery eyes, she smiled at her daughter. "Because we're together and safe." She nodded, grabbed Alysa's hand and they went upstairs.

"It's an early night, Dog." Petros turned out the lights as he reached the top of the stairs.

Charlie barked and settled in his basket.

The dusk is here down by the sea
A summer's day, a nice cool breeze
And as the sun be sinking lower
A silence with its awesome power
The hour, the day is ended

Peter Duggan

Made in the USA
Charleston, SC
12 October 2015